THE MUTANT PRIME

The
Mutant
Prime

KAREN HABER

Introduction by Robert Silverberg

A FOUNDATION BOOK

DOUBLEDAY

New York London Toronto Sydney Auckland

A Foundation Book
PUBLISHED BY DOUBLEDAY
a division of
Bantam Doubleday Dell Publishing Group, Inc.
666 Fifth Avenue, New York, New York 10103

Foundation, Doubleday, and the portrayal of the letter F
are trademarks of Doubleday, a division of
Bantam Doubleday Dell Publishing Group, Inc.

Front jacket artwork by Jim Burns

Special thanks to Lou Aronica, Janna Silverstein,
David M. Harris, and Alice Alfonsi

Library of Congress Cataloging-in-Publication Data

Haber, Karen.
The mutant prime/by Karen Haber; introduction by
Robert Silverberg.—1st ed.
p.   cm.
"A Foundation book."
I. Title.
PS3558.A255M8   1990
813'.54—dc20   90-2978
CIP

ISBN 0-385-24722-2
ISBN 0-385-26648-0 (pbk.)

For Bob, of course

INTRODUCTION

T HE SEASONS MOVE ALONG. The outsiders who have lived submerged among us for so long move into even greater prominence. The world has grudgingly begun to accept the concept that a subculture of not-exactly-human beings with superior mental abilities has existed on our world for hundreds of years, hidden away right in our midst, dwelling virtually invisibly in a worldwide secret ghetto of its own making.

And now an even more unnerving possibility presents itself to an uneasy mankind: the possible emergence of a supermutant, a genetic freak gifted with extrasensory powers that make him as superior to ordinary mutants as the mutants are to the normal population.

That's the premise of the second volume of this quartet of *Mutant Season* books. The characters of Volume One are some fifteen years older now. The rhythms of their adult lives seem set, for better or for worse. The mutant Michael Ryton, locked in a difficult marriage with his turbulent mutant wife Jena, has moved into control of his family's aerospace engineering firm. Michael's troubled sister Melanie, a mutant in whom the mutant powers never developed, has begun a new life for herself as a journalist. Kelly McLeod, the nonmutant woman whose youthful romance with Michael Ryton ended in anguish for them both, is now an officer in the Air Force space service.

And then comes a sudden bewildering telepathic warning: *BEWARE THE SUPERMUTANT! BEWARE THE SUPERMUTANT!* A startled world turns to its television screens and hears a silent voice telling a frightened anchorwoman, *"I can talk to everybody in your audience without opening my mouth."*

PERHAPS THE POSITION of the mutants in the American society of the early twenty-first century as this second volume opens can be seen as similar to that of the American blacks not long after the civil rights victories of the 1960s. The legal barriers that had stood in the way of their advancement into the mainstream of American life had been overthrown; the official position of the government was one of absolute equality of opportunity; the majority of the citizens now gave lip service, at least, to that concept.

But what would happen next—for the blacks in the post–Martin Luther King period and the mutants of tomorrow— was far from certain. Would the once oppressed underclass (in the case of the blacks) or the carefully camouflaged special minority (the mutants) be able to consolidate its victories and move on to true integration with the majority faction? Or would the progress of the minority seem so threatening to the majority that a reactionary movement of new repression would arise?

The experience of the blacks in the 1970s and 1980s was a mixed one: gains on the one hand, losses on the other, old problems replaced by new dilemmas. A substantial number were able to find room for themselves in areas—housing, employment, politics—from which they had formerly been largely excluded. Others, less fortunate, discovered that although they were now legally entitled to ride at the front of the bus if they cared to, they were still forced to contend with repression of a more covert kind and their lives were not significantly better than they had been in the old days of open discrimination.

On balance, though, fundamental and probably irreversible changes in the American racial situation did take place in the two decades after the civil rights era. And the United States of America of 1988 saw the surprising spectacle of the Jesse Jackson presidential campaign—the first time a black political figure had seriously sought the nation's highest office.

Though few political analysts saw much likelihood of Jackson's winning the nomination of his party and none envisioned him as being capable of attaining the presidency in 1988, the mere fact of his candidacy, and of his obtaining a substantial number of white votes in the primary elections, were both development that would have been unthinkable in the America of only a few years before. In the vocabulary of *The Mutant Season* and its successors, Jesse Jackson as plausible black presidential candidate can be seen as a kind of supermutant, a figure unexpectedly rising above the supposed limitations that contained his race and breaking a path into startling new territory.

The mutants of Karen Haber's *Mutant Season* books have already made the leap into national politics. Volume One of the series gave us Eleanor Jacobsen of Oregon, the first mutant member of the United States Senate—ultimately the victim of a bizarre assassination plot hatched by a fellow mutant with presidential ambitions. By the time of Volume Two, the presence of mutants at all levels of power in industry and the government is taken pretty much for granted; and though there has not yet been a mutant President or even a mutant presidential candidate, no one would regard it as astounding for such a figure to appear in the next few years.

But the analogy between blacks and mutants breaks down here.

Both groups, the real ones of our world and the imagined

ones of these novels, are minorities that have had a hard struggle against the fears and prejudices of the majority race that surrounds them. Gradually, after years of careful planning, they have come forward into a situation of *equality of opportunity.*

Equality of opportunity is one thing, however, and equality of ability is another. It has been the position of many white supremacists that blacks are less than human, that they are a life-form inherently inferior to whites. Therefore the chief goal of the blacks in twentieth-century America has been to obtain recognition of their fundamental humanity—to demonstrate that they are something more than beasts of burden suitable only for service as slaves, to show that they are, in fact, full members of the human race, entitled to the same legal privileges as the whites who brought their ancestors in captivity to the New World. It is not an issue seriously in dispute any longer, except in South Africa, where the black-white conflict is still in an earlier phase.

The mutants are *more* than human, though. Perhaps all they want politically from the America of the early twenty-first century is equality, but there is no getting around the fact that they are an advanced form of the human species, or perhaps some new species entirely. No well-meaning political rhetoric can hide the uncomfortable truth that the mutants are capable of telepathy, of telekinesis, of all manner of astounding things beyond the understanding of mere normals.

For the two races to be able to live in peace, side by side, thus becomes an exercise in harmony that makes our recent real-world civil rights campaigns seem like kindergarten stuff. No one but the most confirmed racist would try to assert, nowadays, that the blacks are an inferior form of the human race who must be confined to their own districts, their own lunch counters, their own restrooms, their own sections of the bus. They differ somewhat from the majority population in their physical appearance, yes—but that is no reason to deprive them of any of their rights of citizenship.

The mutants, though, are not only a minority group—and in a generally conformist society like ours, minorities are always in danger of some oppression—but are undeniably *superior.* True, their only demand is for equality, the right to live as they please without fear of persecution or discrimination; but the real problem for the nonmutant majority is that equality isn't the essential issue. What the normals need to do is to arrive at an acceptance of one stunning, gigantic fact: *They're better than we are.*

The first volume of the *Mutant Season* books showed the United States of the near future doing a remarkably good job of overcoming the not very surprising bigotry and fear that the revelation of the mutant presence in its midst would create.

But now, with the superior mutant minority just barely assimilated into American life, to have to come to terms with the realization that an even more potent human form may have emerged, an actual supermutant—

It may be asking a little too much.

—ROBERT SILVERBERG
Oakland, California
October 1989

THE MUTANT PRIME

1

THE DOME was clear and crystalline, and the deep black bowl of space pressed up against it, the sharp light of stars pricking the airless void. Then the stars disappeared behind a filament of fine white lines: a deadly cobweb. Kelly McLeod stared at it in horror. The unthinkable had happened: One of Moonstation's main domes had cracked.

Death should make some sound, she thought. Even in the vacuum of space—a musical note to herald the end.

Instead a shrill klaxon split the air. The clank of safety doors slamming closed added a grim percussive counterpoint to the siren's wail. Kelly tucked her dark hair under the collar of her orange pressure suit, sealed the helmet, and moved toward the main corridor.

Too late, she thought. I'm probably too late.

She walked as quickly as the cumbersome suit would allow. Sweat matted the hair to her forehead, her neck.

Thank God the shuttle trolley was connected to the south port. No safety doors to cut through. And no corpses. Yet.

The dome had been deserted because of the early hour: Kelly had drawn night shift, and for once, she was grateful. She was halfway to the airlock when she saw someone, unsuited, clinging to a steel fiber handhold. It was Heyran Landon, the mutant commander of the shuttle, her immediate superior. Where was his pressure suit? Had he heard the alarm and bolted from his quarters without thinking?

No time for questions. Kelly cast about the hallway for the suit depot. Every corridor had one; emergency preparation was a fact of life on Moonstation. Ah, there it was, red light blinking on the left, halfway down the wall. She pried it open, pulled out an orange acrylic oxygen mask with its robe, and managed to wrap it around the suffocating man. He nodded weakly, golden eyes half-shut through the mask. Mutants were rare enough in the service without adding Landon to the casualty list.

Part of the dome imploded with a muffled roar. The air around them became a pale blue gale rushing out into the vacuum. Life-giving atmosphere roared past, pulling papers, screens, furniture in its wake. Kelly dodged a pink wallseat torn loose from its moorings and grabbed at the handholds attached to the walls. At least they didn't give.

Hastily she hooked Landon to her belt, slid her arm around his back, and towed him, handhold by handhold, toward the airlock. But even in the lowered gravity she was fighting the pull of escaping atmosphere, losing ground.

Would they make it? It wouldn't be hard for her to hold them there, webbed to one of the walls. But the oxygen supply was finite. Landon's would run out in six hours. Rescue was possible . . . all of the domes couldn't have blown. But she and Landon were expected to be part of the rescue force.

She clung desperately to the scalloped handhold, a dull throbbing building in her arm above the elbow. Dammit, why hadn't she worked out more? Three months on Moonstation duty had weakened her, despite rotation and time off.

Just as she decided to web them in and wait for help, Kelly felt a gentle push, as though someone had come up behind her and was leaning against her shoulders. She twisted around to look. The corridor was empty. The push became stronger, more insistent.

Telekinesis.

The hair on the back of her neck prickled.

Half-conscious, Landon was using his mutant powers to propel them down the hallway.

The airlock loomed before her, the round black doorway rimmed by double rows of blue acrylic seals around the seams. Before she had time to reach for the manual controls, the doors opened, she and Landon swept through into the trolley, and the doors sealed tight behind them. Kelly collapsed onto the nearest webseat. Landon sprawled next to her, seemingly unconscious. But they were safe.

Strapping Landon in, Kelly checked the trolley pressure readings. They were normal. She scanned the dome interior and subsidiary corridors for life readings. Found none. Other domes had blown as well.

I can't think about that now. I won't.

She scanned the pressure readings in the building.

Unstable.

Let's get out of here.

She pulled the trolley away from the airlock and placed it in a low orbit. The radio began to squawk: transmissions from the dormitories below ground. She switched on the shuttle transmitter, wide band so that the French and Russian shuttle stations would catch it.

"Moonstation Control, this is Trolley Four, Captain McLeod reporting. Dome C has imploded. Repeat. Dome C is gone. Related living quarters are at risk of violent decompression. Pressure suits are suggested for all inhabitants. Please supply your coordinates. I will request rescue assistance from the Dubrovnik and Brittany orbiters."

"We read you, McLeod. Stand by for transmission."

Kelly saw movement out of the corner of her eye. Landon sat up carefully and pulled free from the oxygen mask. His thin face was pale.

"Are you all right, sir?"

"I thought I dreamed it." He gazed around the trolley, taking in the screen, webseats, blinking radio. His eyes met hers. "I'm fine, McLeod. You saved us both."

She handed him an orbit-ready pressure suit. "I think *you* saved us, sir. I'd be willing to bet a promotion that you gave us a telekinetic boost right through the airlock."

"So I didn't dream that, either." He stood up slowly, as though every bone in his body ached. Just as slowly, he donned the gray fiber suit.

"I'd never have been able to get us both aboard," she said. "That was some push."

"Nonregulation. But it worked." A slow smile lit up his features for a moment and faded. He turned toward the trolley controls. "Let's get busy. Somebody's got a hell of a problem on their hands. I wouldn't want to sort out the blame for this mess."

"Yessir. Me neither." The trolley's blinking green LED screen registered reports from the surface of casualties from chain-reaction decompression. Don't think about that now. Kelly took a deep breath and switched on the radio.

"LYDDA, when will you stop hiding? What are you afraid of?"

Narlydda leaned back against the blue enameled wall of the satorifoam pool—a luxury her artwork had earned her—and gave him a scornful look. Skerry had been her lover now for three years, but sometimes he presumed too much.

"Afraid? Do I seem afraid?" She lifted one long, greenish-tinged leg half coated in iridescent foam out of the bath and watched sparkling dream images float upwards from the froth towards the skylight: a lavender horse with mane of fire, a fuchsia daisy with a yellow woman's face at its center.

"Yep. Oh, don't laugh. I know you, lady. The bravado. The mask of aloofness, not to mention your elaborate disguises. And the frightened mutant peering out from behind them all, unwilling to take credit for her work. Especially now that you've gotten that fat commission from the Emory Foundation."

She blew sparkling foam at him. "Credit? Dear man, I take plenty of credit for my work. And Eurodollars. Diamonds. Selenium crystals. Real estate."

"Okay, so you've made a fortune. And welcome to it—you're damned good. The darling of old and new money." It was true. Everybody from the Nouveau Brahmins to the Seventh Column chip runners wanted a Narlydda original.

"Don't forget my simultaneous retrospective at the Getty/Whitney and the Hermitage." She grinned triumphantly. "Before the age of forty-five, I might add!"

"Stop preening, Lydda. I've told you before what I think of your work. All I'm saying is you're hiding your mutancy behind the name. The elusive Narlydda, who never attends openings. Is never photographed, holographed, videoed, or seen. You were tough even for me to track down. And I'm good."

"Very good." She gave him a sly look, an invitation. But he ignored it.

"Don't you think you've carried this too far? Face it—you're scared to admit that the world-famous Narlydda, artist of sky and space, is a mutant. So you cheat all of us from sharing in the legitimacy, the reknown."

"Cheat you? That's not how I see it." She stood, stepped out of the foam, and stalked toward the wall-mounted sonic dryers. She was a tall, lanky woman, naked in the filtered sunlight, with an odd green cast to her skin and hair, save for a silvery white thatch at her forehead.

The dryers hummed, removing all traces of the dream foam. Nearby, a basket of ripe peaches sat on a low glass table. Narlydda selected one and floated it into her grasp, took a bite, swallowed. "Is this the face, the body, the skin, that the public wants to see behind the marvelous Narlydda's work?" She finished the peach, tossed the pit into the compactor. "Not bloody likely. You know better, Skerry. The critics would kill me. They'd relegate my *oeuvre* to a mere curiosity. Mutant kitsch."

"Bull. It'd shake everybody up. A good idea, if you ask me."

"I didn't." She said it archly, but there was fire behind her words.

"What's the use of art if it can't stand a little controversy? Especially in this effete, technohybrid paradise? We can't always count on the Japanese-American Consortium for scandal."

He was using one of her own arguments against her.

Narlydda sank down onto the cushioned deck. "I can't believe you're that naive. The art critics will only approve so much controversy. Otherwise, they might lose control of the market. And as for collectors . . . well, they do what the critics tell them."

"Don't you have any faith in your work?" His look was steely.

"Of course I do. I'm damned good. But what are you suggesting, Skerry? That I shoot the golden goose? Thumb my nose at the art establishment? Make fools of them? I'm plenty independent, but I'm not stupid." She slouched against a soft yellow pillow. "Fifteen years ago, when I got started, Eleanor Jacobsen had just been killed. Then old 'Mutant Uber Alles' Jeffers was unmasked as a lunatic fanatic." She gave a mock salute. "And thank God for that."

"Thank me."

His voice was flat. She paused, uncertain. Surely he was joking.

"Well, I thought it was a bad season for mutants," she retorted. "And a good time to lay low."

"You weren't alone. I remember." He paused, lost in some private memory. Then he shook it off, returned to the offensive. "But times change."

"Oh, sure. I grant you that things are better than before.

But even now, we still make normals nervous. Admit it, Skerry. You know it's true."

He nodded grudgingly. She smiled, a point won.

"Besides," she added, "I like my privacy. I don't want to be bothered by all those critics and journalists. And I'm too old to go back to being a poverty-stricken artist."

"So much for artistic integrity."

"Stuff if, Skerry!" She stood up. "I've got plenty of artistic integrity. Narlydda is a free agent. Nobody tells me what to do or how to do it. As for cheating the mutant community, I donate plenty to our genetic research and storehouses. You can't accuse me of being stingy or uncaring. Even if I don't attend clan meetings. And since when are you so concerned about the mutant community, lone wolf?"

Skerry climbed out of the pool and stretched out on the biplast deck. His thick, graying hair was caught in a ponytail at his neck. Hallucinatory images of red concentric circles and black waves danced around his muscled body as the foam evaporated.

I've always been involved," he said calmly. "Behind the scenes. That's my style."

"Well, what's so different from what I'm doing?"

"At least I don't hide behind the mask of a normal."

Above the bubbling silvery foam, the image of a small woman formed. She was pink, naked, standing on a seashell, hands modestly clasped over her privates. Her dark hair was pulled back into a chaste bun. A banner ran from her left shoulder across her breast, to her waist. Blinking yellow neon letters spelled out the name ANNE VERLAND. The woman's eyes flashed from gray to gold as her skin flickered back and forth between pink and green.

Narlydda laughed and clapped her hands. "Very good. I think maybe you should be the artist. And I see you've been boning up on your art history. Botticelli would be amused."

"I'm glad somebody would be."

"Don't sulk," she said. "It's boring. What difference does

it make if I've got a computerized alter ego? I paid a year's income for that simulacrum, and Anne Verland has been worth every credit. Half the art critics from Metro L.A. to Gdansk think Anne Verland *is* Narlydda anyway. And that software's so clever, sometimes even I believe it."

She stretched like a cat in the sun, took a long step, and leaped into the air, tumbling above Skerry's head up towards the arched skylights in a series of complicated, graceful arabesques. Still airborne, she performed an extended backwards somersault and came to rest in midair, floating on her back above the sparkling pool. Tiny seahorses, winking orange and green, floated up to meet her.

"Terrific," Skerry said sourly. "I know somebody at Ringling Brothers/Sony who could use another telekinetic trapeze artist. And then you won't have to hide behind a pink-faced computer program. Or skin dye."

"No thanks. I prefer to work with a net."

"That's what I'm afraid of. But this Emory Foundation commission is big—really big. You may not be able to hide anymore."

"Then I'll run instead."

"I'm not kidding, Narlydda!" Skerry's eyes flashed golden fire. "Dammit, you know how I feel about you. I wouldn't be here otherwise. But it's time to decide where your loyalties lie and who you are." He reached for his clothing.

Gods, she thought, he could be tiresome. She took a deep breath. "You're probably right. May I decide over tea?" Even as she said it, she regretted the words. She'd merely intended to nettle, but she'd overshot and now Skerry looked furious.

Silently, he pulled on a bright purple tunic, leggings, boots. Then he turned to her. "You probably need a little more time than that," he said. His tone was deceptively light. "And you'd probably prefer to spend it alone. Well, fine, Lydda. Take all the time you need. Take your whole bloody life." He strode away from her toward the door.

"Come back when you've calmed down," she called after him. "I promise to decide by then."

But her words fell heavily on empty air as the front door shut behind him.

THE NEWSROOM HUMMED like a hive of insects. Curious, horrified insects. The noise broke through Melanie Ryton's concentration. She looked up from the latest facts on orbital factories to see half of the newsroom staff gathered around the mobile scanner in the center of the room. Everybody from glamorous, bald-headed Nesse, the anchorwoman of the evening news, to Ray Goldfield, the stringy-haired part-time intern, was staring at the amber mech and its wrap-around screen.

Something's up, she thought. Something bad. Maybe San Diego finally had the 7.6 they've been expecting and fell off into the sea. I thought the ground felt wobbly this morning.

She slipped into her red boots and joined the crowd.

Disaster on Moonstation, a message tape announced in yellow letters. The casualty figures scrolled in: Fifty dead in subsidiary Moonstation explosion after Dome C cracks. Moonstation administrator dead. Sabotage a possibility. . . .

Randall Camphill, executive editor and producer, strode out of his glass-walled office. His short salt-and-pepper hair glinted. So did the diamond stud in his right earlobe. He plowed through the crowd until he was at dead center. Then he turned on the professional baritone voice that had made his fortune, first as a news anchor, then as a network executive.

"Listen up, people. You're paid to cover the news, not watch it. We've got to get on this, and fast."

Melanie held her breath.

Camphill's icy gray eyes swept the group. "Nesse, of course," he said, giving the nod to their star. She grinned. Her bald head gleamed. "Benjamin, Saroya . . ."

His gaze fell on Melanie, paused, moved on. "Richardson and Cross." He nodded. "Get moving. I've got a shuttle scheduled for you in half an hour. You'll find your mechanicals onboard."

He turned off the voice, turned back towards his office. Melanie followed him.

"Mr. Camphill?"

"What is it, Ryton?"

Her heart pounded. "What about backup? Couldn't they use someone else to help with background?"

He nodded slowly. "You're probably right. Good thinking, Ryton." He looked over her shoulder to a stocky, dark-haired man in a blue suit. "Ferron, you go along to help with the transmission and research." He disappeared into his office.

Stunned, Melanie stared after him.

"Tough break, Mel," Ralph Ferron said. His tone was sympathetic, but his dark eyes twinkled. He brushed past her on his way to the door. "You know how Randy C. loves to bait and switch. Don't feel bad. I'll bring you back some Moon dust."

"Thanks." Just what she needed. Melanie slammed the green acrylic cover of her deskscreen in frustration. Randall Camphill specialized in arbitrary decisions, like most petty tyrants. How could she catch his attention long enough to convince him she deserved a chance at the anchor spot? She'd been with Cable News for five years, working her way up from the research staff to reporting as a correspondent. She worked hard, long hours, weekends, whatever they asked, and enjoyed the work. But how much harder could she work? If she gave all her reports while standing on her head, would Camphill even notice?

She dialed up Tri-Com on her deskpad. Might as well check out the competition. Her screen pulsed with yellow and green light. Then the image solidified into a blond-haired, green-eyed Brazilian, Tri-Com's star reporter, Lucia

Silva, interviewing a trim, brown-haired man in a purple Shuttle Corps uniform. A nameline ran beneath his image: Shuttle Commander Heyran Landon. Landon's eyes were golden, glittering.

A mutant shuttle commander. Melanie felt a surge of surprise.

I didn't know there were any mutants in the Corps, she thought. Interesting. And won't Randall C. be pissed off when he sees how Tri-Com scooped us.

Melanie pulled off her boots and sat cross-legged in her chair, a slim figure in a soft black jumpsuit.

"Audio."

The screen volume rose to a comfortable level.

"Commander Landon, why were the casualties so few?" Silva asked.

The mutant shrugged. "I'd have to say that the timing of the explosion had something to do with it. Most of the Moonstation inhabitants and visitors were asleep, safe in their own pressurized quarters. When the dome went, there weren't many people around. Most of the casualties were due to failures of safety door seals and related pressure leakage."

"And here's the other half of the rescue team," the reporter announced. "Captain Kelly McLeod."

A dark-haired woman in a purple uniform trimmed with gray stared steadily into the camera. Kelly McLeod? Her old friend from Piedmont High was on Moonstation, a hero of the disaster? Melanie twisted in her seat and grabbed her lapscreen. Maybe there was still a chance for her to get in on the action after all.

"DID YOU HEAR about the Moonstation disaster, boss?"

Michael Ryton looked up from his desk, his face bathed in amber screen-light. In front of him was a five-year comparison of third-quarter profits. For a moment, he stared at his secretary, Lari, without recognition. Then her short red hair and snub nose came into focus, and behind her, the smooth blue-green walls of his office at Ryton, Greene and Davis Engineering.

"What disaster?"

"The main dome blew. Or one of them."

"Jesus, no! The entire industry will go under." Michael turned to his deskscreen, flush against the sleek blue surface of his desk, and began punching buttons. "Survey contracts, Moonstation," he snapped. "Specifics on dome construction." He turned back to Lari. "I think Aubenay's group got the contract on the domes. I hope so."

The computer hummed, beeped. Michael scanned the screen.

"Hmmm. Still searching." He ran his hand through his short blond hair. "That's not a good sign."

Lari frowned.

"Fifty people died," she said quietly.

"Terrible," Michael said, staring at his screen. "Keep me posted. Also, tape and transmit any statements by NASA brass, other space engineers, especially any EEC firms . . ."

"I get the idea."

"Thanks, Lari." He wheeled around in his chair to the subscreen.

"Get Jena's shop." Might as well tell her he'd be late. He wanted to check all the files relevant to Moonstation before the government did the research for him. Government scrutiny of documentation had gradually increased ever since the Japanese-American Consortium had joined France and Russia as a partner in Moonstation. If the industry survived this disaster, government surveillance would only increase.

Circuits whirred. He could hear the screen ringing. Then his daughter Herra appeared onscreen. Jena must have shifted the phone so that it would ring at home instead of at her import shop.

"Hi."

"Where's your mother?"

She shrugged coolly as only a fourteen-year-old could and levitated a strand of long blond hair over her shoulder. Herra was beautiful, just like Jena. And knew it.

"Do I keep track of her? Mutant Union meeting, maybe." Her voice was one step beyond bored.

"Again? She's certainly turned into a true believer."

"I guess. Listen, Dad, I'm waiting for a call, and—"

"Forgive me for interrupting."

Michael broke the connection. His head was pounding.

Gingerly, he massaged his temples, then reached into his desk drawer for his alpha boosters. He'd only just learned about the Moonstation disaster but it had already given him a headache.

The computer chimed, three quick bells. He turned toward the screen, scrolled through the information twice, nodded grimly. His stomach began to constrict into a hard, tight knot.

Aubenay had indeed manufactured the seals—ceramic acrylics—and substructure for the Moonstation dome, ten years ago. But Ryton, Greene and Davis had provided the kiln and casting facilities, and had acted as consultant on construction. The work had been supervised by James Ryton, Michael's father.

"Legal, get me legal," Michael said. "Hurry."

2

THE ROOM was dark, quiet, illuminated only by a silvery spotlight. The light was trained on a thin male figure in white, bleaching all color from his shock of blond hair and pale skin. He was floating in the air, seventeen feet up, five inches away from the sloping, black-lacquered ceiling.

Silently, the petals of the circular door slid open, creating the illusion of an unblinking eye in which the iris was dark, the pupil transparent. And in the center of the pupil, a woman stood.

"How do you feel, Victor?" she asked. Her upturned face was stained silver by the lamp's glow. But the silvery veneer did not mask the strong nose and brow, the plump, voluptuous lips, nor the strong, restless nature beneath the skin. Hers was a fierce, predatory face, softened only by the fleshiness that came from wine at lunch and dinner, rich desserts, and other savory gourmet rituals of the international business elite. Tavia Emory camouflaged her bulky figure under elegantly flowing robes, layers of slithering microthin silk. Her deepset eyes sparkled gold. She was not mutant. But oh how she longed to be. And Victor Ashman knew it.

He floated down the air toward her, pedaling backwards

for comic effect until he stood lightly upon the gray woven-rubber carpet.

"I'm fine, Tavia. Much better."

"I'm so glad to hear it. After last time . . ."

"That's over with," he said quickly. "There's nothing to worry about. I'm stronger than ever." He smiled, showing even white teeth almost silvery in tone. "But when are you going to release me from house arrest?" His tone was light but his smile did not reach his eyes.

"Don't be ridiculous, Victor." She dismissed his complaint with a wave of her hand. "As my special guest, you have the run of the house. You're free to come and go as you please."

"Inside, yes. In fact, there are a few places I just might want to visit." He trailed a long finger down her neck, toward her cleavage. Tavia shuddered lightly.

Pleased, Ashman withdrew his hand. "But the front door doesn't respond to my voice command. Or to telekinesis. What have you got in it, my dear? Mental dampers like the ones they use in the storehouses?"

She ignored his question and, with a flounce, sat down on a large woven bronzed leather chair suspended by air streams. She pointed across the room at a green alabaster tripod table covered with amethyst cabochons of varying sizes. "If you're so strong, try to lift that table by the wall. Without knocking anything off of it."

Ashman stared intently, and the alabaster table soared toward the ceiling, each purple gem on its surface in place as though glued.

"Now levitate."

Eyes closed and lips compressed into a tight line, he floated upward until he was the silvery center of the table's orbit.

"Very good! You've made real progress." Her voice throbbed with rich satisfaction.

"Yes. I told you so." The table wobbled a bit in its orbit around him, slanting dangerously. Hissing, the amethysts slid toward the table's edge. Ashman made a small sound in his throat, halfway between a grunt and a whimper. The table righted itself, cabochons still firmly attached.

"Nice recovery."

She watched him for a moment more. Then, growing restive, she moved toward the wall panel.

"Lights!"

The room was bathed instantly in a golden glow.

Tavia Emory stood near the door, hands on her hips.

"One more test," she said. "Tell me what I'm thinking."

Still floating above her, Ashman closed his eyes. Smiled a tight, pained smile with his thin, colorless lips.

"You're thinking that you'd like to have a statue of me carved by Narlydda. Perhaps in synthetic amethyst. And that as long as you've given her that commission, you might as well select the subject too."

Tavia Emory clapped her hands gleefully. Her silken, copper-colored robes whispered as she moved.

"May I set myself down now, madam?" Ashman asked, bowing pompously from midair.

"Oh, of course, silly. Come sit here by me, Victor." She sank down onto the wallseat and patted the cushion next to her.

Ashman lowered the table and lowered himself to the capacious bronzed satin cushions. Curled on his side, head supported on one hand, Ashman watched her through half-closed eyelids.

"And just where is our young friend Yosh?" he asked. "Have you tired of him and sent him away? Does that mean there's a chance for me?"

"Yosh is visiting Narlydda in Mendocino. They're collaborating on the Moonstation Memorial."

Ashman arched a thin, perfect eyebrow. "I didn't know our musician was a sculptor as well."

"Well, you do know that Narlydda works in various media. She wanted the help of a musician familiar with spun ceramics—controlling its tonalities in pressurized environments."

"And he can answer her questions?" Ashman's look of surprise was genuine now. "I thought all he could do was tootle on that glass flute of his. Well, good for him. A breakthrough for his career, I suppose. And while he's away?"

Tavia smiled. "I love it when you flirt with me, Victor. It means you really feel good." She grabbed his hand impulsively. "Oh, we're going to do such wonderful things together, you and I."

"Tell me again." He leaned back against the pillows. "As if I haven't heard this before. Indulge me, Tavia. It's my favorite bedtime story."

"Once you're ready, we'll contact the mutant councils, the world governments and the media. Give them a demonstration of what you can do." She shook her head in amazement and delight. "You'll be such a rallying point, Victor. Such a symbol of hope and unity. If only Richard had lived to see this. He dreamed of the day when mutants and nonmutants would be drawn together. Finally, we're ready!"

Ashman smiled an almost-feline smile. "Your words are like poetry, Tavia. You convince me every time you say them." Gently, he kissed her hand. "Thank you."

She stared at him, mouth open, nonplussed. "For what?"

"For giving me hope. And more."

MELANIE BUZZED at Camphill's office door.

"Come."

The door slid back to reveal a semicircular room whose far wall was a clear slab of transparent plastic glass through which the filtered sunlight poured, casting an incandescent arc on the spotless white carpet. Everything in the office was white. Melanie slipped off her shoes. Randall Camphill reveled in little power games, and one of his favorites was requiring everybody on staff to remove their shoes at the door to his office. If he'd asked, his entire staff would have disrobed as well. Camphill's word and whim was law at Cable News, at least until he was promoted or deposed in an executive coup.

The curved walls of his office were lined with monitors, each tuned to a different news broadcast, each flashing pink, brown, yellow faces, white smiles, blue titles.

A good disaster really brought out the experts, Melanie thought. This one had even knocked the Soviet elections right off of prime time. She watched as a familiar face appeared on the lowest row of monitors: a woman in her late thirties, her dark red hair expertly coiffed. Senator Andrea Greenberg, known for her pro-mutant policies and pro-business stance. An unusual combination.

"What is it, Ryton?" He was seated behind his massive glass desk in which a thousand filaments of gold and purple swirled and twinkled in the sunlight.

"Mr. Camphill, I've got a story idea."

"About?"

"The Moonstation disaster. A closer look," Melanie said quickly. Camphill had a notoriously brief attention span. "We've heard from the scientists and politicians. We know that everybody thinks we should close Moonstation down or that we should plunge on deeper into space. Why don't we narrow the focus? Get away from the theorists and generals. We could do it with a feature on Kelly McLeod. The shuttle pilot who gave the first alarm. I went to school with her and I think I can give this a really personal spin."

Camphill shook his head. "Sorry, Ryton." He shifted in his high-backed white leather seat. His eyes stayed focused on a monitor to his left. "I just don't see the angle. Okay, so you and this lady shuttle jockey were chums. As far as I can see, she's just one more face in space. Been interviewed by everybody, including us, and five minutes ago makes it old news. Besides, that mutant shuttle commander has more star power. A cold character, if you ask me, but the audience just gobbles him up and begs for more. You didn't know him when you were a kid, did you?"

"No." Just a few other mutants, she thought.

"Too bad. If you could give me a fresh angle on him, well, I might go for it. You're a bright kid. If you come up with anything, flag me, and maybe we'll get Nesse in on it." Briefly, he looked at her, winked, then turned toward the wall of monitors behind his chair. The audience was over.

Melanie grabbed her shoes and, barefoot, stalked toward her desk. The last thing she wanted to do was give Lea any new angles. So Camphill thought that mutants had star power, did he? Maybe he'd like to see mutant gold up close. She could pop out her blue contact lenses and give *him* a wink. Maybe that would convince him she was anchor material.

Disgusted, she sat down heavily and reached into her drawer for a tab of Valedrine. Her hand closed on the pink plasticpak, but a flashing newsbyte pulled her attention to her deskscreen and its swirling yellow title.

"Reclusive artist Narlydda has received the Emory Foundation's commission for a series of multimedia works to be sited at Moonstation plaza. Details at five."

Narlydda! Melanie froze. What if she were to find *her?* That would grab Randall Camphill's attention . . . and maybe even win her a promotion.

Valedrine forgotten, she hit the audio button.

"Get me the Emory Foundation headquarters," she said.

A moment later, the Emory Seal, half fleshy Roman muse, half silvery moon rocket, splashed across the screen as though freshly painted, accompanied by a regal trumpet fanfare.

Emory Foundation was the brainchild and trust of Tavia Emory, and a memorial to her late husband, Richard, a space industrialist killed in the Soviet shuttle accident of '23. Five years before his death, he'd been the first businessman to establish orbiting polymer factories as adjuncts to the French and Soviet space stations. He'd made billions. Emory Foundation was the machine through which Tavia turned Emory Industries profits into good works, social position, and power. She strewed hospital wings and artistic commissions about as though they were party favors.

"Emory Foundation," the mech receptionist droned. "Your call will be answered in the order it has been received. Please don't hang up."

Melanie waited two minutes. Five. Finally, a human face stared at her. Curly brown hair. Olive complexion. Golden eyes.

"Emory Foundation," she said. "How may I help you?"

"Melanie Ryton, Cable News, calling about the Moonstation Plaza commission. I'd like to interview Narlydda for our weekend feature."

"Ah, yes, Ms. Ryton. Let me transfer you to public relations."

The Emory seal reappeared, then vanished. And Melanie was looking at yet another mutant, a young man of about twenty-five. His head was half shaved in the retropunk mode. An inlaid green and silver mutant unity earring dangled from his left ear. His eyes glittered.

"We have a taped release we can give you," he said. "It's a review of Narlydda's work, with quotes from her and the curators of last year's museum retrospectives. We feel it encapsulates her philosophy about art—and that of the Emory Foundation."

Melanie put on the professional smile which meant no thanks. "I'd prefer to interview the artist."

The young mutant didn't reply for a moment. A worried line creased his forehead. "I don't think that will be possible."

"Why?"

"We're under strict orders not to give out the artist's personal phone number."

"I see." Melanie frowned. "I'll get back to you." She broke the connection. She'd just have to look elsewhere.

THE SURF BOOMED in gentle percussion. Kelly pulled a pink conch shell out of a tuft of straw-colored dune grass and stared at it in surprise.

"I didn't think you could find these anyplace but a shell farm," she said. "Or a museum."

Heyran Landon looked up from his own beachcombing, every inch the commander, even when wearing a black thong swimsuit and sitting on a pristine white Caribbean beach. His skin was naturally tan—it hardly seemed affected by the sun. His golden eyes sparkled at her in a way she found disconcerting.

"A few places yet are left," he said. "To the very rich."

"Or heroic." Her wry expression made him chuckle.

"Especially to heroes after their rugged debriefing." He patted her shoulder. "Chin up, Kelly. You'd think there was something wrong with being a hero instead of a casualty. Relax. Enjoy the privilege that being a hero brings."

"It's only chance that separates us from the casualties. We were in the right part of the dome. So we lived."

"Bullshit. We lived because of your quick wits." Landon dusted sand from his palms. "And that's exactly what I told the brass. There'll be a promotion in this for you, Kelly. At the very least."

"If there's any service left, after the investigation. Today, a space hero. Tomorrow, a commercial pilot." She shook her head. "I just can't help thinking of those who died. . . ."

"Bad case of survivor's guilt, if you ask me. Look, there was nothing else you could do. Either of us could do."

"Do you really believe that?"

"I have to, to stay sane."

She pulled at a clump of seaweed. Then she tossed it into the frothy blue-green water. "I hope they dismantle whoever's responsible for the explosion."

"Oh, don't worry about that. They'll have a public burn-ing, make no mistake. And if they can't find somebody to play the goat, they'll invent him. Or select a 'volunteer.' Whatever they have to do to keep the public pacified. And keep the space program flying."

Kelly chuckled. "You're awfully cynical."

"I prefer to think of myself as a seasoned service veteran. Sounds much better than cynical." He paused. "It's good to see you smile, Kelly. Take my advice and soak up a new attitude before the investigation begins next Monday at Armstrong. This private playground is the perfect setting for it." He gestured down the length of the sparkling beach lined with palm trees. "At least it's a breather from that damned media circus back home."

"It's beautiful," Kelly said. "But what paradise is patrolled by dogs and guns?"

"These days, any paradise that wants to remain unspoiled. And free from reporters and video jocks, or should I say jerks? So lean back and enjoy it. That's an order."

"Yessir."

Kelly watched the sunlight dance on his light brown hair. An attractive man, she thought. A prickle of desire brought a swift, automatic rebuke. Down, girl, she thought. He's your commanding officer. Not to mention married. And half of the reason you're attracted to him is because he reminds you of Michael Ryton. Admit it.

She'd spent fifteen years putting as much physical space and work as possible between her and Michael. Pursued by unhappy memories, she'd run right into the Air Force, and from there to the shuttle corps. The last thing she needed now was to get involved with another mutant, much less a shuttle commander. Quick, think of something to say.

"When is your wife arriving?"

"Tomorrow." He looked at her thoughtfully. "Have you invited anybody to join you here?"

"No." She tucked a strand of dark hair behind her ear.

She'd considered asking Grant Tessalt. After all, she'd had a casual affair going with him for six months. But somehow she'd felt uncomfortable about asking him. She didn't particularly want to be alone. But she didn't want to be with Grant. Even if he was a major.

"Maybe you should reconsider," Landon said. He sat down in the sand and stretched. "Once the investigation starts rolling, you won't have much time for personals."

"Do you think it'll be that tough?"

Eyes closed, Landon nodded. "A lot of people are going to sweat before this one is over. Remember the hammering you got at headquarters? Just be glad you're on the side of the angels. For starters, I expect to see complete reshuffling of the Moonstation administration. And NASA as well. They'll be looking for somebody to hang, be it service, contractors, or the usual congressmen."

"I always enjoy a good public hanging of a congressman."

Landon smiled. "Me too."

His teeth were white, even, perfect against his tan. Kelly forced herself to look away, down the beach to the water where the blue-green breakers swelled.

"Heyran, can I ask you something off the record?"

He opened his eyes, raised an eyebrow.

"Sure."

"Why did you join the service?"

"It beat laying bullet train rails."

"Not by much. Come on, you know what I mean. I can count the number of mutants in the service on one hand, and still come up with spare fingers."

Landon grimaced. "You want to know why the exotic mutant asked what he could do for his country? The whole story?"

She nodded.

"It's simple," he said. "I was the sacrifice thrown to the military lions by the Western Mutant Council."

"What?"

Landon's expression was no longer playful. He stared out over the waves.

"Yeah. I was interested in mathematics. Planned on a career in solid-state computers. But my crime was that I was too steady. Too dependable. The military was clamoring for a pet mutant, and I was a safe choice: just enough telekinetic ability to be interesting, but not enough to toss a satellite at somebody. So the council decided I had a bright future in the shuttle corps. Provided a nice wife for me." He shook his head, lost for a moment in memories. "Know what the most surprising thing of all is?"

"What?"

"I've been pretty happy with this life. When I'm not grappling for dead bodies on the Moon, that is. Or ducking reporters." He looked at her, shading his eyes from the sun. "Shocked?"

"No," she said bitterly. "Mutant councils can be merciless."

Landon stared at her. His eyebrows curved upward in surprise. "You sound as if you speak from firsthand experience."

"Me?" She shrugged quickly. "No. No. Just picked up the impression from newscasts, I guess." She shoved thoughts of Michael back into the subbasement of her memory.

"I see."

With elaborate casualness, Kelly looked away. She sifted sand between her fingers, chased a small green crab with her toe.

Landon watched her for a moment. Then he stood up and stretched again. "Well, guess I'll go for a run. Want to come?"

"No thanks."

He trotted off down the beach, a slim, muscled figure silhouetted against the white sand, legs pumping. Kelly watched him go. For a moment, she imagined him without the bathing suit, in bed, suspended above her, eyes glittering. Quick, think of something else.

She looked out over the blue-green water swelling gently. Maybe she *was* being a fool. There was hard work ahead. And if she had company, perhaps her dreams wouldn't be so haunted by silent explosions in zero-G. Nor would her days center around her handsome, forbidden commander.

Don't be such an iron woman, she told herself. Give in. Get yourself a little comfort. She walked up the beach to the sleek wooden beachhouse and requested Grant's number from the wallscreen.

3

B RIGHT SUNLIGHT made patterns on the white floor-
boards and lavender rug. Narlydda looked at the wallscreen.
Nine o'clock. Time to key up the old art machine and get
going.

Her light easel stood in the corner by the broad picture
window. She turned her back on the view of rugged coast-
line and plugged in her brush. From the palette, she selected
a bronzed mix touched with green and sketched the curve of
a man's arm onto the screen.

Good, she thought. Model it just so. Now a bit of texture,
here and here. Maybe a bit more umber for shading.

She was sweating, the silken rose-colored robe sticking to
her back. Barely pausing in mid-stroke, she shrugged out of
the robe. Naked, she stood, a slim celadon figure framed by
the easel. She preferred to work this way. The room was
warm, especially with the sunlight spilling through the windows. And on foggy mornings the walls provided radiant
solar heat.

This is the way Skerry first saw me. Bursting through all
my defenses to find the naked artist.

Across the room, the wallscreen rang.

Go away. Leave me alone.

She sketched fiercely, but with one ear cocked, waiting for the simulacrum to take the call. On the third ring, it did.

"You've reached the studio of Narlydda," said a smooth female alto voice. "How may I help you?"

"Narlydda? Is it really you?"

The simulacrum Anne Verland paused. Narlydda could almost imagine the computer humming as it selected a quick response from its standard menu.

"This is not Narlydda. I am her business associate, Anne Verland."

"Oh." The caller sounded disappointed. "Well, please tell her my name is Wendy Thomas and that I just love her work, I'm her biggest fan. I've got holoprints of the *Lunar Web, Spanninger's Congress* and *Seventeenth Mile.*"

"Thank you. She will be pleased."

The caller rang off.

"I wonder how they get my number," Narlydda said.

"No system is completely sealed," the simulacrum responded.

Narlydda turned toward the screen. A rather prim-faced young woman with pale pink complexion, narrow lips, and gray eyes stared back at her. Anne Verland, faithful computer watchdog. Worth every Eurodollar she'd paid IBM/Bergen.

"That's true," she said, "but we do a pretty good job of keeping the riffraff out, don't we, Anne?"

"Yes, Narlydda."

"How does it feel, to be a ghost in the machine?"

"I'm sorry, Narlydda. I don't understand. . . ."

"No, you're not programmed to understand." Narlydda's golden eyes twinkled. "Never mind, Anne."

"Do you require further service?"

"Not right now, Anne. Thank you."

The screen shut down.

Narlydda turned back to the portrait. Her curiosity made her monitor most calls, even if she didn't want to talk to three quarters of the people calling. But it was time to stop teasing the computer and get back to work.

She'd planned a bronze and crystal figure, with elegant holographed details to capture the fleeting expressions that would play upon the face, the movement of hair, the rise and fall of the chest, breathing. On the light easel, a figure of heroic proportions had taken form, half aquatic creature, half man. Well-muscled across the chest, with large shoulders, bulging biceps. Long brown hair caught behind the neck in a ponytail. A clipped brown beard. Graceful finned tail curving up behind him. A beautiful merman. Narlydda stared at the sketch, shaken. It was Skerry, to the life.

"You're in love," she muttered. "At your age. Damn fool. It's the last thing you need right now. Especially when the object of your affections isn't talking to you."

The doorbell chimed a high, ethereal triad, notes floating in the air for a moment. The doorscreen showed a young Japanese man with long, sleek hair and dark eyes, wearing a tan leather jacket over a gray silk jumpsuit. A purple jewel glittered in his cheek.

Anne Verland flickered back to life. "Identity?" she asked.

"Yosh Akimura. From Emory Foundation. Narlydda's expecting me." His voice was a pleasant tenor.

You're early, Narlydda thought, and grabbed up her robe, settling it firmly around her. I haven't had time to put on skin dye, or even a mask. She hesitated. Oh, what the hell.

She hit manual override and unlocked the door. "Come on in."

Humming gently, the door slid back into the wall, giving the young musician just enough time to enter before it automatically slid back into place, locked.

Yosh nodded in admiration. "Nice system."

"It should be. Cost at least one sculpture."

He smiled. Then his smile faltered for a moment as he took her in. "Narlydda?"

"The real thing. Take a good look, young man. Not many

29

people have the opportunity." And I hope you're happy, Skerry, wherever you are. She leaned over her desk and picked up a pad. "Please read the top sheet and sign it. It's legally binding; a contract that you will not reveal to anybody in any way anything you've seen here. Just a formality, since Emory Foundation has a legal agreement that applies to each and every employee. Still . . ."

"You're into detail," he said. "Pen?"

She handed one to him. He signed with a flourish. She tore the top sheet off and fed it into the deskscreen.

"There. Well, so much for formalities. Come see my preliminary sketch, Yosh. Since we're going to be collaborating, I'll even ask your opinion."

Yosh chuckled, but the sound died in his throat as he stared at her light easel.

"You like it?"

"That's not the term I'd use." He paused. "It's very potent. Powerful. And beautiful. Sort of reminds me of Michelangelo's *David*. But not really."

"I'll accept that," she said, pleased by his comments. Well, so be it. Skerry would become the centerpiece of the Emory Foundation's Moonstation plaza. A mutant merman on the moon. "Sit down, Yosh. Something to drink?"

"No thanks. I'm ready to get started whenever you are."

"Eager beaver, huh? Well, I'm not quite ready to discuss materials, but—"

The screen rang.

"You've reached the studio of Narlydda," said faithful Anne Verland. "How may I help you?"

"Melanie Ryton," the caller replied. "Cable News. I'd like to interview Narlydda for our weekend features."

The screen showed a young woman of about thirty, blue-eyed, although somehow there seemed to be something vaguely Oriental about the eyes. Her straight, silky dark hair was blunt cut at chin level and just brushed the edge of her yellow, high-necked tunic. Her expression was all business.

"Cute," Yosh said. "Wish she were calling me."

"Well, she'd probably rather talk to you than to my answering machine," Narlydda said. "Not that she has a choice." The image Melanie Ryton saw on her screen was Anne Verland sitting at her workstation, auburn hair pulled back into a bun. She, too, was all business. "I'd love to know how these media vampires find my number. Maybe I'd better change it again."

"Narlydda is not available for interviews," Anne Verland said. "We have a tape available from her museum retrospective last year. . . ."

"I'm not interested in that." Melanie Ryton's tone was brisk, aggressive. Narlydda didn't care for it at all. "We want to give the Emory Foundation commission full coverage, and Narlydda's participation is crucial."

"I'm sorry," Anne repeated. "Narlydda is not available for interviews."

Good girl, Narlydda thought. Stonewall 'em.

"Can I reach her at this number later?"

"Narlydda does not answer this phone."

"This is her corporate number. Is there any other number where I can reach her?"

"Narlydda does not give out her private number."

"Then how can she be reached?"

"Narlydda does not give out her private number."

"You've already said that. Look, I've got to talk to her."

"I'm afraid that won't be possible."

"May I leave a message for her?"

"Narlydda does not return calls."

Ms. Ryton sighed in exasperation. Narlydda almost felt sorry for her, pesty though she was.

"I'd like to leave a message anyway."

"As you wish."

"Please tell Narlydda that I must speak with her. It's a matter of life or death—because I'm going to get killed by my boss if I don't get this interview. All right?"

"Your message has been recorded."

"Thanks. My number is 1213478712354. Ask her to call, day or night."

The connection was broken.

Yosh whistled. "Tough lady."

Narlydda chuckled. "Nice going, Anne. She was pretty insistent."

"Aggressive. Yes. Reporters are often that way."

Yosh gaped. "Your 'answering machine' is a simulacrum, isn't it? I didn't think any of those were commercially available yet."

"I have good contacts in software." She smiled slyly. "Anne is loyal, obedient, reliable. Almost everything I require in a companion." Almost.

"What is she programmed for?"

"Phone and door, grounds surveillance. But she can do much more."

"Such as?"

"Anne," she said, "what do I look like?"

"You are approximately one and three-quarter meters in height, sixty-five kilograms in weight. You are forty-three years old, born in Oregon, of mutant ancestry, telekinetic skills highly advanced. Appearance: light green complexion, dark green hair with white patch in front, long nose . . ."

"That's my description, give or take a few kilograms," Narlydda said wryly. "But what do I look like to you?"

Anne Verland paused. Narlydda could almost hear the computer circuitry buzzing, straining over the unexpected question.

"I don't understand."

"Never mind." Narlydda stared at the simulacrum. Should she put a portrait of Anne on the Moon? Immortalize her electronic amanuensis? It was an amusing thought. "Anne, how do you tell when there's a real emergency on the line?"

"Voice analysis is usually sufficient."

"What do you do then?"

"Notify the appropriate authorities or resources in the caller's vicinity."

Yosh cut in. "While they're still on the line?"

"Yes, it's a subsidiary connection, easy to make even while I speak with the caller."

"And does the subsidiary connection also see Anne Verland on the screen?" he asked.

"Of course."

"Don't you ever get confused about which Anne is which?"

"All of them are me," the computer replied serenely. "Narlydda had me programmed with multiple image capacity."

"Yes," Narlydda said. "Although half the time I forget what I've programmed you with."

"Would you like a printout . . . ?"

"No thank you."

The screen shut down.

"She's very good." Yosh shrugged off his jacket, reached into the pocket, and pulled out an envelope. "I brought you a personal message from Mrs. Emory."

He handed her a sleek blue micropackette. Narlydda clipped it into the wallscreen.

The Emory Foundation seal filled the screen. Then it dissolved to the image of Tavia Emory, dressed in golden silk and smiling her predatory smile. Her eyes twinkled with golden light.

"I didn't know she was mutant," Narlydda said.

"She's not."

"Narlydda," Tavia said, "Now that you're part of the Emory family . . ."

Like hell, Narlydda thought.

". . . I wanted to personally invite you to come visit. We'll be holding a small reception in your honor on the twelfth, to celebrate the Moonstation commission. I'm very excited about this work, and I hope to discuss it with you.

33

I'm sure many of your admirers will be on hand. And perhaps we'll be able to arrange a little surprise." She seemed to look away, off camera for a moment. Then she was back, focused like a bird of prey. "Until the twelfth. . . ." Tavia Emory faded away.

Narlydda reached for a fresh stylus. "Please convey my regrets to Mrs. Emory," she said.

"Are you sure?"

"Even if I planned to go out, I'd hardly be interested in some silly reception in the desert. Tell her thank you, but I'm just too busy in the studio. Mrs. Emory should know that I never attend these things."

"You spurn Tavia at your own risk," Yosh said.

"Tavia? You sound as if you know her quite well."

"I do."

They stared at each other for a moment. Then Yosh looked down.

"She usually gets her way," he said.

Narlydda crossed her arms. "So do I."

MICHAEL RYTON stared at the federal summons blinking on his deskscreen. He was being "invited" to attend an investigation into the Moonstation disaster on Monday, January 5, at Armstrong Airbase.

A preliminary head hunt, he thought. And they've just gotten around to me.

"Legal," he said. "And transmit screen message."

The deskscreen bisected the image field, retaining the summons in the lower half. Above it, Bill Sutherland's ruddy face appeared.

"Trouble, Mike?"

"You see the summons."

Sutherland nodded. "So your hunch was right. Too bad. Well, let's see." He leaned back in his chair, studying the screen. "As far as I can tell, you're probably in the clear. But your old man is damned lucky he's in the storehouse."

"You may be alone in that opinion."

"Hardly. Best defense these days."

"You mean he could be held liable for the disaster? How?"

"Well, let's just say that the record of his lobbying efforts to reduce safety regs for space engineering would make a convenient noose."

"But he was right! Dammit, Bill, those regulations were ridiculous. A waste of time and taxpayers' money, more cosmetic than effective. Besides, they didn't even relate to this project."

Sutherland shrugged. "With enough safeguards, the dome might not have blown, right? Even if nobody in the business would have manufactured that many fall-back systems. I'm a lawyer, not a space engineer, but I know how Federal investigators think. Where were the safeguards? And after the reporters are finished with you, what's left won't be worth much in this industry. When the dust settles, the Koreans will be the only ones building domes. You'd better come up with a rock-solid defense of the manufacturing process and materials."

"I wasn't even working on this project."

"I know. But you're the boss now. So, retroactively, you're responsible."

Michael sat back in his chair, thunderstruck.

"Shit."

"Yeah."

"I think you'd better plan on attending this with me, Bill."

"Of course." Sutherland gave him a wry, sympathetic look. "Cheer up, Mike. Things could be worse."

"How?"

"You could be François Aubenay."

"Keep reminding me of that." Michael rubbed his jaw, numb with shock. "Thanks, Bill. I'll get with you later."

Half the screen turned black.

"Save and store message. Research."

The summons disappeared, replaced by a view of the research department over Penny Lansdale's shoulder. She smiled at Michael, lines raying out from the corner of her golden eyes. But the smile faded as she saw his expression.

"What's wrong?"

"Bad news, Pen. Drop what you're doing. I need you to compile a detailed analysis and report on File R9C."

Penny turned to her auxiliary screen and requested the file. A moment later, she looked up. Her expression was grim. "Our assist with the Aubenay Moonstation contract. I remember it."

"I thought you were here then," Michael said. "Good. I need a solid defense, Penny. They're looking for somebody to hang. We've got to convince them that our neck is not the right size for their noose."

"Is it that bad?"

"Worse."

Her eyes widened. "I'll get right on it, Michael."

"Thanks, Pen." He cut the connection. What next? Might as well share the good news with Jena.

Dourly, he called her shop. She answered on the first buzz, her image bright in a turquoise tunic. Behind her, the walls of the store sparkled with precious objects.

"Expecting a call?" he asked.

Something about his body language must have broken through her self-absorption.

"Don't play games, Michael. I was near the screen, that's all. What's wrong?"

"Federal summons to the Moonstation investigation," he said.

"What? Why are they calling you?"

"My old man did some subcontracted work on the dome."

"He did?" She frowned in irritation. "Are we at risk?"

"Looks that way. I'll have to go to the West Coast next week. Want to come?" He managed a hearty tone. "You can get in some shopping."

She fiddled with her hair nervously. "I—I can't, Michael.

I'm expecting a shipment of Gabonese reed glass. I don't trust anybody else to unpack it. And who would watch the store?"

"Your staff."

"And Herra?"

"She's old enough to stay alone. She's hardly ever home anyway." For a moment, he stared at her. Blond hair framing her face, golden eyes glinting, she was as beautiful now as when he'd married her, fifteen years ago. Beautiful, selfish Jena. He admired her from a distance, as if looking at a holopainting.

"I don't want to argue, Michael, but it's out of the question. I'd like to be supportive, but I just can't go."

Just as he'd expected. He wasn't even angry, really. "If that's how you want it. I'll talk to you later."

The screen went black.

He'd stopped arguing with her long ago. Stopped looking for a way to bring them closer.

The room felt stifling. He peeled off his green silk jacket. Still sweating, he jumped up, paced to the sleek blue-green wall, then back to his desk. When would Penny finish that analysis? He was halfway across the room again when the phone buzzed.

Lari's voice came over the speaker: "Mr. Ryton? Your mother, line two."

Sue Li stared serenely from the screen, face framed by white hair. Her golden eyes were calm.

"Michael, I wanted to touch base with you about the mutant council meeting in Mendocino. Reservations and all that."

"Sorry, Mom. Skipped my mind."

"Big contract?"

"No."

"Something wrong?"

"Yes." He let out his breath in a high, irritable hiss. "I've been subpoenaed to attend an investigation on the Moonstation disaster."

As always, in times of trouble, Sue Li's face was as impassive as Buddha.

"Did you build anything for them?" she asked.

"Yes."

"Was the explosion your fault?"

"I don't know yet. But I don't think it was anybody's fault."

"No, of course not."

Her calm drove him crazy. "Just hope that nobody digs up the records of Dad's lobbying efforts."

Sue Li shook her head. "I told your father not to get involved in that."

"Well, he doesn't have to worry about it, does he?" Michael said sharply. "He's not the one who'll be testifying."

Pain flickered across his mother's face. He felt as if he'd just stabbed her. Stupid, he thought. "Sorry."

For a moment, she said nothing. When she spoke again, her voice was even, measured.

"Never mind. Is Jena going with you?"

"No."

Again, silence. Then Sue Li smiled gently.

"Then I'll keep you company. And we can both go to the mutant council meeting out there."

"Mom, I don't know if I'll have time for that . . ."

"When does the investigation begin?"

"The Monday after the council meeting."

"So you'll have plenty of time. At least you'll come with me to Dream Haven and see your father." It was not a request.

Michael dreaded visiting his father at the storehouse even more than he dreaded the investigation. He took a deep breath. "Of course. We can fly out together. I'll rent a skimmer or take the bullet train to Armstrong."

"And I'll notify the council to provide housing."

38

"Fine. I've got to go, Mom. . . ."

"See you next week, then."

JENA RYTON paced the length of the Piedmont auditorium, heels clicking against the polished gray acrylic floor. She paused, combed her hair, then nodded at her reflection in the window. She'd kept her figure, thank god. And had hardly a wrinkle to show for being a mother. And wife. She tapped her foot impatiently, admiring the glossy blue shine of her boot leather. Wade Walters had asked her to meet him after the officers of the Mutant Union's Eastern Division met, but he was late. She really should get home, especially tonight. Poor Michael. She honestly pitied him, up to his neck in a federal investigation. What a mess.

"There you are," Wade said, coming around the corner, an easy roll to his step, dark hair gleaming, mustache jaunty. As if he'd been the one waiting all along. He had his nerve. For a moment, she considered turning around and stalking away. But then he had his arms around her and she forgot about her anger, about her husband, about everything.

"I thought you'd never get here," she said, and kissed him lightly. The pressure of his body against hers was a maddening delight.

"Stand you up? Not a chance. That union meeting just took longer than I expected." Wade's grip on her grew stronger.

"Anything important happening?"

"The usual bureaucratic bullshit. More hat-passing by the Eastern Bloc rep. Dr. Sarnoff from Leningrad explaining why the Russian mutant population is so much smaller than that in the United States, and why, therefore, we should support our economically deprived Russkie brethren with dollars." He kissed her again.

Jena closed her eyes, savoring his touch. Once, long ago, she had felt this way with Michael, when they were both kids, before Herra was born. Where had that magical feeling gone? Leached out by routines, by diapers and business deadlines? For years now she'd shuffled numbly through the seasons: through clan meetings, Mutant Union activities, teacher-parent seminars. When Wade arrived last year, fresh from the West Coast, with his charming smile and a certain recklessness that matched her own spirit, she felt the attraction instantly. She'd fought it for a while. But only for a while. He made room for her. He wanted to see her. He'd brought her back to life. Even his voice was an aphrodisiac.

"Come over to my apartment," he said. "I'm finished for the day."

She pulled away from him reluctantly. "No. No, really. I can't. I've got to get home." Should she tell him about the investigation?

He didn't bother to cover his disappointment. "When am I going to see you?"

"Michael's going out of town next week. We'll have time then," she said. "Walk me to my skimmer."

"All right."

He opened the car door for her. Then he got in beside her. "Wade!!"

Telekinetically, he sealed the doors and pushed the seat down. She began to think of the other things he could do with his power, and felt her resistance ebbing.

Thank God the windows are opaque, she thought. He had her half out of her clothing, spreadeagled on the backseat like a teenager, moaning with delight. Just this once, she thought. This one affair. And when it's over, I'll be good. I'll be a good, faithful wife to Michael. I promise. I can do it. I know I can.

Then he was on top of her and she stopped thinking.

4

MELANIE set the computer to autoscan and scrolled impatiently through her file on Narlydda. She'd tracked her quarry to a corporate address and phone number, but the trail ended there. No trace of Narlydda's actual residence or studio. No phone number. It was as if she didn't exist. And that woman, Anne Verland, hadn't been much help. Maybe there really wasn't any Narlydda. It was all an elaborate scam by some Korean corporation, using computer graphics and a post office box in Northern California.

A shadow fell over the screen as somebody stood close behind her, blocking the overhead light. She whirled around to see Ralph Ferron grinning down at her.

"On deadline?" he asked.

She smiled. "Only my own."

He settled easily into the red float chair by her work station. His dark eyes watching her closely.

"What's up? You've been haunting the screen like one of Camphill's ghoulies on the late shift."

"The roving eye never rests." She smiled. "Deep background on a story."

"Tell me about it?"

She hesitated. Ralph was her favorite person at Cable

News. But she didn't want to give the scoop away. No, she wouldn't even tell him.

"Not yet." She watched his face fall in disappointment. "But soon. I promise. Why don't you tell me about the moon?"

"Swarming with security folk and media vultures. Like Metro L.A. without air."

"Or pollution."

"I knew there was some reason I liked it." He reached into his pocket. "Here."

A plaspak of dark sand shot through with odd sparkles landed with a thud on her keyboard.

"What is this?"

"Moondust. I never forget a promise."

"You're sweet." Melanie was tempted to give him a hug, but that would only cause trouble. She knew that Ralph liked her. More than liked her. And she'd seen what happened with office affairs; at worst, they were a temporary distraction from the job. At best, they led to serial marriage, lasting just long enough to deflect both participants from the inside track. Well, no thank you. Melanie wasn't interested in marriage, children, or even a weekend fling. What she wanted was to find Narlydda and show Randall Camphill that she was ready for the main news desk. If she could just get his attention with a big story—after all, she was as pretty as Nesse. Prettier, really.

"How about a break? Want to get something to eat? A new Malagasy place opened near La Brea."

She ignored the eager entreaty in Ralph's voice. "No thanks. You go." Please, she thought. Don't make me hurt you.

"Can I bring you anything back?"

"Uh, yes, a sandwich. A choba and sardine sandwich. That would be great." She gave him a big smile and he went away cheerfully. Sweet Ralph, she thought. The last thing you need is a nice mutant girlfriend to break your heart.

The screen blinked in front of her. Maybe she'd try art supply jobbers. And after that, fine art foundries.

"Ryton?"

The voice on her intercom was Randall Camphill's.

"Right here, boss."

"Drop what you're doing. I want you to get over to Armstrong Airbase and help cover the investigation of the Moonstation disaster."

"You do?" Melanie nearly dropped her remote scan control.

Camphill chuckled. "Yes, I do. You've been hot to get in on this disaster since the beginning. Well, here's your chance."

"Yessir." She grabbed up her screencase and headed for the door.

Ninety minutes later, when Ralph Ferron returned to the office with her sandwich, she was at the shuttleport, boarding a flight to the Mojave.

THE CABINS WERE NESTLED into a small hollow by the lake, gray, weathered redwood soft against the bright green foliage: sword ferns and pine trees, azaleas and bay laurels. Sue Li sniffed the air with pleasure. Dream Haven almost looked like a rustic resort. Until you noticed the blue-robed figures shuffling along pebbled paths, accompanied by gray-coated attendants. Or saw the groups gathered on benches under the trees, never speaking.

Sue Li had brought James here ten years ago. Oh, she knew she should have brought him sooner—he'd been unable to function for some time before she steeled herself to the inevitable. But she'd kept him at home, hoping that love and familiar surroundings could fight the relentless mental flares, that if she only held on long enough, the mutant scientists would discover a cure.

After James's second suicide attempt, her two sons had convinced her that she had done all she could. So she packed up her husband like a precious artifact and brought him across the country to be kept in a lovely redwood cabin in the green hills of Mendocino. Nearby, the cold blue Pacific Ocean relentlessly pounded the boulder-strewn shoreline. Here, at Dream Haven, the inmates led their half-lives in the twilight of drug therapy as their loved ones waited for the relentless pounding of their hearts to cease, to release them all from kindly bondage.

Beside her, Michael stood stiffly, remote in his gray suit, frowning slightly. This was probably harder for him than for her. And she wasn't finding it easy.

She adjusted her red cape and moved toward the matron at the first cabin.

Who? came the mental query.

James Ryton, Sue Li replied.

The woman nodded and withdrew into the building. Moments later, she led a stooped, shambling, gray-haired creature out to meet them.

Sue Li had last seen her husband six months ago. He had not looked good then, but these new changes were severe. His face was furrowed by lines. His skin had gone putty-colored. He neither looked at them nor away from them. Michael's eyes widened in shock.

I should have prepared him for this, somehow, she thought grimly.

"James? Can you hear me?"

A slow nod, his eyes unfocused, wandering.

She knew that the narcophalion depressed the speech center, but it was the best drug they had to combat the mental flares. And it usually stopped the awful screaming of the advanced cases.

"Do you know who I am?"

The same nod. But this time the eyes came upon her, moved to the left, returned. Stayed.

"Here, see, Michael's come with me."

The golden eyes never moved from her face.

Michael moved forward. "Hi, Dad. It's good to see you. Let's take a walk, and I'll give you an update on the business."

The older man's lips curved upward in what could have been a smile. The ghost of a smile. Sue Li thought her heart would break at the sight. She took a deep breath, cast a glance at her son, and moved forward to take her husband's arm.

"I STILL THINK you're asking for trouble, mating ceramic, metal and polymer," Yosh said. "The sculpture is going to be in a pressurized location on Earth and on Moonstation, but what about the trip up? I can't vouch for the acoustics if the thing cracks."

Narlydda looked up from a screenful of forging schematics, impatience scrawled across her face. "I'll let Emory Foundation worry about getting it there in one piece," she said sharply. "Your job is to make sure it sounds the way I want it to. Like a space harp."

"*If* it doesn't crack, it will sound fine," Yosh retorted. His face was flushed. "Those solar-activated chips will keep my divertissement recycling in random combinations—as you requested—through each moon day. To vary the harmonic texture, I've inserted three diminished themes in minor keys which repeat at unequal intervals." He turned his back on her. Gods, she could be irritating. And every bit as difficult to deal with as Tavia. He was glad this job was nearly over.

Behind him, he heard Narlydda sigh.

"Hey, don't get so upset," she said. "I know I'm prickly, but if we're both busy being temperamental, nothing will get done." Humor danced in her golden eyes. "Besides, it's my house. So I get to be the prima prima donna."

"You said it." Yosh's anger receded. He could never stay angry long anyway. He smiled quickly at the mutant artist—he'd almost grown accustomed to her unusual coloring—and sat down next to her at the desk.

"Do you think Mrs. Emory will like it?"

"Tavia will *love* it," Yosh said, mentally crossing his fingers.

Narlydda rolled up the sleeves of her lavender silk shirt. She always fussed with her clothing when she was pleased.

"Will she really?"

"Of course."

The artist turned suddenly and gave him a long, cool, penetrating look. "What is it between you two, if I may ask?"

"What do you mean?"

"You're blushing. And you know perfectly well just what I mean."

Yosh felt embarrassed and irritated. "I'm the musical consultant for Emory Foundation."

"Is that like being the court musician?"

"Come off it, Narlydda. If I'm court musician, that would make you the court artist, wouldn't it? Or would you prefer to be jester?"

Her smile froze. He'd scored a point.

"No, thanks," she said. "Sorry." Her voice was thin.

He stood up, anything to reduce the tension.

"Come on, let's break for lunch."

The screen rang. Narlydda jumped. She'd reacted this way for the past three days, each time the phone rang.

"Expecting a call?"

"Yes."

They both listened in silence while Anne Verland took the call. It was another taped fanfare from Tavia Emory entreating Narlydda to come for a visit.

"That's the third invitation she's sent," Yosh said. "Are you sure you won't reconsider? What's so terrible about a visit to Phoenix in the winter?"

"Nothing. But I know how tiresome these receptions can be. And I'd have to go in skin dye, wear a mask—I'm not exactly this free and easy with other people, Yosh. That's part of my mystique—who is Narlydda? What does she look like?" Halfheartedly she struck a flamboyant pose. Then, deflated, she sank down onto a wallseat. "Besides, I'd just hate to be out of town until I hear from . . . somebody."

"Oh." Yosh shifted from foot to foot, uncertain. He didn't want to pry into her affairs. In fact, he was edgy, restless, anxious to be gone from the fog and chill of the Mendocino coast, and Narlydda's uncertain moods. "Well, I've got to get packed. My shuttle leaves at four."

When he walked out of the room, he looked back for a moment. Narlydda, oblivious to him, was tracing the outline of her merman sculpture. Tears were slipping down the celadon curves of her cheeks.

MICHAEL HAD SEEN HIS FATHER just over a year ago, and remembered the visit as less than pleasant. By comparison to this, it had been a picnic. James Ryton just didn't seem to be the same man. Barely human. More like an animated corpse. By the time the visit was over, Michael was white-faced, tight-lipped with anguish. With relief and pity, he watched his father be led away by an attendant.

"That wasn't fun, was it?" his mother said.

He glared at her. "It's like he's walking dead," Michael snapped. "Is that what's waiting for me?"

"You know there's no way of telling. . . ."

"No, our blessed geneticists can't quite figure that one out, can they? So this hangs over our heads." Furious now, he levitated a large rock out of his way as he strode along the wooded path. It fell heavily, splitting the blackened trunk of a lightning-struck tree in two.

Sue Li hurried after him. "Michael, wait."

"He'd be better off dead!" Michael said, kicking branches out of his way on the path. "We all would be."

"Don't say things you'll be sorry for later."

He stopped abruptly and sank down on a weathered wooden bench, his face wet with tears.

47

His mother patted him on the shoulder. "I didn't think he'd look so bad. Next time, I'll come alone."

"No, that's okay." Michael took a deep breath. "With Jimmy in Argentina, I guess I've got to show the old family spirit." He wiped his eyes.

For a time, they sat together in silence. Not for the first time, Michael envied his mother's serenity and acceptance of what was. She could sit quietly in the forest and stare at the silver-leaved gooseberry bushes in the soft gray fog as though nothing had happened. As though she had not spent an hour with the wreckage of a human being: her husband. How does she do it?

Beside him, Sue Li stirred, shivered in the mist, and resealed her red cloak.

"Have you heard from Melanie recently?" she asked.

"Not for at least six months, and then it was just a note on e-mail concerning her dividends from Ryton, Greene and Davis. She's very busy with her job at Cable News." He shrugged. "Aside from her share in the company, I guess she's just not interested in family matters."

Sue Li's lips jerked downward. "I really mishandled that one," she said sadly. "Poor Melanie. I should have been more sympathetic. After all, it's hard to be a null. Why wasn't I kinder to her? Oh, if only we could go back." Sue Li shook her head, as if throwing off a demon, and her placid mask was back in place. Almost.

"Would you really redo your life if given a chance?" Michael asked. "How do you know it would come out any differently? Maybe Melanie's better off pretending she's a nonmutant."

"Maybe that's what she was meant to be," Sue Li said. "But I have so many regrets. I'm sorry now that I didn't encourage you more."

Michael stared at his mother, shocked by the admission. "What do you mean?"

"Oh, that time when you wanted to marry Kelly McLeod

and ran off." Sue Li closed her eyes with sorrow. "I came after you."

"That's what you had to do."

Her eyes flew open. "Was it? So that you could endure a loveless marriage that had the Mutant Council's stamp of approval? Oh, you can't fool me about the way things are between you and Jena, Michael. I was stupid. And a coward. Better you should have run, and found happiness with Kelly McLeod. She was such a nice girl. Jena would have had the child, no matter what. The genetic material would have been preserved, passed along. And the clan would have provided for Jena. These days, it scarcely matters if the mother is married."

Michael put his arm around his mother and hugged her tightly. "Don't blame yourself. None of us know if what we're doing will be the right thing, the proper path. The community was threatened. It had to be preserved. Now I believe that, too."

"But at such a price, Michael. Such a high price."

"I try not to think about it." He looked at his watch. At the white-trunked eucalyptus trees.

"Will you go to Armstrong Airbase now?" she asked.

"No. Just have to get together with my legal counsel to discuss the file." He forced a smile. "Do you want me to take you back to the hotel?"

"No. I think I'll walk a bit. The storehouse jitney can take me to the station later."

"I'll see you before the Mutant Council meeting tomorrow."

Michael kissed his mother on the cheek, then hurried toward his rented skimmer, grateful to get away. He glanced in the rearview mirror. Behind him, in the gathering fog, his mother was the only spot of color, of life, in all the terrible calm of Dream Haven.

5

"ALL JOIN NOW in meeting," the Book Keeper said. She was a short, gray-haired woman with a generous bosom. Regal in her deep red high-necked tunic, she radiated authority throughout the room. Conversations faltered, halted. Dozens of mutants in glittering silk, ragged jeans, metallic tunics, yellow shrink suits, and green sun robes drifted toward the vast meeting table and took their seats. Their skin tones varied, from deep tan to palest cream, with a few startling shades of celadon and violet thrown in by that old genetic jokester, mutant DNA. Only the eyes were the same, all of them the same. Golden and glowing. In fellowship, the mutants joined hands to begin their year-end meeting.

"Crank her up, Bekah!" called a young mutant with short black hair, gray skin, and a nose ring. His quip was met with chuckles and nods.

"We welcome our cousins from the East Coast," she said, and smiled at Michael and Sue Li. Around the huge table, a hundred golden eyes gazed upon them with acceptance and affection.

Michael nodded in acknowledgment. But he felt a little uncomfortable. How odd to be with a different council for the meeting. He had hardly gotten used to seeing somebody else officiate at the Eastern Council after Halden died. In fact, Chemen Astori, a slight, chipper half-Filipino, did a fine job of leading the Eastern clan. But this West Coast Council was different: looser, unpredictable, notorious for progressive thinking. Rebekah Terling had been Western Council Book Keeper now for ten years. Michael thought she seemed capable if a bit aloof. But he couldn't call his West Coast brethren aloof. They sat comfortably, at ease, joking and clowning as the Book Keeper called for order. It was all very informal, friendly, and good-natured. But strange.

The door to the meeting hall slid open, pushed by a blizzard of twinkling lights, glimmering particles flashing blue-green, silver-gold.

"Ho, ho, ho," said a sardonic male voice from the center of the whirlwind.

The particles coalesced into a tall, muscular, white-bearded figure wearing a flowing red-and-green robe with cuffs lined by white fur. On top of his head was a green candle, flame guttering as he moved.

"I am the ghost of Christmas present," the apparition intoned. "So be good, for goodness' sake."

The group broke into applause and laughter. The "ghost" bowed deeply, scattering wax everywhere, and slowly, the festive robes darkened, shrank to become a black silk kimono sashed in red at the waist, red leggings, and black leather boots. The beard turned brown, streaked by gray. The candle vanished. There were lines at the corners of the mischievous golden eyes. But the grin was familiar as ever.

"Skerry!" Michael cried.

His cousin turned and his smile broadened. "Kiddo! What are you doing here?"

He embraced Michael heartily, pounding him on the back, practically knocking the wind out of him.

"Thank you for joining us, cousin Skerry," Rebekah said. "I was wondering how you could top last year's performance." Her tone was dry, but not without humor. "Very impressive. But please don't delay us further. A place is ready for you."

Even as she spoke, a floatseat levitated away from the wall and settled down next to Michael.

We'll talk afterward.

With a wink to Michael, Skerry nodded and sat down.

"I will read from the Book, the fifth refrain from The Waiting Time," Rebekah said. "Please join with me." And in a lilting alto voice she led the clan over the familiar words.

> And when we knew ourselves to be different,
> To be mutant and therefore other,
> We took ourselves away,
> Sequestered that portion of us most other,
> And so turned a bland face to the blind eyes
> Of the world.
> Formed our community in silence, in hiding,
> Offered love and sharing to one another,
> And waited until a better time,
> A cycle in which we might share
> Beyond our circle.
> We are still waiting.

There was silence as Rebekah closed the book.

"We are still waiting," the clan intoned around her.

She looked up, a ghostly smile playing at the corners of her mouth.

"Perhaps we will not have to wait much longer," she said. "Please share that hope with me now." She closed her eyes and lowered her head.

The familiar linkage caught them all in its gentle embrace. Michael felt the affectionate mindtouch of his mother and the vibrant energy of Skerry beside him. Then self-awareness faded as the groupmind asserted dominance: a loving harmony of shifting chords and thoughts in which all was accepted, forgiven, understood, and healed.

Michael floated freely in the current of the groupmind, at ease, at peace. He scarcely noticed as the internal melody shifted slightly into a minor key, something discordant sounding there for a moment. Then resounding. A wailing, strident echo shattered Michael's calm. It echoed from head to head in hot orange tones, amplified with each mental bounce. Harmony shredded. Clan members clutched their heads in pain, wrenched from the circle of intimacy. A sharp, insistent thought pounded at them like a drum, tearing asunder the shared moment.

BEWARE THE SUPERMUTANT! BEWARE THE SUPERMU-TANT!

"Who is causing this disruption?" Rebekah demanded aloud, above the mental din. "What is the meaning of this?"

Michael stared around the room. Beside him, Skerry jumped to his feet. His mouth was set in a grim line. Squinting, he surveyed the assembled group, slowly narrowing his focus to a tiny, wizened old woman.

"Leita!" he exclaimed. "It's you. I knew it."

She laughed. The sound was low and chilling.

"Crazy old bitch! Either you stop this feedback or I'll stop it for you!"

The noise eased, faded, vanished. "You don't frighten me, Skerry," the old woman rasped. "You and your parlor tricks. None of you can scare me." Leita was on her feet now, almost skipping around the table. "But you're scared, aren't you? The supermutant is coming. In fact, he's here. Is he of us? Which clan? Nobody knows." She cackled like a witch.

"Stop talking in riddles," Rebekah said. "What supermutant, Leita? What do you see?"

"Oh, you're not going to start believing her loony predictions now, are you?" Skerry rolled his eyes. "I've seen normals who had better accuracy."

Rebekah ignored him. "Leita, what do you see?"

The old woman stopped her odd skipping dance and sat down. Her voice took on a crooning tone.

"He's come. Turn on your wallscreen, Bekah. He's sitting there, bold as day. There's a ring of power around him would burn any mutant esper trying to get through." She gave Skerry a sidelong glance and smiled with open malice.

"Screen on," Rebekah said. A patch of wall behind her came to life, rainbow colors resolving into a news bulletin. Anchorwoman Nesse of Cable News was interviewing a pale young man. His hair was so blond it almost looked white. And his eyes—they were a startling shade. Not brown, nor blue, not green nor hazel. Not even mutant gold. They were icy, opaque silver. The shimmering iris was banded by violet.

Michael shivered. The man looked unearthly.

Skerry whistled tunelessly. "Holy shit," he said. "Where did he come from?"

Every golden eye in the room was trained on the screen.

"Audio," Rebekah requested.

"Mr. Ashman, just exactly how can you claim to be an evolved form of mutant . . . a 'supermutant,' as you say?" Nesse asked.

"Easily," the man replied. He had a soft tenor voice, almost girlish. "For example, you're thinking that I'm probably some kind of glory-seeking hoaxer. And you're also wondering how you can turn this into a scoop that'll further your career without making you look like a naive fool, but you're not sure if it's worth the risk and—"

"Thank you." Nesse's face was red. "Well, apparently, you can read minds, but many mutants have telepathic abilities, or so we've been told. What makes you special?"

This time, the man remained silent. He smiled. And every piece of blue furniture on the set except his chair levitated out of camera range.

"Mr. Ashman, please let me down." Nesse's voice sounded shrill. Panicked.

He nodded. The furniture, with anchorwoman in place, floated down and gently settled back into place.

"Well, that was interesting." Nesse straightened her tunic and ran her hand over her bald head self-consciously. "But we've all heard about doubly talented mutants. At least, some of us have. What else can you do?"

I can talk to everybody in your audience without opening my mouth. In fact, even as you hear this in your mind, Nesse, every person watching this, mutant and non, is also hearing my voice in their head, regardless of where they are, on the planet or in space.

Ashman stared pleasantly into the camera.

"Omigod," Michael said aloud.

Ashman's words perched in his mind. He began to sweat. His pink shirt was sticking to his back. That mindspeech had been direct, clear, as though Ashman had been standing across the room. Slowly, very slowly, the sense of psychic invasion dwindled. His pulsebeat calmed.

"Bad news," Skerry said. *"Very* bad news."

Onscreen, the young man with silver eyes smiled.

6

SCREEN OFF. Opinions? Suggestions?" Pale but controlled, Rebekah looked around the room. The clan was silent. Michael thought they all seemed stunned. Even Skerry had nothing to say. His expression, for once, was sober.

"We've got to find out who this guy is," Michael said. "Where he came from."

"He doesn't even look mutant, not like us," said Sue Li.

"He isn't like us," Leita said. "That's the point."

"What kind of crazy mutant would expose himself on the news?" asked a young woman with olive skin and wildly curling blond hair. "And with silver eyes? He's a fake. Has to be."

"Or crazy."

"He'll cause trouble for all of us. The normals won't be able to handle it. They'll lynch him."

"Just so long as it's him and not us," Skerry said.

"We've got to find out who he is," Rebekah said. "And right away. Any volunteers here?" She stared pointedly at Skerry.

"Oh no." He stood up, holding his hands out in warning. "Don't look at me, Bekah. I just remembered an important appointment in Tangiers . . ." Even as he spoke, Skerry seemed to fade away until all that was left was his voice, trailing behind.

Rebekah leaped to her feet. "Skerry, come back here! How can you run out like this when we need you?"

The wind whistling in from the open door was the only answer she received.

"I'll go catch him," Michael said. He grabbed his gray jacket and hurried out into the dusk.

Rebekah called after him. "Be careful out there. It's easy to get lost."

The fog gave a soft, spectral feel to the twilight. In a moment, Michael was far from the meeting hall, on a sloping path leading into wooded canyon.

"Skerry? Come on, don't go away," Michael called. "I haven't even had a chance to talk to you."

No answer.

Michael levitated over a stand of red-trunked manzanita and landed in a clearing ringed by towering eucalyptus trees. Their clean, balsam scent was powerful in the still air.

"Skerry! Dammit, I know you can hear me."

Michael walked deeper into the woods. It was no use. He'd never locate his elusive cousin. The path divided and he hurried on along the left-hand fork. He passed gooseberry bushes glowing in the dusk. The silence was unnerving. He looked behind him. Which way had he come? He levitated upwards, but below him was a canopy of pines and eucalyptus.

Cursing, he landed and tried to retrace his steps. Surely the path was over here. No. Well, here then. If only he had mindspeech, he could call out to the clan. Or night sight, so that he could see beyond the trees. Just as he was beginning to consider shouting for help, he felt a mental prickle.

Stop bashing around. These are all protected native plants.

"Skerry?"

No. If you're looking for that other esper, he's about two miles away, heading south fast. Hold on, I'll call him for you. There. He's coming back.

"Who are you?"

The linkage faded. In its place, a buzzing came, almost electronic. Like a swarm of angry metal bees.

All right, I'm back.

"Jesus, you are a pain in the ass," Michael said. He sank down on a rock. "First I get lost in the woods looking for you, then the old man of the forest tells me to keep off the grass."

Jason? He's all right.

Michael looked over his right shoulder. His left. All he saw was darkness. "Dammit, Skerry, materialize. I'm tired of talking to phantoms."

Don't be so touchy.

The buzzing took on a rhythmic quality, almost musical, and then it *was* musical: the "Flight of the Bumblebee." Suddenly, a thousand golden insects beat their wings against the night sky, flying in formation, coalescing, until in place of the bees was a bearded, grinning mutant. Skerry.

"Could you turn off the soundtrack, please?"

The woods were silent.

"Thanks."

Skerry sat down next to him. "Well, did you have Jason call me back just so you could criticize my musical taste?"

"Get serious. You *know* why I came after you. I think you should go check out that guy Ashman. He's strange. Scary. Don't you care?"

"Of course I do." Skerry's tone was sharp. "But I don't like being ordered around. Skerry do this. Skerry do that. Quick, Skerry, save the supposedly free world from itself." He made a sour face. "I'm getting kind of old for this stuff. Isn't there any other member of this clan who can go check out this so-called supermutant?" He paused and gave his cousin the once-over. "You look like you're in pretty good shape for a desk jockey. Why don't you go?"

Michael grinned. "Don't be ridiculous. Besides, I've got enough problems already."

"Such as?"

"The Moonstation disaster."

"What have you got to do with that?" Skerry's tone was incredulous.

"My old man helped build parts for the dome that blew."

"So?"

"So I've been invited by the government to discuss this at Armstrong Airbase on Monday." Michael forced himself to sound genial, unconcerned.

"Jesus, a congressional investigation?" Even Skerry was impressed. "Think they'll nail you?"

"If they can. But I'm not going to give them any help."

Skerry patted him on the back. "That's the spirit. Okay, so that's one catastrophe. What else? No, wait. Let me guess. The gorgeous wife."

Michael nodded curtly.

"Where is she, by the way? And the bambina?"

"Back home in Piedmont. The bambina is almost fifteen. And just like Jena."

"A looker?"

"Of course." Michael's voice was acid. "And just as self-absorbed."

Skerry chuckled. "I'm glad you said it instead of me. But who told you to marry her?"

"The Mutant Council, remember? There was this slight case of pregnancy. . . ."

"You've gotten sarcastic in your old age, kiddo." Skerry stood up, stretched. "Not that I blame you."

Michael followed his lead. "Oh, go ahead and blame me. I think I was a fool not to follow your advice and take off years ago."

"The road's not for everybody, Mike."

"No, especially not for mutants who put community before their own best interests." He gave a self-mocking smile.

"And I've given the precious community my daughter, for all the good it will do them. I've no doubt she'll have herself sterilized before she's nineteen. She's already had a contravention block."

"Just as well, unless you're eager to be a grandpa."

"No thanks." Michael stared up at the stars twinkling above them. They were cool, silvery. Like Ashman's eyes. He turned to his cousin. "Are you afraid of this supermutant?"

"No. Just tired." His voice had a hollow ring to it. "Come on, let's get out of the woods." Skerry began walking uphill at a healthy pace.

Michael hurried after him, eager not to get lost again.

"Do you think he's for real?"

"No. If I did, then I might be scared. He's probably just some jumped-up multitalent."

"Not like any other multi I've ever met," Michael said.

Skerry stopped walking. "What do you mean?"

"Well, his control. I can't levitate and use my telekinesis at the same time. I don't know anybody else who can, either. But Ashman didn't seem to flinch, even when he was mindspeaking while levitating an entire set full of furniture."

"Hmm. Good point." Skerry stroked his beard. "Can you ever switch back and forth long enough to appear to be doing both?"

Michael snorted. "Maybe if I trained from birth, like that mutant girl in the Moscow circus. Jesus, that's hard work, Skerry. I don't know who could do it." He paused. "But if your hunch is right, I'll bet he can't use multiple skills for long. It's too hard. Like holding up a heavy weight in each hand. Sooner or later, one of your arms starts to shake."

"I see what you mean."

The meeting hall loomed up in the darkness, its halogen lamps casting yellow circles on the path before them. The doorway glowed with recessed lighting, like a beacon.

"Well?"

Skerry hesitated. "I don't know. I need to think about it. Besides, I've got some things to take care of right now."

"Things?"

Skerry shrugged. "Some business, which will keep me out of town just long enough, I hope, to make me feel like kissing and making up with a certain lady I know."

"Had a romantic spat with some chip runner?"

Skerry's eyes flashed with anger. "Don't ask stupid questions, Michael. I've got a short fuse these days." He shook his head. "Dammit, I miss her."

"Who?" Michael was wildly curious—Skerry so rarely talked about his women. "Is she involved in business with you?"

"None of your business and no."

"Sorry." Well, maybe he'd never know, Michael thought. There had always been mysteries about Skerry. Probably always would be. He could live with that.

"So leave me alone. It's my concern and I'll decide what I will or won't do."

"Suit yourself. But you tell Rebekah."

"She'll figure it out on her own. She's all right—a little pushy. But so was Halden. Book Keepers always are." Skerry nodded and turned to Michael. "Listen, I'll be checking in with you during the investigation. If you need my help—or somewhere to run—don't hesitate."

"Let's hope it won't come to that." Michael squeezed his shoulder. "Besides, you're pretty hard to find sometimes."

NARLYDDA HAD WATCHED the news broadcast with cool fascination. Again, she scanned the tape. Ashman's face was peculiar: almost genderless, with a sharp nose, thin lips, high cheekbones, and of course, those eerie, silver eyes.

"Hold," she told the computer. The image onscreen froze. She leaned over and grabbed a sketchpad. Quickly, with great economy of line, she captured the supermutant's triangular face, his short, silvery hair, elongated bone structure.

If he's really the supermutant, then he probably knows I'm doing this.

Impulsively, Narlydda added horns and a halo to the sketch.

There. Let him really get an eyeful. The sketch pulled loose easily from the pad. Should she fax it to her agent? Send it to the L.A. *Times* editorial section? For a moment, she was tempted. Then she crumpled the sketch and threw it in the corner. He was probably a sham. But an interesting one. What would he be like in person? Shy? Aggressive?

Why not find out? Emory Foundation was hosting Ashman and handling his publicity. Well, maybe it was time to take Tavia Emory up on her persistent invitations. Besides, Skerry had been out of touch for over a month. Narlydda turned toward the computer. "Anne, get me Tavia Emory."

KELLY SAT in the rec lounge, watching the wallscreen in amazement. This Ashman, could he really be what he claimed? An evolved mutant?

"Jesus, do you believe this?" Ethan Hawkins, first officer of the shuttle *Brinford,* sat down next to her. His dark face was somber. "I don't know whether to laugh at him or go hide under the bed."

"Me neither."

"Have you seen Landon around?"

"No. But I'd love to hear his opinion." Kelly shivered. "This guy gives me the creeps."

Hawkins nodded. "Me too. He's got to be a fake. Got to be."

"But what if he's not?"

"If he's not, he'd better hide his ass. Every scientist is going to want a piece of it. And every army as well." Hawkins took a sip of coffee and nodded slowly. "If I were Mr. Ashman, I wouldn't be so free about advertising my wares."

• • •

JENA LOLLED in bed, naked, wrapped in orange sheets, watching a tape of the supermutant interview. Across the room, Wade was on his private screen with Mutant Union officials. She barely noticed; her attention was riveted to the silver-eyed Ashman. Her cheeks were bright, her eyes flashed. I've got to meet him.

Wade sat down beside her and stroked her cheek.

"Show you a guy with silver eyes and you get all excited," he said. "Not that I mind."

She shook off his roving hands. "He's fascinating. Wade, I can hardly believe it. After all these years of talk, talk, talk, we've finally gotten a supermutant!"

"We?" Wade lifted an eyebrow.

"Well, he's got to be related to some clan, doesn't he? Oh Wade, who is he? Where did he come from?"

"That's what we're trying to find out."

Jena grabbed his shirt in excitement.

"What do you know? Tell me. Tell me."

"You were at the council meeting." Wade shrugged. His tawny hair slanted down across his forehead into his eyes. He brushed it away impatiently. "We're all stumped. But after tomorrow, maybe we'll know a little more."

"What do you mean, after tomorrow?"

"A group of top Mutant Union officials is going to meet with Ashman and interview him. We'll try to learn what we can."

"Oh, Wade, take me along!" Jena jumped up, throwing off the sheet.

"Don't be ridiculous."

"It's not ridiculous at all. I'm a dues-paying Union member. Why shouldn't I go?"

"It's for union officials only."

Jena pouted. "Why can't you bring me along as a companion?" She put her hand on his thigh, slowly moving it upward. "You'll get lonely in Arizona. I couldn't bear for you to be lonely."

He grinned at her. "You're relentless, aren't you?"

"Completely." She slipped her hand under his shirt. He leaned back against the silken apricot pillows.

"What about your poor husband at that investigation?"

"Don't let's talk about him now." Jena nuzzled against him, and he cradled her in an easy embrace.

"Why don't you leave him?"

Jena started laughing. "Oh, Wade. Don't be ridiculous. We've been through this before. I couldn't. The council frowns on it. And besides, there's Herra to think of."

His expression turned icy, and he stood up, moving beyond her reach. "You still love him." His voice was sad, almost reproachful.

"Well, yes, I guess I do." She surprised herself with the admission. Quickly, she reached for his hand. Squeezed. "But that doesn't mean I don't want to be with you. We have such a wonderful time together."

Wade shrugged out of her grip. "Look, I've got to go."

"What about the supermutant?"

"It's out of the question."

"But Wade . . ." Flabbergasted, Jena watched the door slide closed behind him. It's not fair, she thought. The most exciting thing to happen in mutant history, and I'm stuck at home.

She turned back to the wallscreen. "Replay."

7

A HOT WIND blew out of the desert, roaring north toward the coastal megalopolis that stretched from San Jose to San Francisco, hundreds of miles away. It set the eucalyptus leaves dancing on their long, viny stems. The manzanita, the dry grasses, all whispered and nodded, accustomed to the vagaries of weather, even in winter. Even in California.

"Strange wind," Melanie said. "Isn't it supposed to be cool and rainy out here in January?

The guard shrugged. "I'm from Pennsylvania, myself. But I've been here long enough to know that anything can happen in the desert. And probably will." He inspected her press credentials and waved her on.

Melanie scanned the empty spaces around the Spaceport. Tawny as a lion's back, a flat, dry landscape with muscular, rolling hills in the distance. The dry lakebed on which Armstrong was built was a perfect site for runways and launchsites. Even the buildings were sleek, low to the ground and sand-colored. Everything looked new, rebuilt in '15 after the Houston/Gulf spill made California the center of shuttle operations in North America.

She hurried into the auditorium where the Moonstation investigation was being held. Her credentials got her a front row seat in the press section. She staked out her territory with the crylight nametag she'd been given, then went looking for a cup of coffee. The hallway ped strip was moving at a good clip when she saw a vending mech rolling past, lights blinking, in the opposite direction. She jumped off the grid and hurried after it, nearly bumping into a dark-haired young woman wearing a purple Shuttle Corps jumpsuit.

"Sorry."

The woman grabbed her arm and stared hard. "Melanie? Melanie Ryton?"

It was Kelly McLeod.

"My God," Melanie said. "Kelly. Is it you?" They hugged briefly, almost out of instinct. Then, suddenly self-conscious, they pulled back, awkward strangers despite their teenage friendship.

"You look so official in that outfit."

Kelly chuckled. "That's the idea. And you don't even look like a mutant with those blue eyes—what are they, contact lenses?"

"Yeah."

"So that *was* you, all those years ago, in Colorado?"

Melanie flushed with embarrassment. "Uh, yeah. I guess I wasn't ready to admit who I was to anybody then."

"Don't worry about it." Kelly laughed easily. "It's nice to see you again, with or without golden eyes. Are you here because of Michael?"

"Michael?" Melanie gaped at her. "What are you talking about?"

"Your brother. He's been summoned as part of the Moonstation investigation. Didn't you know?"

"No. I'm here covering the investigation for Cable News."

"Oh."

They stood in silence for a moment as the information sank in.

"He's in trouble?"

"Looks that way. Haven't you been in touch with him? I would have thought he'd tell you about it."

"Uh, not for a while." Omigod. What do I do now? Melanie began to sweat under her red silk tunic. "Is he all right? Have you seen him?"

"Yes."

"Is his family here with him?"

Kelly looked down. "I don't think so."

"Figures. That Jena always was a bitch. She's the last person I'd expect to be helpful. Has he seen you?"

Now it was Kelly's turn to flush. "Uh, no. I—I guess I don't really want to talk to him. Past is past."

"I guess." Well, that was her business. "Where is he now?"

"I don't think he's shown up yet. They're still doing preliminary questioning. He's probably back at the guest quarters."

"I've got to see him." And she meant it. Suddenly, Melanie wanted to see her brother very badly. To stand with him. Especially if he was here all alone. "Do you want me to tell him you're here?"

"No. Please." Kelly's tone was urgent. "Melanie, please don't say anything. Remember how badly you wanted to leave your past behind? I understand how you felt. Can't you understand that there are parts of my life that I never want to think about again? And your brother is one of those parts."

Well, that was direct. "All right. I guess you have your reasons. I won't mention you. But I'd better run if I want to catch him before this session starts, and I have to be back in the press gallery. Can we meet later? I want to hear all about the rescue."

"And I want to talk to you about this strange supermutant guy."

"Ashman?" Melanie rolled her eyes. "I'm sure he's a fake."

"Well, whatever he is. Let's talk soon. You can reach me at the Shuttle Corps dorm. I'm in room 19A."

Melanie was already halfway down the hall. "Good. I'll catch you later, okay?" Without waiting for an answer, she waved at the purple-clad figure and raced for a payscreen.

In a different segment of North American desert, Tavia Emory was not having a good day. She bustled along the carpeted corridor of Emory Headquarters, ignoring the desert view through the filtered windows, wishing she were anywhere else—in her private quarters, floating in her lap pool. But no time for that now. She'd already had Security eject three free-lance video jocks who'd somehow found their way into the guest wing. Then Ashman had refused to meet the delegation of government officials from the Pentagon, claiming fatigue. Dr. Sarnoff was with him now. Maybe that would help. Meanwhile, a group of mutants was camped on her doorstep, demanding to see the supermutant. In all the fuss and chaos, she'd even forgotten to put in her gold contact lenses. Gray-eyed, she gazed upon her mutant visitors, envying them the obvious marks of their mutancy. The only bright spot in all of this was that Narlydda had finally accepted her invitation. So much for Yosh. He'd told her to forget about Narlydda. Well, she'd remind him of that later.

Tavia entered the reception hall. The Mutant Union delegates were gathered by the window. A short, gray-haired woman in forest green—what was her name? Rebekah?—approached once again.

"Mrs. Emory, surely you can appreciate our position," she said.

Tavia gestured impatiently. "Of course, of course. You know I'm sympathetic to you. But as my aides have told you repeatedly, Mr. Ashman is not seeing anybody today. He simply has too full a schedule."

"We'll wait."

Stubborn woman. Well, why not? Mutants had to be stubborn to get anywhere. And she'd rather have Ashman talk to them than to a bunch of generals with ribbons on their shoulders anyway. He wasn't meant to help the military. He would be an agent of peace.

The office door irised open. Ashman stood, white robes glowing, a figure out of a dream or an illustration.

"What are you doing here?" Tavia cried. "You know you should be resting."

Ashman stared at her coldly and turned away toward the group of mutants clustered by the wallseat.

"My friends and cousins, welcome." There was a forced vibrancy to his voice. He moved quickly—too quickly, as though he didn't quite trust his legs—across the dark red carpeting toward the windows. Sat down on the bronzed wallseat and beckoned the others to join him. They gathered around him in a loose semicircle.

"Mr. Ashman, we represent—"

"I know who you are, Rebekah. I'm so pleased you've come."

Her face paled at his words, but her expression remained firm. "Yes, well, we wanted to ask you—"

"Don't worry." He smiled reassuringly. His small teeth were even and neat. "We will work together. I would like to address a meeting of the Mutant Union at the earliest possible opportunity. And the mutant councils as well."

Rebekah glanced at several of the mutants around her.

"Oh, I know you have many questions," Ashman said pleasantly. I can see them bubbling away in your minds. Please, ask me anything. I want to set you at ease."

"Well, I would have preferred to discuss this in private," Rebekah said.

Tavia squeezed her way through the group and sat down next to Ashman. "Now Victor, isn't it a little too soon to talk about meeting with groups?"

"Nonsense. I feel fine." He patted her hand affectionately.

"Tavia is such a mother hen," he said, chuckling. "But feel free to speak in front of her. She is absolutely trustworthy."

Tavia didn't like the tone in his voice. What was happening to him? A moment ago, he'd seemed on the verge of fainting. Now, his voice was strong, vibrant. He glowed with charisma. The mutants seemed stunned to silence. Then the woman named Rebekah spoke.

"Well, yes, we do have many questions," she said. "To begin with, to what clan do you belong?"

"Every clan. And none."

"Is that a riddle?"

"It's an answer." Ashman smiled beatifically.

"Why didn't you come to us first?"

He levitated a hammered copper bowl of fruit across the room, selected a yellow apple, then passed it in front of the group. "Please have something. Oh, go ahead." As the bowl floated before them, the apple began to peel itself, the skin twirling off in golden curls, disappearing in midair. When no one made a move, Ashman sighed and set the bowl back down on the table before him.

"It didn't seem appropriate to contact you. Or necessary. I knew that you would come to me."

"I see." Rebekah exchanged a meaningful glance with a tall, dark-haired man next to her. "As I was saying, about meeting," she continued. "We would like to invite you to a special council meeting in two weeks."

"I'd be delighted," he said. "I hope to preside at future meetings, of course, but I suppose preliminary arrangements are in order."

"Preside?" Her face paled.

"Oh, let's not talk about that now." Ashman waved his hand in dismissal. "We'll have time to discuss all this later, I'm sure," Ashman said. "I have no doubt we'll all be able to work together as a family." He nodded. The group around him seemed fascinated, Tavia thought. Almost hypnotized. Then, like a door closing, the spell seemed to end. Ashman's skin turned a pearly gray. Beads of sweat stood out on his forehead. He seemed to sag in his chair, energy ebbing.

Tavia took control. "You'll have to excuse him," she said. "He needs to rest now. Please come back sometime next week." She smoothly ushered them toward the door, through it, down the hall, and into the waiting arms of her public relations staff. They would see the Mutant Council out. Tavia turned and hurried back to the reception hall. She found Ashman pacing back and forth.

"Victor, are you all right?"

"Fine." He looked furious. "You had no right to make them leave, Tavia. I wasn't finished with them yet."

His words sent a chill through her. "But I thought we agreed . . ."

"I've decided to take a more aggressive approach," he said. "Beginning with making decisions about what's best for me." He locked his gaze with hers.

For a moment, she struggled. How dare he? After all she'd done for him. Taken him in and . . . but his silvery eyes were lustrous, compelling. She couldn't take her eyes off them. Silver, rimmed by violet. Beautiful. Peaceful. Well, he probably knows best.

"I was told you needed me," a deep voice, strongly accented, announced.

Dr. Sarnoff stood in the doorway, his full, dark mustache adding a doleful touch to his already stern expression. He was a small man, almost swamped by his blue lab coat. "I was busy in your laboratory, Mrs. Emory. . . ." He paused, observed them with glittering golden eyes. "Victor, you are straining too much." He turned to Tavia. "And you are pushing too hard. Leave him alone."

"I only want what's best for him."

"Then don't argue with him," Sarnoff snapped. "Or me." He gestured for Victor to accompany him, and the two men left Tavia sitting by herself on the wallseat.

The wallscreen buzzed. "Mrs. Emory? Narlydda is here."

Thank goodness, Tavia thought. At least she had time to put in her contact lenses. She stood up, straightened her turquoise silk robes, and hurried toward her office. "Wait five minutes. Then show her in."

NARLYDDA ENTERED the sumptuous office, marveling at the luxurious materials in evidence: solid burled-teak desk, actual leather on the bronzed wallseats and cushions. The walls appeared to be covered in thin yellow silk. And the floor was a marvelous abstract mosaic of ceramic metallics, glinting in tones of rich treasure.

She adjusted her silver sunburst demimask. The lower portion of her face was bisected by skin dye patterns in white and red, which gradually coalesced to form an elaborate butterfly that framed her red-stained lips. Her hair was hidden under a red and black Noh wig. She'd encased her long, lanky body in black leggings and a woven robe of red velvet and mirrored chips. When she moved, she reflected silvery light in every direction. Drama was expected from great artists. Narlydda did not intend to disappoint her public.

A large-boned, bulky woman in turquoise silk stood up as she entered. "Narlydda. Such a pleasure to meet you. I'm so delighted you've come."

Narlydda took her hand. Her grip was powerful. In keeping with the rest of her. Tavia Emory had a strong face. Her short, gilded hair did not soften her hawklike features.

Interesting face. I'd like to sketch her.

Her eyes glowed with the gold of mutancy. But surely Tavia Emory was a normal. How peculiar.

"I'm delighted our schedules meshed," Narlydda said. "You have a marvelous complex here."

"Thank you. I hope you'll make yourself at home."

Narlydda accepted the drink offered. Sipped cautiously. Rose plum nectar with a hint of minty alcohol. "Refreshing."

"It's one of my favorites. Please sit."

Sinuously Narlydda lowered herself onto a pile of green leather cushions. "I'm anxious to hear your reaction to my roughs for the Moonstation memorial."

A shadow passed over the Emory woman's face. "Yes, well, of course, we'll have time for that a little later, won't we."

"That means you don't like it."

Tavia Emory's eyes widened.

She's not accustomed to people being blunt with her. Good. Narlydda smiled sweetly.

Tavia opened her mouth to reply. But a high, tenor voice stopped her.

"A guest, Tavia? Are you going to introduce me?"

It was Ashman, the supermutant. Dressed in a flowing white robe, his silvery-blond hair and silver eyes burning with odd light, he looked like an apparition from out of the desert—or somebody's dreams.

"I imagine you already know who I am," Narlydda said dryly. "And I certainly know who you are."

His smile was huge. "Narlydda. I'm so glad you've come." With a child's enthusiasm, he turned toward Tavia Emory. "Oh, Tavia. I knew *she* wouldn't be afraid of me." He grabbed the artist's hand. "We're going to have such a good time."

"We are?" She allowed him to squeeze her fingers for a moment, then gently withdrew her hand from his. "I guess you mean the reception—"

"Yes, of course," Tavia cut in. She seemed a bit flustered. "Tomorrow night. But we can talk about that later. I'm sure Narlydda would like to relax after her trip."

"That would be pleasant." Narlydda was eager to be alone, away from the odd tension in the room. She watched gratefully as Tavia Emory summoned an assistant to convey their guest of honor to her room.

"We'll see you tonight, at dinner," Tavia said.

"I look forward to it."

Ashman was silent.

As she left the room, Narlydda saw the supermutant and Tavia lock gazes.

They remind me of the mongoose and the cobra, she thought. But which is which?

MICHAEL SET his white collar tabs in place, surveyed his image in the hotel room mirror, and nodded. He looked professional, somber, and, he hoped, innocent. He was scheduled to testify in an hour. Time for a quick bite, although his appetite was minimal.

The door buzzed. Probably the room service mech.

But when he slid the door open, a young woman in a red silk tunic stood there, leaning against the bell. She had straight, silky dark hair, blue eyes, and looked vaguely Oriental.

"Can I help you, miss?"

"A fine greeting for your own sister," she said crisply and pushed past him into the room.

"Melanie?!"

He spun around. She was sitting on the corner of the bed, smiling a nervous half-smile.

"Melanie!" He grabbed her by her shoulders and pulled her into a hug. "Gods, how long has it been?"

"Who's counting?" Her voice was muffled. "And could you ease up a bit on the hug? I think I'm suffocating."

He pulled back. "I see that working in video news has turned you into a wise ass." She looked wonderful. So poised, so stylish. The years had sanded away all traces of the awkward younger sister he remembered. He grinned. "What are you doing here?"

"I'm part of the team covering this circus for Cable News. Imagine my surprise when I discovered you were scheduled for center ring today."

"How'd you find out?"

"Uh, the clerk at the information desk told me." Why did her voice sound hollow suddenly? Well, no matter.

"Despite the circumstances, I'm really glad to see you. You look wonderful. Even with blue eyes."

"Thanks." She stood back, staring at him. "Wish I could say the same for you." Gently, she brushed his hair back into place. "You look like you haven't slept in a week. Nervous?"

"Yeah."

"Can they do anything to you?"

Michael shrugged. "You're a reporter. You know how these things can go. Dad had a hand in the fabrication of this dome. And if they can't screw the contractor, they'll go for the subcontractor."

"Who was the main contractor?" Suddenly, her voice was all business.

"Aubenay."

Melanie made a quick note on her notescreen. "I'll keep that name in mind." She looked up. "Where's Jena?"

"Home."

"Is she coming out to join you later?"

"No."

"That's loyalty." Melanie made a sour face. "Are you here alone?"

"Mom's coming down. . . ."

"Mom?" Panic spread across her features. Gone, for the moment, was the cool, sophisticated stranger, and in her place on the beige wallseat was the anxious teenage sister he remembered so well.

"What's wrong?"

Melanie swallowed carefully, as though unsure of her voice.

"I just don't think I'm up to facing her after all this time. What would I say to her? I can't exactly talk about what I've been doing, can I?"

"She'd love to see you." Michael sat down beside her. "I know she would. And what can't you tell her?"

Melanie let out an exasperated sigh. "You don't want to know either. Michael, I've had a few experiences I wouldn't recommend to anybody."

"Like exotic dancing in Washington?"

"How did you know about that?" She looked thunderstruck.

"Remember when Dad was doing that lobbying to relax the federal safety regulations? We got pretty chummy with an assistant of Senator Jacobsen's—Andrea Greenberg."

Melanie's eyes were huge. "Not Senator Greenberg from Maryland?"

"The same. Even then, she had good connections. Anyway, at our request, she did some looking around, and finally found your trail." Michael paused. "So we know about the dancing, and about the stolen skimmer. . . ."

"Does Mom know?"

Michael nodded.

"And Dad?"

"We never told him. And even if we did, it wouldn't matter now." Michael knew he sounded bitter, but he couldn't help it. "He's forgotten most of what he once knew, anyway."

"That bad?"

"Worse. I didn't recognize him the last time I saw him. I don't think Mom did, either."

"You and Mom went to visit him? Where is he?" Melanie's face was pale, and getting paler.

"At Dream Haven. The California storehouse. I thought I told you. . . ."

"The storehouse?" Melanie was on her feet, pacing in agitation. "How bad is he? No, don't tell me. I don't want to know."

So she couldn't share his pain, could she? Suddenly, Michael's fury, pent up for years, came boiling out. "Don't worry. I wouldn't dream of offending you with facts from real life. About your real family. The rest of us will cope while you hide, safe behind those blue contact lenses. At least Jimmy tries to help out whenever he's in the Northern Hemisphere. I don't know what dimension *you* inhabit."

"Oh, Michael, don't be mad at me." Tears trickled down her cheeks. "I know I've let everybody down. I didn't really mean to. But I've been away for so long now, I don't really know how to act with family any longer."

She's telling the truth, he thought. His anger evaporated, replaced by sympathy and even pity for his exiled sister. At least he had the network of the family and the clan to support him. Who did Melanie have? She was alone. All alone.

"Here." He handed her a tissue. "And I'm sorry. I didn't mean to come down so hard on you."

She dried her eyes, professional mask back in place. "I guess I deserved it."

"I shouldn't judge you, Mel." He shook his head. "I'm in no position."

"Don't let this investigation get to you. . . ."

"It's more than that. At least you followed your instincts and left. Despite mine, I stayed. Married Jena. Tried to be a good mutant boy. I was so stupid, Mel."

Gently, she put her hand on his shoulder. "You did what you thought was right, Michael."

"Right. What is right?" he said. "There are mornings I wake up, and I don't recognize myself or my life. I can't believe how I sold myself out."

"Sometimes, there's no choice."

"I suppose." He rubbed his eyes. His watch chimed gently. "So much for regrets and should-haves. It's getting close to showtime. . . ."

"I'll come with you."

"Sure I won't bias your reporting?" he said wryly.

She managed a small smile. "I can't change the facts, even if I want to." Her smile broadened. "Imagine it when I break the story: Reporter's brother guilty of entire Moonstation disaster. Ryton breaks down under questioning and admits: 'I did it. I used substandard glue. Entire Cable News network implicated. Details at seven. Maybe." She started giggling.

Michael caught her mood. Chuckling, he copied her mechanical reporter's intonation. "Entire mutant conspiracy feared." He began to laugh.

"Lock your doors."

"Say your prayers."

They were both leaning against the walls, hooting with laughter.

"Promise you'll come visit me in jail?" he sputtered.

"Every six years or so. Why break my record?"

They clutched their stomachs and slid down in their plush upholstered chairs. Finally, they calmed a bit, wiped their eyes.

"Whew."

"I needed that," he said.

"Me too." Quietly, she slipped her hand into his. "You know I'll be there with you."

"Thanks." He squeezed her fingers.

Together, they stood up, left the room, and walked, hand in hand, toward the elevator.

8

OUTSIDE, the sun was setting behind Camelback Mountain in tones of blood, bronze, and blue-green. Inside, the lighting fell softly, pink and gold, upon the masked partygoers, diffused by a thousand twinkling spotbeams sunken into the arched ceiling of the Emory ballroom. Masked musicians saluted the beginning of night with a flourish of horns and bells. Then the eerie notes of a claviflute cut through the din of the party, sinuous, compelling, half bass rhythm, half ethereal song.

The partygoers froze, transfixed by the music like a flock of iridescent hummingbirds hypnotized by sweet, exotic nectar.

Grateful for the distraction, Narlydda turned away from the space industrialist in orange silk. Turquoise horns jutted outward from the top of his mask toward her like eerie, grasping fingers. He'd spent the past fifteen minutes telling her about his art studies in college.

How beautiful the music is, she thought. And how strange.

Tavia Emory, resplendent in a sculptured gown of gold and silver leaf over flexible ceramic, stood nearby. Narlydda drifted toward her.

"Who is that playing?" Narlydda asked.

"Yosh Akimura."

"The musician who helped me on the Moonstation piece?"

"The same. He's *very* talented, isn't he?" Tavia's voice purred with double entendre.

Narlydda wrinkled her nose at the tone, grateful for the shield of her own pearl and glass mask.

Tavia's face was concealed behind a green and golden shell mask through which her eyes glittered in their golden lenses, adding to the peculiar gilded effect. More mutant chic. But then, half of the people here appeared to be mutants. Were they? It was impossible to tell.

Narlydda adjusted the filter behind her eyeslits. Through it, her own eyes appeared to be green in this light. She scanned the crowd, looking for a sign of Yosh. Finally, she saw the young musician strolling toward her.

He wore green silk, a trailing, long-sleeved tunic, belted in purple, and pants tucked into high boots. His face was unmasked, but half-painted in gleaming swirls of silver and lavender paint, shot through with metallic sparks which glittered as he turned in the light. He finished his serenade and bowed gracefully as the guests applauded. Moments later, the musicians began a popular, rhythmic tune as a circular portion of the inlaid floor intended for dancing detached, hovering on g-fields as guests hopped aboard to swirl gaily around the shimmering room.

"Yosh, your music was lovely," Narlydda said. "I wish I'd asked you to play for me before."

He smiled modestly. "Narlydda? I recognize the voice. But what have you done to yourself?"

"Skin dye. Lasts almost a week."

"Very convincing." He walked around her, nodding. "Is this how you dress all the time?"

"Only around people I don't like. Or trust."

"That's a fine distinction."

Narlydda chuckled. "Oh, there are quite a few people I like whom I wouldn't turn my back on."

"Such as?"

"That would be telling." She smiled a secret smile. "This party must be costing Tavia a small fortune."

Yosh nodded and surveyed the colorful crowd around them. Then he turned back to her. "Good thing she has a very large fortune. Are you enjoying yourself?"

"Not really. I never do at these things."

"Shame." He helped himself to a hypo from the tray of a passing mechwaiter. "I like parties." He injected the stimulant, closed his eyes as it took effect. Opened them. "Don't you dance?"

"Not by myself."

"How about with me?"

"Won't Tavia get annoyed?"

Yosh grinned. "Hardly. This is part of my job. And the guest of honor really should dance, don't you think?"

"I suppose so." Narlydda glanced doubtfully at the rotating platform. As long as we don't fall off."

"Don't worry about that. There are g-fields all along the perimeter: if you started to slip, they'd just pull you back up."

"In that case . . ." She allowed him to sweep her up and onto the dance floor. He was graceful, led well, and seemed to enjoy himself so much that Narlydda began to catch his mood. The platform seemed at least as stable as the shuttle that had brought her here. For the first time that evening, she began to relax.

"Guest of honor?" she teased. "I thought that was Mr. Ashman. In fact, I'd prefer it—at least that way, he could share the burden of good manners that falls upon all guests of honor but somehow never extends to anyone else."

Yosh chuckled.

"But I don't see him," she said. "Where is he?"

"Tavia's toy is probably resting," Yosh said, swinging her

in a complicated loop while weaving around two other couples. "He'll be here later. Have you met him?"

"Briefly."

"What'd you think?"

"He seems like a delicate flower. Fascinating. Not quite real."

"Oh, he's real enough," Yosh said. "There's a spine of steel behind those fainting spells."

"You don't sound impressed."

"I'm not. I mean, I think his skills are impressive. But if that's the next step awaiting mutants, I think I'm really grateful to be normal."

Narlydda spun in his arms again. "Poor Yosh. Surrounded by mutants. Must seem a bit tiresome."

"It is. No offense. I like your green filters, by the way. But I get tired of all these golden eyes. Tavia even wanted *me* to wear those damned lenses. We had a real battle over it."

"And you won."

Before he could respond, the music changed to a fanfare of horns. The dance platform lowered gently until it was level with the rest of the ballroom floor.

Narlydda and Yosh came to rest facing the main entrance. Slowly, the door petals irised open to reveal Ashman, glowing in red silk pants and tunic. His skin was silvery, seemingly translucent. Narlydda expected to see his veins pulsing, silver-blue, just beneath the skin.

Ashman ignored the clamor of the guests and made his way toward Narlydda.

"I'm so glad to see you," he said eagerly. "So glad you're here."

"That's very flattering." Narlydda paused, uneasy. He seemed as guileless as a small boy. "I'd been wondering where you were."

"Were you?" He smiled in delight. "Come talk to me, Narlydda. I want to hear about your work. About you. I think in some ways, we're very much alike." He took hold of her arm possessively. His touch was surprisingly strong.

Tavia Emory bore down upon them. "This is a party, Victor. You mustn't ignore the other guests."

Narlydda flashed her a grateful look. "Yes," she said. "You have so many people here who are so anxious to see you—they're all bored with me already." She forced a yawn. "And I've been up since dawn. I'd really like to lie down. But don't forget our appointment, Tavia. Tomorrow, before I leave."

"You're leaving?" Ashman seemed thunderstruck. "But I thought we were going to take a shuttle ride up to see Moonstation to survey the plaza and—"

"All commercial and private flights to Moonstation have been canceled," Tavia said curtly. "You know that. Even the Emory fleet has been denied clearance. And besides, Narlydda has work to do."

"Yes," the artist said. "I have commitments and work at home."

Ashman looked so crestfallen that she almost felt sorry for him. But the urge to get away was stronger.

"Oh." He looked at the floor sadly. Then he brightened. "Well, maybe I'll see you before you leave."

"Of course."

He waved and, with Tavia at his side, moved on into the crowd.

Relieved, Narlydda watched him go. He was an odd one, all right: spooky, even for a mutant. She looked around, but Yosh had disappeared. A pity. Narlydda would have liked to thank him for the dance, but she didn't see a trace of him in the swirling mix of partygoers. Never mind. She could find her way back to her room alone. In five minutes, she was alone, safe behind the glazed pink-and-gold door.

Parties! The small talk. The patience and bright talk required of her despite the endless, presumptuous rudeness on the part of grotesque strangers. Why had she come here? How she longed for the quiet of her own home.

Gladly, she put aside her party finery and crawled into the huge bed. The covers were pale pink and feather-light. A soothing floral scent wafted toward her from the pillow. She fell into a comfortable slumber, dreaming at first that she was walking along a moonlit landscape, Skerry at her side. In silence, they walked, hand in hand. But as they approached a fork in the path, Skerry released her, moving away on a separate trajectory. "Don't go," she called. "Come back." But he dwindled until he was only a bright spot of light on the horizon. And then gone. But wait . . . he's coming back. Yes, riding through the white haze of the desert, moonlight on him, atop a silver horse. But it's not Skerry. No. The face is pale, eyes silvery. It's Ashman, and before she can speak, he dismounts and pulls her toward him, into his own private world, and he is touching her without touching her. She is silvery green, bathed in moonlight, sighing with delight at his mindtouch, dancing in his arms to strange music. His hands, when they reach her, are gentle, so gentle at first. And then less so, but that's good too. And the small voice behind her eyes which is saying no, no, not this one, stop it, this isn't a dream, that voice is very faint, very weak, and after a time, she doesn't hear it at all. The only thing she can hear is her own blood pulsing as she dances in the moonlight, naked, in the middle of a silvery dream desert, with Ashman.

The California desert air sizzled, even in January. Michael hurried into the building, grateful for its refrigerated cool. He shivered as the sweat evaporated from his body.

I can't believe Melanie's here, he thought. It's good to see her. A welcome distraction from the business of the investigation. Hope I wasn't too hard on her. Hard to know how to act with her.

He walked quickly toward the main auditorium, repeating the chant for calmness. Ahead of him, the black doors loomed like sentinels.

Here goes everything.

Michael took a deep breath, pushed open the old-fashioned double doors, and entered the auditorium. The room was shabby and badly in need of repainting, with a mottled, greenish tint to the walls. Down front, the congressional subcommittee sat in the isolation that authority confers: suspended five feet above the crowd on a curved, raised platform.

"Michael Ryton! Calling Michael Ryton," the wallscreen announced.

Nerves jumping, he hurried down the narrow aisle, aware of every eye in the place trained on him. Michael stood before the video terminals that lined the base of the front platform to confirm his identification. Placed his hand against the palmpad until the fingerprint check was completed. That completed, he took a seat beside Bill Sutherland. The congressmen stared down at him imperiously.

Kate Fisher, the salty consumer advocate and Democratic representative from Rhode Island, presided. Next to her sat Roland Johnston, D-Mississippi, Tami Feldman, D-New York, Jason Jordon, R-Wisconsin, and Darlene Timons, R-Oregon.

"Talk about a packed jury," Michael whispered to Sutherland. "They're notoriously antibusiness."

Bill Sutherland gave him a sympathetic smile.

Kate Fisher glared over her old-fashioned lenses framed in silver and gold chromium.

"Mr. Ryton, it's my understanding that you requested the opportunity to make a taped sworn deposition rather than appear here."

"Yes, ma'am."

"Why?"

"Well, I'm a busy man, and—"

"Too busy to appear before a congressional inquiry? My goodness, that's busy indeed." Representative Fisher smiled frostily. Beside her, Representative Johnston snickered.

87

Michael kept his face impassive.

"Mr. Ryton," Representative Fisher continued. "Your company specializes in space engineering, does it not?"

"Yes."

"You have completed several contracts for NASA, and have constructed Brayton generators for Moonstation?"

"That is correct."

"Has your firm constructed any of the environmental dome units on Moonstation?"

"Only two subsidiary units to store mechs."

She bore down on him. "Will you describe what safety features are standard requirements on these dome units?"

"We use an extruded polymer, a half-meter thick, heat and cold tempered, designed specifically to withstand artificial gravity and atmospheric pressures in vacuum and pressurized environments."

Fisher sighed as though the details bored her. "Were you familiar with the materials used for the dome unit that imploded?"

"Only in passing. The materials were all standard, as far as I could tell."

"Could tell?"

Bill Sutherland cut in. "I respectfully remind the congresswoman that Mr. Ryton was not present during the fabrication of this dome, nor involved in the contract. His father agreed to act as subcontractor for Aubenay—"

"Yes, yes, we know all that," Fisher said. She turned toward her chalk-white deskscreen. "Play back Captain McLeod's testimony."

McLeod? Michael felt a chill. The screens before him came to life with a dozen images of a woman in a purple uniform. She had a heart-shaped face, short, dark hair, and blue eyes. It was a face from out of his past. His dreams. Kelly McLeod.

"I looked up and saw the dome cracking. . . ." the recorded image said. Michael stared in wonder. She hadn't changed in fifteen years. The soft lips. The pale skin. She was still lovely. He closed his eyes. Opened them, and saw her. Not the image, but Kelly herself. She was sitting at the far side of the first row of spectators, wearing a purple shuttle corps uniform, which made her seem official and yet appealing all at the same time. Her dark hair was cut shorter than he remembered, curling around her face. Her eyes, deep blue, sparkled as he remembered. Her face was pale.

Kelly. Here, now. Michael's heart began to pound.

Her eyes met his. Her mouth opened in shock. What was she thinking?

The drone of the recorded testimony ended. Michael became aware of the silence surrounding him. Representative Fisher stared at him severely.

"Have you any response, Mr. Ryton?"

"Uh, no. I don't think so."

"You don't *think* so?"

Michael's cheeks reddened. "Could I hear the testimony again?"

Fisher sighed in disgust. "Replay."

The tape began again: Kelly's clear alto voice soberly recounting the implosion at Moonstation. When it ended, the congresswoman looked at him expectantly.

Concentrate, he told himself. Moonstation. Stress on the dome supports.

"When was the dome last checked for fatigue and for faults?" Michael asked.

Fisher turned to an aide behind her. He glanced down at a notescreen, then replied, "Six months ago, regular maintenance."

"With all due respect, we recommend a twelve-week maintenance survey in vacuum environments," Michael said.

"Mr. Ryton, it's difficult to take your position seriously," Fisher said. "How can you recommend additional safety checks now, considering that you and your father were involved in supporting legislation fifteen years ago that removed safety regulations on space engineering?" Her tone was frankly hostile.

Michael bristled. "That's misleading and untrue. We only lobbied for reduction of certain unnecessary measures. . . ."

"Unnecessary to whom?" Fisher said. "Would the Moon-station casualties still be alive and among us now if those safeguards had been in place?"

"I have no idea."

"No idea?"

Bill Sutherland broke in. "I again respectfully remind the congresswoman that Mr. Ryton was neither the primary contractor, nor the engineer assigned to this project. Without additional information . . ."

"And I again tell you that we're aware of these facts," Fisher said sharply. "Nevertheless, Mr. Ryton, you refuse to see a connection between your lobbying efforts and corresponding relaxation of industry standards which might have resulted in this tragedy?"

"Absolutely," Michael said. "The measures we addressed concerned the engineering of generators and factory equipment. Not environmental domes."

"But didn't they have long-term effects upon industry standards?"

"I doubt it. But more specifically, I don't know."

"How convenient." Fisher gave him a look of pure malice. "Nevertheless, these fatigue flaws to which you allude sound like an attempt to shift attention away from the materials your firm generated. Couldn't the materials have been flawed to begin with? The engineering substandard?"

Michael's face turned red with anger. "They never would have been allowed out of the plant. As my lawyer has said repeatedly, my firm was a subcontractor for this dome. I suggest you interview the primary contractor." He glared back at Fisher. It was Aubenay's dome, and his problem.

Fisher subsided abruptly into icy professionalism.

"Very well, Mr. Ryton. Thank you. You may go. For the time being."

Wearily, he rose from his seat. He glanced across the room, hoping to catch Kelly's eye again. But the seat in which she had been sitting was now vacant. She was gone.

MELANIE LEFT THE PRESS BOX quickly. A headache was rapidly gaining strength behind her eyeballs. She rubbed her forehead and wondered where she'd put her alpha blockers. The interrogation had been brutal, with all the signs of a real witch-hunt, just as she'd feared. And her brother was the prey they were after. Michael had defended himself well, but she was worried just the same. Even if he was innocent, once her compadres in the media got finished with him, he'd be lucky if somebody let him make screen components in Little Korea, much less manufacture Moonstation domes. And what was she going to do about this story? How could she report the public "lynching" of her brother in glorious, living videotape?

Her lapscreen buzzed. She flipped it open.

The image of Randall Camphill appeared, staring at her.

"Ryton, we're sending Ralph Ferron to relieve you," he said. "I want you in this office, pronto."

Melanie nearly dropped her screen. "Relieve me? Why?"

"I want you to accompany Nesse to Emory Foundation."

"Emory Foundation!" She stared at her boss in confusion.

"Yeah. I finally worked out an agreement with Mrs. Emory to do a series of interviews with her and that supermutant, Ashman."

"The strange guy with the silver eyes? You're kidding."

"No. Get back here. Now."

"But——"

"But what?"

She'd almost said "What about my brother?" She stammered for a moment. "Uh, the investigation is heating up. . . ."

"Ferron will cover it." Camphill's eyes were icy. "Unless you'd prefer I sent somebody else to Scottsdale?"

Melanie shook her head fervently. "No, no. Of course not, chief. I'm on my way."

"Good." His image vanished.

Well, so much for watching her brother be chewed on by the congressional lions. A small voice in her head told her she was being disloyal, that she should have refused the assignment and stayed. Maybe so. But to refuse Randall C. was certain death careerwise. She knew that. And besides, she was confused enough about her feelings toward the family. Maybe a cooling-off period was a good idea. Michael would be fine without her. She'd leave a message for him and try to return as soon as she could. That supermutant had to be a fake. Maybe she and Nesse would wrap up this story quickly, and she could get back here by the end of the week. Sighing with relief, Melanie bundled her equipment together and punched in a request for a taxi. Sometimes her life felt like one long, revolving shuttle ride.

9

KELLY McLEOD opened her eyes and stretched in the morning sunlight. Nine o'clock. She just had time for breakfast. In the corner of the room, her message screen blinked in blue letters. She hadn't bothered to check it last night. Yawning, she padded over to it and hit the replay switch.

The image of Melanie Ryton appeared. She looked nervous. "Kelly, I've got to leave—I've been reassigned to a different story. I didn't get a chance to tell Michael, I can't find the screen code for his hotel, my shuttle is about to leave, and besides, I can't afford to let anybody know how we're connected. So please keep your eye on him for me. If you need to reach me, try AF7951-CABLENEWS. I'll try to get back as soon as I can. Thanks." She nodded and the image faded.

"Damn," Kelly muttered. Melanie's got to be kidding, she thought. The last thing I want to do is keep an eye on her brother. I thought I'd made that clear. She has a hell of a nerve—funny, I don't remember her being that way in high school. Seems like she's made up for lost time. Well, regardless, Michael would just have to look after himself, because Kelly would be far, far away.

She dressed quickly in a standard purple shuttle corps uniform. Hair neat, a touch of lipstick, and she was ready. As she walked toward the commissary, Kelly reviewed her plan. She would ask Landon for a leave of absence until the sub-committee had finished its preliminary investigation. If they hanged Michael Ryton from the shuttle's landing gear, at least she wouldn't be around to see it. She'd given her testimony. What more did they need from her?

After a quick cup of coffee from the commech, she hurried to her shuttle commander's temporary quarters in the next building. Luckily, Landon was in, and his assistant, Marc Hershman, buzzed her ahead.

"Colonel?"

Landon looked up from his screen. "Come in, McLeod."

She set her jaw in determination, walked in, and sat on the narrow red chair in front of his desk. The room was filled with pink memorypaks and triple-column printouts. Screenwork. The bane of every shuttle jockey's earthside rotation.

"Sir, I request a change of assignment." Her voice shook on the last word.

He stared at her a moment, eyes glittering. Kelly had the uncomfortable sensation that he could look right through her.

"What do you mean?"

She shifted uneasily in her seat. "Sir, I don't think that I'm really being useful now that my testimony is on record, and I could be working—"

"You are working."

She nodded quickly. "Yes, I know. But I don't see why—"

"You know your duty, McLeod."

"Then I request leave."

He leaned toward her. "Why the sudden wanderlust?"

"It's personal."

"I assumed that." His expression softened. "What's going on, Kelly? Something wrong? You and Grant not getting along?"

"What difference would that make?" she asked sharply.

Landon sighed. "You're not helping me out, Kelly. I can't release you without a damned good reason. Now stop wasting my time. And yours."

Kelly hesitated. Could she trust him?

"Come on, Kelly. Or else I have to deny your request automatically."

She had no choice. When she spoke, her voice felt tight in her throat. "I knew one of the witnesses."

"I see. Who?"

"Michael Ryton, sir."

Landon's eyes widened. "Ryton? How well?"

"Very well, sir. If you know what I mean."

Landon sighed. He reached across the tan acrylic desk and turned off his screen.

"Why didn't you tell me this before?"

"I didn't know he was going to be here."

"You saw the list of those subpoenaed."

"Yes." Kelly looked away from Landon's glittering eyes. "But I thought maybe he wouldn't come."

"What? Ignore a government summons and risk a citation for contempt of Congress?"

She shrugged. "You told me yourself that mutants are independent. Unpredictable. I didn't think he'd come. I prayed he wouldn't. Maybe I just thought if I ignored it, it would go away."

"Terrific." He stood up, ran his hands through his short brown hair. "Well, I don't think this compromises anything, really. Have you talked to him?"

"No. And I don't want to."

"I thought not. Don't suppose you'd want to tell me the details?"

Kelly forced herself to meet his gaze. "We were sweethearts. Childhood sweethearts." She closed her eyes. "Gods, I can't believe I just said that."

"What's wrong with it if that's the truth?"

"Makes my skin crawl." She gave him a tiny smile. "Anyway, we wanted to get married. But the Mutant Council had other ideas. So he married a nice mutant girl and had a nice mutant baby. And I joined the service. Thought it was time to see less of him and more of the world."

"A good idea." Landon's tone was sympathetic. "I'd almost accuse you of being foolishly optimistic, trying for intermarriage. It's still considered shocking in certain circles these days."

"Well, I learned the hard way." She paused. "Speaking of certain circles, what does the Mutant Council think of this supermutant?"

"He's disturbing. We don't know what to make of him. And now that he's accepted the protection of the Emory Foundation—he's under lock and key in Scottsdale—we've got to ask permission to talk to him."

"I'll bet the military brass are going crazy."

Landon nodded.

"Everybody wants a piece of him. The military. The CIA. The research labs. If I were Ashman, I'd stay out in the desert."

"Will they get their hands on him?"

"Eventually." Landon shrugged. "Unless he can also make himself disappear." He toyed with his screen key for a moment, then looked up. "All right, Kelly, I'll grant you a leave until this circus is over. But don't disappear completely. Stay in touch."

Kelly jumped up. "Thank you. I didn't think—"

"Save it." Landon smiled. Then his face turned somber. "I don't know if you can outrun your past, Kelly. But you saved my life, and the least I can do is try not to trip you up now."

"Thanks." Giddy with relief, she walked out of his office as though floating through a low-g field.

I was lucky when they rotated Heyran Landon onto my duty roster, she thought. Bless his golden eyes.

She spoke quickly into the black mesh callbox. "Elevator, down."

If she hurried, she could pack and catch a morning shuttle back to the East Coast. Visit the folks.

The red-enameled elevator doors slid open with a sigh and Kelly entered the cab. She was so preoccupied that she scarcely noticed the other occupant of the elevator until the doors closed and he turned around. A slim blond man in a sober gray suit.

"Hello, Kelly."

The tenor voice was familiar. It had echoed through a hundred memories and nightmares. It belonged to Michael Ryton.

"Stop dancing around, Tavia, and admit it. You just don't like my sketch." Narlydda sat opposite the hawk-faced woman in a spacious office flooded by sunlight. Tavia shifted a moment, straightening a seam in her green silk caftan. Then she looked up, golden contact lenses gleaming.

"It's not that I don't like it, Narlydda. I wouldn't exactly use that term. No, your work is so very, very fine that I would never say I didn't like it." She smiled. Was there just a trace of condescension there? "What I would say is that I think this has perhaps been, well, misconceived."

"Misconceived?" Narlydda sat back in the plush leather chair and glared through the eyeholes of her half-mask. "How so?"

Tavia picked up a hammered bronze paperweight and shifted it from hand to hand. "How I envy mutants their abilities," she murmured. "If I were a marvelous telekinetic, I would juggle without hands." She put the paperweight down. "So many wondrous mutant abilities. And now there's Ashman." Her voice grew louder, more imperative. "I think it's important to honor all mutants for their achievements, don't you?"

"Of course. I thought that was what I was doing." What was she driving at?

"Honor them all. *Especially* Ashman."

Their eyes met, locked. For a moment, Narlydda was tempted to give Tavia Emory a demonstration of telekinesis by pushing her backward out of her chair. Finally, Tavia looked away.

"You want me to do a sculpture of Ashman?" Narlydda said.

"I thought I'd made that obvious."

"You've made nothing obvious, Tavia. I thought this commission was for a Moonstation memorial, not a private portrait."

"This will hardly be private. . . ."

"My fee triples for portrait commissions, regardless of their intended use or siting," Narlydda said sharply. "But I have no intention of changing my conception of the memorial. I think it's perfect as is."

"That's a pity. There are so many other artists who are easier to work with. . . ."

"Then I suggest you contact them immediately. I reject this commission. Get yourself another artist."

Before Tavia could reply, Narlydda was out the door, striding toward her room.

I don't need her or her money, she thought furiously. I'll order a taxi and get out of this claustrophobic fiefdom before I start knocking down walls. And as soon as I'm home, I'll call Tri-Com and Cable News.

She grabbed her green leather travel bag. Thank God she'd packed before breakfast. But as she turned toward the door, she felt a wave of dizziness come over her. Head spinning, she sank down onto the bed.

Sleep.

The mental command was direct, compelling, inescapable. Narlydda slept.

When she awoke, the walls had changed color. No. She

was in a different room, and the walls were a soft, padded blue-green velour. But where was she? Where was the door? Narlydda staggered to her feet. She felt fuzzy-headed. Drugged. A drink of water, that's what she needed. She reached telekinetically for a glass sitting on a low table across the room. The glass just sat there. Narlydda tried again. Then, desperately thirsty, she strode across the room, grabbed the glass, and gulped down its contents.

The water was wonderfully cold. In a moment, her head began to clear.

How odd, she thought. Why can't I levitate anything? Everything in here seems nonresponsive to telekinesis. Am I still asleep? No, that water was real. Could the walls be lined with mental dampers? I've heard about that stuff. But I thought it was controlled carefully, used only in storehouses to keep inmates from injuring themselves or others. And what use is it here, except to keep me under control?

She took a deep breath. "Let me out!" she cried. "Hey! Somebody, where am I?"

No answer.

Weakly, she kicked at the wall. There was a mech inset near the bed, programmed to provide food and drink. She saw that a luxurious bathroom opened onto the room at the far corner. But no door. No window. What had happened?

Don't be afraid.

Narlydda yelped. The mindspeech was loud, almost painful.

I apologize for the volume. It is difficult to control. . . .

"Ashman?"

"Of course."

"Let me out of here."

If I do that, then you'll go away.

"At least give me a doorway. A window. A peephole. Something!"

A line appeared between turquoise panels and deepened

until an entire segment of wall had slid back, revealing a doorway.

Come.

Narlydda walked out into a corridor lit by yellow tube bulbs. There was a door on her left that led through a narrow passageway into what seemed to be a different wing of the building. She crossed a pink-walled corridor and entered a long, dimly lit chamber. At the far end of the room, a thin, white-clad figure sat on a strange acrylic ebony chair whose ladder back rose up behind him for at least two feet. Ashman sat enthroned, bathed in a pool of silvery light.

"What time is it?" she asked.

"Three o'clock." His voice echoed in the empty room.

"In the morning? I've been out that long?"

"Morning. Afternoon. What does it matter?"

She put her hands on her hips and tried to bluff him.

"You'd better let me go, Ashman. People will start to look for me."

He laughed, a peal of high notes with just a touch of tension—or hysteria—in them. "I like you, Narlydda. You're so brave, especially when you're frightened. And I'm lonely." He beckoned her toward him. "Talk to me."

Obediently, she perched on a pile of red velvet cushions near his chair.

"What are *you* doing here?" she asked. "Really."

"Mrs. Emory is my sponsor."

"Sponsor?"

He shifted in his chair. "Difficult to explain. She has provided a shield for me. Which I appreciate."

"Are you a native of Arizona?"

"Now that's a leading question." He waggled his finger at her in mock reproof. "And I brought you here to ask you the questions."

"I'm not going anyplace, am I?" she said acidly.

"I'm fascinated by the unusual."

"Then you must spend a great deal of time gazing into the

mirror." She wanted to say more, but his silvery eyes held her, transfixed.

He stood up, walked toward her. "I'm lonely," he said. "I like you."

Her heart began to pound.

Ashman placed his hand under her chin and drew her face up. His hand felt like parchment. "Yes, you are very unusual. Strong. Beautiful."

She searched for her voice. Found it. "Thanks again. But isn't this very sudden?"

"Don't play games with me." He shook her gently. "I feel such a strong attraction to you, Narlydda. Much stronger than with Tavia. But of course, she's only a nonmutant." The words were tinged with gentle contempt. His eyes glittered with strange light. "I must know you."

Suddenly, Narlydda felt afraid. She wanted to pull back from his spidery touch and run, get away, but his grip on her was deliberate and steely.

He drew her closer. Closer. Their lips met and she was swept into an unwelcome communion of brutal, overwhelming power. He was inside her head deeper than anyone had ever been, rummaging casually through her intimate memories, her vulnerabilities, her fears. She recoiled in anguish against the violation but his arms held her imprisoned. Oh God no, please, get out. But still he roamed her depths, relentless, probing for her private essence, examining, savoring the humiliation this invasion caused her. Getoutgetoutgetout. Narlydda convulsed with a wordless, agonized mental shriek.

Ashman chuckled and released her.

Narlydda fell back in a heap by his feet and covered her face with her hands. Her head pounded. She felt naked. Flayed.

"Before we ever met, I'd suspected you were mutant," he said. "Your work has an additional depth and dimension to it. No normal human artist could manage it. And you hide yourself, playing games with the public. You like your games, don't you, Narlydda? Maybe I'll teach you some new ones."

Desperately, she cast about the room for an object to toss. She'd kill him now, if she could.

Don't even try it.

Damn it. He had her outgunned. Narlydda began to tremble. What did he plan to do with her? But as she watched him, Ashman's eyes grew dull. His skin took a waxy pallor and he slumped suddenly into his chair.

"What's going on here?" a strident female voice demanded. Ceiling lights flared to life, revealing a long, narrow room whose walls were paneled in dark wood. There were no windows. Tavia Emory stood in the doorway, hands on her hips.

"My screens showed an intruder here. But I thought you'd left hours ago."

"Tavia," Ashman muttered almost to himself. "Would have expected that you'd have been in bed hours ago."

Narlydda spun around. "Your precious supermutant has kept me prisoner here against my will."

"What? Why would he do that?" Tavia said. There was contempt in her expression. "You're crazy. Look at him. He's weak as a kitten. What have you done to him?"

"Done? To him?" Narlydda began to laugh nervously, almost hysterically.

The Emory woman moved as though to hit her. Narlydda pulled back. But Tavia Emory was frozen in place. Only her eyes darted, fearfully, from side to side, glittering in their fraudulent gold. She seemed incapable of movement or speech.

"No, Tavia," Ashman said quietly. *"I summoned her."*

Tavia made whining noises in the back of her throat.

"Speak."

"Victor, let me go. I promise I won't hurt her."

He nodded. Tavia Emory toppled onto a pile of blue cushions. Her face was pale, ghostly with fear.

"Victor, is it true? You forced her to stay?"

He nodded.

"Be reasonable, Victor. Please, listen to me. You can't keep Narlydda here. . . ."

"Be quiet!" he yelled. "Won't you be quiet? Must I silence you again?"

Terror silenced her. Mutely, she shook her head.

"I'm so tired of being told by you what I may or may not do," Ashman said. "You think I'm a toy, but you're wrong, Tavia. You have no idea what I am. And how alone. But how could you? You're just a normal."

Tavia cringed as though struck by a blow from his hand.

"You parade me around like a peacock, taking me out for show and tell, then put me away again in my cage. Well, I'm tired of it, Tavia. And most of all, I'm tired of *you.*" He took a deep breath and stretched, hyperextending his long, bony fingers. "Narlydda will stay here until I say she can go. Perhaps she will decide that she likes it so much here, with me, she won't want to go."

"Fat chance," Narlydda said. She regretted the words almost as soon as she'd uttered them. The look on Ashman's face was frightening.

"Don't make me angry," he said. "I'm getting tired, and that's when I lose control." He rubbed his eyes. "See how tired Tavia is getting? She's gone to sleep already."

Indeed, Tavia had slumped down upon the green wallseat cushions as though anesthetized.

Ashman smiled a tiny smile.

"It's late, Narlydda."

Like grains of sand draining through her fingers, the room began to dissolve, fragmenting into sparkling particles, green and white, white and red, reforming around her in the now-familiar turquoise walls of her cell.

Dizzily, Narlydda fell back onto her bed. Had she ever

really left it? A squawk from above drew her attention. A parrot with silver plumage swung from a high perch near the ceiling. The bird had Ashman's face.

There will be time for us later. When I'm stronger.

It grinned and vanished.

Narlydda huddled on the bed. Her hands quivered. She was beginning to get frightened.

THE GROUP gathered around the floating round table was somber and silent. The only sound was the strident echo of buzzing cicadas, penetrating the room from the depths of the neighboring canyons which surrounded the meeting hall. Steam from freshly brewed coffee permeated the air with its sweet, bitter chocolate aroma. But the brimming yellow cups sat untouched before the fourteen mutants at the table.

"We've got to proceed slowly," Wade Walters said. "We don't know what we're dealing with here."

Rebekah cast a cold glance in his direction. "I think we've got a fair idea of the threat. Time is a luxury we can't afford, Wade. I know what I saw in Phoenix, as do you. I'd hate to have my suspicions confirmed at our expense."

"That's recidivist thinking, Bekah," Torey Summers said. He shook his head and the mutant unity earring in his left earlobe swung wildly, casting reflections upon the paneled walls. "Old-fashioned paranoia. Why can't we accept Ashman as a startling new development, but a welcome one?"

"Torey, I don't care what your opinion of my thinking is. You weren't there. Ashman, whoever and whatever he is, is dangerous. Or will be."

"I agree with Bekah," Chemen Astori said. "We haven't got a genetic map or footprint on Ashman, nothing from the East or West Coast Councils, so we can't trace him. It's like he popped up out of midair, out of a magician's hat. I've asked the Russians to trace their files: nothing. Ditto the Europeans. He's not part of the council or the union. Yet he speaks of working with us and presiding over us. Who knows how powerful he really is? Has anybody gotten close enough to try an esper probe?"

"He was shielded the entire time we were there," Rebekah said. "And seamless. I've never felt a shield like that before."

Wade frowned. "This is crazy talk, from a bunch of frightened little mutants. Why would he pose a threat to us?"

"Not a threat," said Rebekah. "But he's uncontrollable."

Chemen Astori nodded energetically. "What if he could compel our most powerful espers? Teach them to meld, work in unison? Or our telekinetics? How would the normals react? What if they attacked him?"

"Or he attacked them," Rebekah said. She looked around the room as eyebrows arched. "That's right. Think about it. We have to consider the need here to protect nonmutants from, at best, an unscrupulous sport. And more likely, a dangerous renegade."

Torey leaned toward the Book Keeper. "Why are you convinced Ashman's hostile?" he demanded.

"I'm not convinced he's hostile. At least, not yet. But he's not part of us, and therefore we have no reason to expect his cooperation. He chose not to reveal himself to us first. I think he's testing the parameters of his current situation. Which, as I remind you, is quite favorable. He has the support and protection of one of the wealthiest women on Earth —a known admirer of mutants."

"I'd call her a collector," Torey said.

Around him, several clan members smiled wryly.

"That's putting it politely," said Rebekah.

"I never thought I'd have to worry about protecting normals," Wade said ruefully. "Especially from a supermutant."

"Well, face it. We have a responsibility here. To our community. To the future." Her expression darkened. "I think we must prepare for the possibility that we might need to eliminate Ashman."

There was a stunned silence. The assembled mutants

stared at the Book Keeper, then, uneasily, at one another. Finally, Torey spoke. "Murder, Bekah? Is that what we do?"

She spun on him. Her golden eyes flashed with anger. "Anything in self-defense. *Anything*. The community must be protected. Dammit, I'm frightened and worried. And if any of you had been paying attention during our visit with Ashman, you'd be worried too. But I refuse to sit here twiddling my thumbs, waiting. Let's vote. All those in favor?"

Yes.

All right.

If we must.

Slowly, the mental tally produced twelve in favor. "Opposed?"

Two votes were opposed: Torey and Wade.

"Congratulations," Wade said drily after the final tabulation. "And now what?"

"Who will do it?" Torey asked.

Rebekah looked at the others gathered at the table. Her throat felt dry.

"I'll talk to Skerry," she said. "If I can find him."

10

N ESSE? Right this way."

Lorten, Tavia Emory's media liaison, led the Cable News reporters down a long, deserted white marble corridor. She was clad in a neat blue jumpsuit with an Emory Foundation patch on the right breast pocket. Lorten walked quickly, and both Melanie and Nesse hurried to keep pace. They turned a corner and came to another hallway, this one lined in pink granite, and equally empty. The pink carpeting muffled their footsteps as they walked past dark reception consoles and empty offices. The only sound was that of their own breathing. Melanie began to wonder if there was anybody home at Emory Foundation.

At the end of the corridor a door stood open and Lorten marched them through it into a spacious room paneled with blond wood and jade green enamel. The furniture was oversize: plump bronzed floatsofas set into sculpted acrylic frames. A chant for two voices, tenor and baritone, was playing over the roomscreen's audio system. The sonorities blended, bounced apart, came together again in a minor key. A mutant chant. In the silence of the building, it filled the room with the resonance and impact of a full operatic chorus.

A woman with pale, pale skin and short, frosted hair, gold-tipped at the ends, sat slumped near the window, facing a wallscreen.

"Mrs. Emory, Nesse from Cable News."

The woman sat up as though jerked by invisible strings. Her face had a sharp, predatory cast that reminded Melanie of an eagle: strong nose, chiseled cheekbones and a high forehead. Her golden eyes glittered. But there were dark circles under them.

"Ah, Nesse, yes? So glad you could come." She held out her hand to the newswoman. She turned, rather jerkily, Melanie thought, toward her.

"And this is?"

"My assistant, Melanie Ryton."

"Hello." Tavia Emory smiled an empty smile.

"Hello," Melanie said, and took her hand. You bald-headed bitch, Nesse, she thought. Since when am I your assistant? Tavia Emory's hand was ice cold. She released it quickly.

"Please come sit down." Tavia gestured toward the sofa. "Lorten. Coffee."

Melanie stared at her. Something was wrong here. But what?

"I see you've noticed the eyes."

"They're hard to miss."

Tavia Emory smiled and a bit of color came into her cheeks. "Contact lenses. Custom-made. Could I pass for a mutant?"

"You fooled me."

She laughed tinnily and patted Melanie on the shoulder. "I like you, Melanie. I can see we're going to be friends."

Melanie smiled as Nesse flashed her a look of undisguised fury. "Aren't those mutant chants in the background?" she asked, pressing her advantage.

Tavia Emory's head jerked suddenly toward the speakers,

then back to face her guests. "Chants? Oh. Yes. How did you recognize them?"

"I've had a bit of experience with mutants," Melanie said. What was wrong with this woman? And didn't Nesse see it?

"Aren't they fascinating?"

"Yes," Nesse cut in. "Tell me: What do you find most interesting about them, Mrs. Emory?"

"Oh, their skills. And their subculture." She gave the reporter what seemed intended as a sly look. "Living among us for generations, in hiding. Just imagine."

I don't have to imagine, Melanie thought.

"Sounds kind of claustrophobic to me," Nesse said.

"Well, I suppose." Tavia Emory frowned, coppery brows coming together. "But that's my point exactly. Hiding. Watching. Waiting. It sets them apart. Makes them special."

"Yes, of course," Nesse said. "Do you mind if Melanie sets up my cam stand while we talk?"

"Not at all."

Tavia Emory seemed to retreat into a meditative state as Melanie scooped up the travelcam and triggered the gray tripod at its base. Three limbs extended, spread, and ratcheted up five, ten, fifteen inches, until the camera stood four feet from the floor, its yellow eye focused on Tavia Emory's pale face.

"Nice piece of equipment."

Melanie peered through the lens and hit the autofocus. "It's all set."

"Thanks, Melanie." Nesse flashed a dazzling smile. "We probably won't need you until later."

"I guess maybe I'll go take a walk in the desert."

"Take your time." Using the remote, Nesse triggered the cam, and when the light stopped blinking, addressed the lens.

"I'm talking with Tavia Emory, president of the Emory Foundation," she said. "Mrs. Emory, thank you for joining us at Cable News."

Tavia lifted her chin. Her eyes sparkled with sudden alertness. "My pleasure." She smiled expertly into the cam.

"As you know, the supermutant Victor Ashman had made various claims about his powers. May we have your reaction to him?"

"Well, Nesse, I'm just very impressed. This man is a marvel. He is what he claims to be, a superior, evolved mutant. A bright symbol for us all of what humanity can attain."

Nesse leaned toward her. "How interesting. Mrs. Emory, would you tell us a bit about your interest in mutants, and the mutant movement?"

"Of course," she said eagerly. "I've *always* been fascinated by the skills and abilities of mutants. We should cherish them as our 'younger brothers and sisters' in the family of humankind. They have much to teach us. And we have much to learn." Her voice had gotten high and thin, as though she were on the verge of tears.

"I understand that Mr. Ashman is your guest."

"Yes. Emory Foundation has extended him the protection he needs: otherwise, he'd never have any peace. Mr. Ashman may stay with us as long as he wishes."

"And in return?"

Tavia Emory gave Nesse a wooden look. "In return? We'll have the pleasure of his company, won't we?"

Melanie began to get restless. She'd intended to watch the interview, but this Emory woman gave her the creeps. All these rich people must use strange drugs, she thought. And it certainly throws off their reaction time.

She left the two women pinned down by the camera's unblinking eye and walked out into the pink marble corridor. It was deserted, save for a green mechmaid crawling down the window wall on its twelve spidery legs, leaving a sparkling trail behind it. Its motor gave a soothing singsong whir as it moved.

Still, Melanie burned with humiliation. Somehow, she would get even with Nesse for calling her an assistant. She rounded a corner and found the plush bronze carpeting leading away in three tantalizing directions. In the distance, she could hear a bass thrumming, as if a giant heart were beating deep beneath the foundation of the building.

Eeny-Meeny-Miny-Mo. She chose the left corridor. Most doors she passed were closed and locked.

It was like a small city, Melanie thought. But where were the inhabitants? Every desk had an Emory seal, every office door was painted Emory blue, but where was everybody?

To amuse herself, Melanie tried each door she came to, zigzagging down the corridor. The first five didn't respond to her touch. But a hundred yards down the hall, a sixth door opened at her request. Melanie walked into a small room whose walls were lined with screens. There was a main screen keypad on a stand behind the door. Quietly, she closed the door and stared at the gray matte faces of the screens. Curiosity nibbled at her conscience. The Emory Net was probably full of all sorts of goodies. She'd love to take a peek, but did she dare?

What the hell.

She touched the keypad gingerly. The screens sprang to bright, flickering life, bands of green, of orange, jittering across the room in a wild ballet of color, jumping from screen to screen, from wall to wall.

"Code?" the screen demanded in a mechvoice punctuated by clicks.

Uh-oh. Think fast. Melanie searched her memory for something that might serve as password into the Emory Net. The screen waited ten seconds, then flicked off.

An image danced in her memory of golden, glittering contact lenses.

Melanie touched the pad again.

"Code?"

"Mutant," she whispered.

"Thank you." The flickering images stabilized into a bright green, full-screen menu. "Make your selection."

Melanie scanned the list, ticking off Mutant Council, Victor, Lorten, Fac 1, Fac 2, Moonstation Plaza.

"Moonstation Plaza," she said.

"Getting."

The information that appeared was disappointing: a list of sites and measurements.

"More."

The screen obediently scrolled through a list of names that Melanie recognized as artists renowned for heroic sculpture. In the middle of the list was Narlydda's name.

"Stop," Melanie said. Narlydda. Hmmm. "Get me all related files on Narlydda."

"Getting."

The screen filled with specifics on a proposed statue.

"More."

A series of taped messages featuring Tavia Emory flew by at double speed, invitations of some sort.

"More."

Suddenly, a sketch appeared. A muscular merman with long hair and a beard.

God, he looks familiar, Melanie thought. I wonder who the model is. Nice sketch. Then she paused. This must be Narlydda's study for the Moonstation commission. If she had a copy of this, she could scoop everybody else with it: nothing had been released.

"Print," she said. "Photo ready."

"Printing," the screen announced. In a moment, a thick sheet of glossy white paper extruded from a slot in the wall that ran the length of the screen system.

Hands shaking, she grabbed the print. It was perfect. The merman in black and white. She rolled it up quickly and put it in her screencase.

"Save?" the screen asked helpfully.

"Save," Melanie said.

She noticed that one of the screens to her left did not carry the merman sketch image, but rather was a list of numerals.

On closer inspection, it looked like an address, phone code, and fax number. Whose? It had to be Narlydda's. Melanie felt a little light-headed. She wanted to laugh. After all her scouting around, here was what she'd been looking for. She had to have that address.

"Print left screen," she said.

"Copy?"

"Left screen."

"Copy?"

This wasn't going to work. And she couldn't waste time searching for the proper command.

"Hold," she said. Reaching into her screencase, she fished out a pen and pad. Hastily, she scrawled down the information.

"Save?"

"Save."

The screen hummed. "More?"

Melanie was tempted. But she'd been in here long enough.

"End," she said.

The screen went black.

Wow, she thought. I can't believe it. Narlydda's real address. Her private phone number. The Moonstation sketch. Melanie hugged herself with delight.

Her exultation was cut short by an odd whispering sound behind her. She turned to see the door irising open.

But I thought I locked that!

A woman stood in the doorway, her eyes glittering with mutant gold. She was tall and lanky, with cropped dark hair save for a thatch of white at her temple. Her skin had an odd quality to it. It was green. But aside from that, it was also transparent. Melanie gasped. She could see right through her.

A ghost? How could this be?

"I don't believe it," Melanie said, and reached toward the apparition. Her hand went right through the green woman. In response, the ghost gave her a reproachful look.

"Ex-excuse me," Melanie said. "I mean, who are you? What are you?"

The woman's mouth moved as though she were attempting to say something. But no sound came from her lips.

Fear took a firmer grip on Melanie. Her hands began to shake. "What are you trying to tell me? I'm sorry, I don't understand. I can't hear you."

The woman shook her head despairingly and faded slowly from view. The door closed and locked with a click.

Melanie sank down onto the small wallseat and closed her eyes.

Ghosts. Emory Foundation is haunted by green mutant women. Melanie took a deep breath. Then another. Finally, her pulse subsided to its normal, steady chugging and she sat up.

Don't be silly, she told herself. There's no such thing as ghosts. Maybe one of Tavia Emory's staff was projecting and got lost. But maybe it's time to go find Nesse and go home. Now.

She grabbed up her screencase and moved toward the door.

Footsteps. Outside, in the corridor, somebody was moving toward Melanie's hiding place. And punching at the doorpad repeatedly. Melanie closed her eyes. But the lock held.

I want to go home.

Melanie pressed against the wall as the footsteps receded. She waited until she couldn't hear even the faintest echo of them any longer. Then, quickly, she opened the door and slipped through. It closed with a snap behind her. Clutching her screencase to her chest, Melanie ran in the opposite direction from that of the footsteps, around a corner, down the right-hand split of two converging hallways. The halls were deserted as before. No phantom green women. No faceless pursuers. No mutant receptionists with golden eyes. She was alone, wandering through Emory Foundation. And soon she was totally lost. Out of breath, she paused by a door, tried to enter. It slid open.

I'll just wait here until somebody finds me, she thought. Surely Nesse will come looking for me to take down the travel cam. She needs me to do that, at the very least. Or maybe I can call the main switchboard and somebody will answer.

She closed the door and turned to see a handsome young Japanese man in rich brown leather jacket and pants staring at her curiously from his perch near a window. His long black hair was caught loosely behind his neck by a knotted red thong. Expressionless, he studied her for a long moment. Then he smiled. His eyes met hers with frank interest.

"Hello," he said. "Lost?"

His voice was a warm, vibrant, baritone. She felt the hair on the back of her neck tingle. She wanted to hear that caressing voice again, right away.

"Not lost," she said.

He smiled easily. "Well, then found?"

She smiled back. "Maybe." His eyes were deep hazel, dark, and magnetic. Quick, she thought, say something. "I'm a tourist. I've been taking in the sights."

"The *son et lumière* doesn't start for another couple of hours," he said, standing up. "My name's Yosh. Would you like a guide?"

Dust motes danced a *pas de deux* in the morning sunshine that poured in through the front bay window of Narlydda's house. Outside, the grounds were immaculate, faithfully maintained by whirring silver mechs. Inside, the house was filled with emptiness, from white timbered ceiling to lavender tiled floors. The only sound was that of the screen, when it rang. And ring it did, but there was no one home to hear it. No one but faithful Anne Verland. On the third ring, she answered.

"You have reached Narlydda. She is unavailable. How may I help you?"

The message was from a Mendocino art gallery inviting Narlydda to an opening. Anne shunted it into an auxiliary message file. The main bank was full. Although Anne's total memory capacity was immense, Narlydda had subdivided it for convenience. But Narlydda had not asked to check messages in seventy-nine hours. That was odd.

A routine survey of the house revealed that nothing had changed in five hours. The gardenmechs made their rounds and fed Bluebeard, Narlydda's malamute. But where was Narlydda? Not on the lawn nor in the back garden.

The swimming pool was clean, sparkling blue. Empty. The foam bath twinkled with rainbow iridescence.

Anne was not programmed for curiosity. But she was programmed to spot anomalies in schedule. Smoothly she scanned all circuits. Her emergency line was clear. Narlydda had not summoned any help, or for that matter, any sort of transportation. Therefore all must be well. She would make her presence known eventually.

The main circuit at the front door buzzed with a prefix code for immediate clearance. The doorscreen showed a muscular, brown-haired mutant with a beard. In a nanosecond, Anne Verland summoned his name from the depths of computer memory. Skerry. Narlydda had tagged all communications from him as top priority.

"Narlydda? Lydda?" Silence. "Anne, is she at home?"

"I am not authorized—"

"Screw authorization," he said. "Code 5YCadmium Yellow."

The front door slid open. He strode in and headed for the main wallscreen.

"Access to data files is open," Anne told him.

"I want a scan of the past week, double speed."

Anne Verland complied.

"Hold."

She froze the image for him: Narlydda walking out the door, an overnight bag in her hand. "More." The scene switched to the outside and showed her getting into a bright blue skimmer that displayed the Emory Foundation logo.

"Seems she went for a little trip. That's not like her." He cracked his knuckles meditatively. "Anne, how long has she been gone?"

"Almost a week."

Skerry swore. "I knew I should have gotten back here sooner. Any messages from Emory Foundation?"

Obediently, Anne replayed Mrs. Emory's invitation.

"And Narlydda took her up on it?" He shook his head in amazement. "I thought this was supposed to be an overnight visit. Get me Emory Foundation. Ask for Narlydda."

After a brief pause, Anne responded, "No answer."

"Try again. Try thirty times if you have to."

Anne got through on the ninth try.

"They inform me that Narlydda left several days ago."

"What? Then where is she? Get me that Tavia Emory woman. Tell her it's the head of the Mutant Council calling."

"But that's not true . . ."

"Do it!" His golden eyes flashed with fury.

Again, Anne was silent. But only for a moment. "I'm sorry. They report that she is ill and unable to come to the screen."

Skerry frowned. "Hmmm. Strange. And not good strange. Try Rebekah Terling, 7089877767375."

"Ringing."

A moment later, Rebekah peered at him. Behind her, a wallscreen showed neat parallel lines of stock quotations in glowing yellow numerals.

"Skerry? I've been looking for you."

"I know. Sorry to interrupt you at work, but it's important. I want you to tell me anything you can about Emory Foundation."

"Emory Foundation? Why?"

"Never mind the reason. Didn't you just go there?"

"Yes. We saw Ashman."

"And?"

"Why the curiosity now?" she snapped. "You weren't interested when I asked for your help. But you seem to think it's fine to interrupt me in the middle of work to badger me with a string of cryptic questions. Honestly, Skerry, I'm getting tired of your games."

He cut her off. "Look, I'm sorry. Maybe I was wrong. I was too hasty at the meeting. Come on, Bekah. Tell me."

"Ashman was friendly, all right. Too friendly. Wants to address both the mutant councils and the union. Said something about presiding."

"I can't say I'm surprised. What did you do?"

"Stalled for time, but in the end we had to agree. What else could we do?"

Skerry shook his head. "You're asking for trouble."

"Well, you certainly seem to be an expert on the topic," Rebekah said coldly. "Did you call me merely to offer advice?"

"No. Sorry again." He held up his hands. "I've got a friend who may be in trouble at the Emory HQ, Bekah."

"A mutant friend?"

"Yeah."

"Do I know her?"

"Not yet."

Rebekah's expression softened. "Then I look forward to meeting her. What kind of trouble, Skerry?"

"I don't know yet."

"What are you going to do?" She gazed at him intently.

"Head for Arizona."

"That fits in perfectly with our plans."

He looked at her sharply. "What plans?"

Her eyes were candid as they met his. "The Mutant Council voted that Ashman represents too great a threat to the mutant population."

"You want me to kill him? No way." Skerry crossed his arms angrily. "I won't be the clan executioner. We don't even know who this guy really is. Or what he is."

"I'm not asking you to do anything any of us wouldn't do."

"No? Then you go kill him! Or have pretty-boy Wade Walters get himself a laser rifle. . . ."

"Wade thinks we can work with Ashman."

"Maybe he's right."

"I don't think you believe that for a moment." Rebekah paused, rubbed her forehead wearily. "Skerry, you know you have special skills that I lack." Her voice was soft, wheedling. "And I'm worried. Ashman is too dangerous. Too ambitious. It radiates out of him in waves."

"Mutant paranoia, Bekah. I thought we were waiting eagerly for a supermutant to come set us all free."

"It's the wrong time. The wrong man."

Skerry's eyes glittered angrily. "Oh yeah? How do we know that?"

"I met him. I know."

"Subjective. Do you have any proof? No, of course you don't. Well, drop it for the moment. What about Emory Foundation?"

"Corporate headquarters on the outskirts of the Phoenix/ Scottsdale metroplex." Rebekah shrugged. "Lots of glass and acrylics. Lots of mutants, too."

Skerry looked at her sharply. "Lots of mutants, did you say?"

Rebekah nodded. "Tavia Emory has a classic case of mutant envy. She's surrounded herself with mutants. I half expected to see some mutant heads, stuffed and mounted on the wall. She even wears gold contact lenses."

"Interesting." Skerry smiled bitterly. "Well, Rebekah, it looks like a trip to Scottsdale has been added to my plans. But I'm not saying I'm going to take this Ashman on."

"I understand." She gazed at him for a moment. "Skerry, be careful."

"I didn't know you cared."

"Stop fooling around! You know that my concerns are well founded. I've been waiting to have a call returned from Tavia Emory for two days. She's usually the soul of promptness. Especially when it's mutant business."

"I don't think she's taking any calls right now," Skerry said. "And don't worry about me, Bekah. I've gotten too old to take stupid chances. But if I see this Emory woman, I'll ask her to get in touch."

"Thanks," Rebecca said drily. "Keep me posted." She waved and turned back to her stock records. The screen went dark.

Skerry studied Narlydda's brightly lit studio for a moment. A rose silk robe lay discarded on a cushion. He reached down and gently touched the glossy fabric. "Thanks, Anne."

"You're quite welcome. Do you require any further assistance?"

There was no answer. And where he had stood, the sunlight cast bright circles upon the lavender carpet.

"KELLY? Please, say something," Michael begged. "Anything."

She stood across from him in the elevator cab, a slim figure in a purple uniform. Her eyes were wide, and the expression on her face was one of chagrin.

"Stop the elevator," she said quietly. "Let me out."

"Wait. Just let me talk . . ."

"Let me out. Stop it."

Summoning his mutant skills, he slowed the cab until it stopped dead in the shaft. The emergency buzzer blared angrily for a moment, then squawked and was silent. Its red light paled, faded, went out.

Michael waved his hand. "All right, I stopped it. That's what you asked me to do, isn't it?"

The hoped-for smile never materialized. Instead, Kelly thrust her chin out in determination. Her eyes sparkled with anger. "Don't play mutant games with me, Michael Ryton."

"This isn't a game." He took a step toward her, all playful pretense dropped. "Kelly, listen to me. I just want to talk to you."

"Go away." She shrank from him into the corner. The shiny cab walls reflected duplicate Kellys, a multitude, all pulling away from him. "Leave me alone."

"Kelly, please!" He'd scared her. That hadn't been his intention at all.

Her voice rose. "I can't believe this is happening. Let me out."

Michael felt his telekinetic control slipping. With a groan, the elevator cab lurched, then continued descending to the lobby. The doors slid open.

"Wait," he said.

"I have nothing to say to you." She glared at him bitterly, angrily. Thre was something close to hatred in her eyes. Then she turned and stalked away in the direction of the Shuttle Corps housing.

Michael cursed and reached for her with his mind. Caught her, strained to pull her back toward him.

She swung around. Her eyes were blazing.

"Let go of me, Michael!"

Her stride had slowed as though she were caught by an invisible hand.

Michael felt the air heating up between them as she struggled in his telekinetic grip. Her features were contorted in anger and fear.

"Dammit!" She took a step as if moving through molasses. But she couldn't get free of his pull.

Around them, people stopped to stare.

"Lady, do you want me to call the police?" asked a red-clad messenger with spiked hair to match.

Kelly shook her head. "No." She stopped struggling. Arms crossed in front of her, she floated a foot off the pavement, watching Michael warily.

"I'll let you go if you agree to have a drink with me," he said. "Just a half hour, Kelly. Please."

"And if I don't, what are you going to do, keep me here all day?" Her tone was mocking. "I know even telekinetics get tired—you can't hold me forever."

"You're right." In defeat, he released her.

She took two steps toward him, her hands balled into fists. For a moment, he thought she intended to strike him.

"Why won't you leave me alone?"

"I just want to talk to you."

"I repeat that we have nothing to say to each other."

"And I disagree."

They stared at one another for a moment. Then Michael smiled.

"Where's a good place to talk?"

Muscles jerked in her jaw. She took a deep breath as though about to shout him down. But instead, she sighed loudly and turned her back on him. When she spoke, her voice was muffled.

"I don't know why you won't leave me alone. You know I don't want to talk to you, yet you insist." She shook her head as though conceding defeat. "All right, then. This way."

He followed her around the back of a hangar and down a steep flight of concrete steps into a half-empty bar below street level. It was dim, cool, and smelled pleasantly of balsam. The walls were lined with gray plank paneling. Each table had its own acoustic baffle shield. Round, silvery mechwaiters circulated. Drinks and hypos glowed atop their lighted trays. The legend above the door said THE OTHER OF-

FICER'S CLUB in dingy pink coldlights. Kelly selected a table in the darkest corner of the room.

"Bourbon," Michael said, seating himself next to her.

"In glass or hypo?" the barmech asked.

"Glass."

"And for the lady?"

"Coffee." Kelly's tone was scornful.

Michael felt weary and foolish. She hated him. What was he doing here? Everything he'd wanted to say vanished. They sat in uncomfortable silence, the bar lights blinking around them, until the mech returned with their order.

After a few swallows, Michael felt the amber liquor burn some courage back into him.

Kelly met his gaze defiantly. "Well," she said. "Talk. It's your credits. And your half hour."

"I wish you weren't so hostile."

"Michael, I told you I didn't want to talk to you. So you insisted: trapped me in an elevator, lassoed me in public with your telekinetic tricks. And now you expect me to be gracious when I didn't want to do this to begin with?" She smiled ironically. "If you think you're going to get a sympathetic ear, you're wasting your time. You're lucky I don't give you a fat lip."

Michael felt his own temper flaring. "Look, all I wanted to do was have a quiet drink and talk about old times."

"Michael, you behaved like an idiot. I'm half tempted to walk out now." She rose from her seat.

"No, wait. Please. I'm sorry, Kelly. I was just so desperate to talk to you. This whole investigation has gotten me crazy. I forgot where I was. Forgive me."

She sat down. "All right. Now what in hell do you want from me?"

"Stop treating me as though I'm a convicted criminal. I'm not. Yet."

"Michael, I shouldn't even be seen with you." She leaned toward him. "I'm on the other side, remember?"

Anger gave fresh color to her cheeks. Her blue eyes were bright, just as he'd remembered them. And her lips looked soft. So soft. His anger faded. Michael wanted to lean over and kiss her. He took another sip of bourbon. "What other side?"

"The government is looking for somebody to blame." She spoke slowly, as though explaining an obvious fact to a subnormal. "And aerospace contractors are the easiest target. Before they're through with you, we'll have ten new laws restricting space engineering."

"Not if I can help it," Michael snapped. "But I still don't see what this has to do with us."

Kelly laughed shrilly. "Us?" Her tone made the word an obscenity. "Don't be a fool. The media would just love to get a cozy picture of Michael Ryton, suspected engineer, and Kelly McLeod, hero of Moonstation, sitting here having a drink."

"Don't be paranoid. Or melodramatic. I still don't see why we can't have a pleasant conversation."

Kelly sighed and leaned back against the pink padded seat. "Maybe I just don't want to. Why shouldn't I be hostile? I don't give a damn what happens to you. For all I know, it's your fault that I almost got killed on Moonstation."

"Don't talk that way."

"Is it true, Michael? Was your company to blame?" Her eyes were icy blue lasers, cutting into him.

"No. We were subcontractors. If there was a stress fracture, as I suspect, it occurred in Aubenay's product, not ours."

"Are you sure?"

"Yes."

She stared at him as though weighing his response. Then she nodded slowly. "Why haven't you told the commission that?"

"I've tried. They're not the world's best listeners once

they've got their teeth into somebody's leg. Besides, I'm not anxious to destroy Aubenay. We do a lot of business together, and when this blows over . . ."

"Blows over?"

Michael grimaced. "Sorry. Poor choice of words. Anyway, I don't want to alienate Aubenay if I don't have to."

Kelly put down her empty cup. "If I were you, I'd worry more about alienating the United States Congress. The subcommittee."

"It's too late for that. They're firmly against the industry and make no bones about showing it. And I'm no magician, Kelly. I really don't know where the failure occurred in the dome. All I know is that we did the job right, and our product was not to blame." He emptied his glass and ordered a refill. "What was it like up there, when the dome went?"

"Scary for the first minute or two. Then I got so busy trying to survive that I stopped thinking about how frightened I was."

"Would you go back up if they let you?"

She considered his question. After a moment she smiled slightly. "Yes."

"Good." He took a sip from his newly replenished glass. "But that's not what I wanted to talk about."

She gestured in a mock bow. "You have the floor."

"Kelly . . . I've missed you."

"Missed me? For fifteen years?"

Michael plowed on earnestly. "The marriage to Jena was a stupid mistake. I didn't know what I was doing—I never should have agreed to it."

"This is all ancient history. Why bring it up now?" She glared at him. "And next you'll be telling me she doesn't understand you."

"No, I wouldn't say that." He smiled bitterly. "I'd say she doesn't have any interest in understanding me."

Kelly shook her head. "You want me to feel sorry for you.

But I don't. You treated me dreadfully. You got what you deserved. Jena was in love with her mirror as far back as high school. If she loves herself more than she does you, well, that should come as no surprise."

"I know. I know. I'm sorry, Kelly. For everything that happened. It was a bad time. And I made a bad decision."

"We all make bad decisions occasionally." She smiled as though at some private joke. "The trick is to survive them. At least you have a family. A center. All I have is the shuttle service. Space."

"You could have married."

She laughed. "No thank you. Marry some dedicated space jockey who I'd visit occasionally between missions? I don't think so. I've seen too many of those kinds of marriages." She turned a hard gaze upon him. "So be grateful for what you do have. It's a little late for regrets, anyway. What about your daughter?"

"Herra? Just like her mother."

"You know, I really hated Jena." Kelly leaned back. Her eyes were focused on some far-away memory. "I saw her once, in town, before the baby came. I was home on vacation from school. She didn't see me. She was so beautiful. So blond and glittering, even seven months pregnant. I felt like she'd stolen my life. My future. And in a way, she did."

"Don't say that."

"It's true, isn't it?" She met his gaze steadily. The anger in her face was gone, replaced by a deeper, sadder emotion. "Michael, I never wanted to see you again."

"I know." It was a whisper. Michael watched the soft lighting glow upon her cheeks. He ached to hold her. "Blame me."

"I do."

He chuckled ruefully. "I don't remember you being this blunt before."

"Thank the service for it. Bullshit is only required when dealing with the brass." Her expression softened. "I didn't think I could ever forgive you. I don't know if I will. But I'm sorry you're in this mess, Michael. I hope you come out of it in one piece." She looked down at her watch. "I've got to go."

"I'll walk you . . ."

"No. Don't. Please."

He watched her leave, a slim, uniformed figure moving away quickly—too quickly—as though eager to get as far from him as possible. Then he signaled for another bourbon.

11

YOSH PUT DOWN his claviflute and turned toward the dark-haired young woman standing in his doorway. He'd seen her earlier onscreen, with that bald woman from Cable News, talking to Tavia. She looked familiar. He studied her now as she stood before him. Loose yellow silk tunic and leggings, soft leather sandals. Bright blue eyes. Soft brown hair fashionably cut. He smiled.

"What's your name?"

"Melanie Ryton. I'm a reporter."

Their eyes locked, mutual attraction pulsing between them. Finally she broke the spell, looked away, tapping her foot.

"What do you do?" Her voice was a rich, lilting alto. Good tonality, he thought.

"I'm a musician."

"For Emory Foundation?"

"That's right."

She smiled. Yosh felt electrified. He couldn't stop looking at her. Quick, think of something to say.

"So, Melanie-Ryton-from-Cable-News, my offer still stands. You're a long way from Tavia's office. Would you like a guide?"

She gave him a sly look. "Actually, I'd rather hear you play something." She smiled again. And as he watched, she sank down on a pile of orange cushions.

Yosh grinned back. "My pleasure. I've just finished composing something I hope you'll enjoy." He reached for his flute, never taking his eyes from her.

THE AUDIENCE had overflowed the auditorium seating. There were rows of mutants standing, shoulder to shoulder, up the aisles and around the back of the hall. Jena had never seen a Mutant Union meeting so packed. All eyes were trained on the Mutant Union officers onstage. And all everybody wanted to do was talk about Ashman the supermutant. She watched eagerly as Wade Walters took the microphone to address the crowd.

"Friends, as you know, Dr. Sarnoff was going to discuss the end of experimentation on mutant subjects in Russia and Eastern Europe. Unfortunately, he had been called away on urgent business. Therefore, we will throw this meeting open to debate. The subject before us is Victor Ashman. Is he friend or foe? You all know my opinion. I believe we should cultivate the supermutant. He can work with us to better our lives. Any discussion?"

"How do we know we can trust him?" Kira Remmer demanded. She had run for a seat on the board in the last election but had failed to qualify. "Will he submit to DNA fingerprinting? Will he work with us on mutant rights?"

Wade shook his head. "We don't have the answers to those questions yet. We hope to have them soon. I'm sure Ashman will be eager to work with us."

"Spoken like a true politician," Kira said. She smiled oddly. "You're positive yet you don't have answers. Meanwhile this dangerous enigma is frightening the normals, appearing on television, and seems to have a wealthy woman in his pocket."

"Why doesn't he come to see us?" shouted a violet-haired

man with silver studs on either side of his nose. "He should be here among us if he cares about us at all."

A roar of approval went up from the crowd.

"That's the point," a piercing voice said, cutting through the din. A round-faced man of middle size, tan with dark hair, stood up: Chemen Astori, the East Coast Book Keeper. The hall quieted around him. Astori rarely attended union meetings, but when he did, he proved to be a formidable opponent in a debate. "Ashman doesn't care, and if we fool ourselves into thinking that his laxity in contacting us is just confusion rather than arrogance, we're asking for trouble."

Wade flashed a warning look at Astori, but he ignored him. "To invite him to a union meeting may have disastrous results," he said.

"What kind of disaster?" Kira Remmer demanded.

"Don't tell me you're worrying about floods or pestilence," said a dark-haired mutant sporting a goatee. "What could he do?"

"He could make you think whatever he desired," Astori said. "Convince you to rise up, a mutant army, and depose the normals. Marshal a squad of telekinetics to tear apart the Pentagon. He could tell you that day is night and night is day, and you would all find yourselves sleeping at noon, awake at midnight."

"I don't believe in this, or him," the bearded mutant said scornfully.

"Whether you do or not, he believes in himself. And that's all that matters."

"I agree in spirit with the Book Keeper," Kira said. "But I think we should demand answers from Ashman. He's frightened enough people already."

"What do we need him for?" cried the mutant with violet hair.

"More importantly, what might he need us for?" Astori said. Around him, several Mutant Union members began clapping.

"And I think it's too soon to know," Wade said forcefully. "If we prejudge Ashman and reject him, we may alienate a powerful potential ally. We just don't know enough yet."

"Listen to Wade," a pale-skinned, gray-haired mutant shouted. "Don't slam the door on the future."

A loud chorus agreed with him.

Wade smiled and held up his hands. "It's important to raise all these issues now. And these are all good questions. I'm certain that, in time, they'll be answered. But right now, all I can tell you is that Ashman told me personally that he wishes to address us, and soon. That sounds like he intends to work with us."

The room erupted into applause again.

Chemen Astori shook his head. "I've said what I came here to say." And with that, he made his way to the door and was gone.

Jena watched him leave and thought that the Book Keeper was certainly a bad sport. Wade was right. Ashman could make the mutants stronger, work with them. Maybe she'd even get a chance to meet him after all. She'd have to make up with Wade after the meeting. Wouldn't do to be quarreling with him if Ashman came to visit. Besides, she was lonely. She'd expected to spend more time with Wade as long as Michael was out of town. But Wade was so busy these days. Well, she'd see about that.

Kira Remmer stood up. "I move that we request a special meeting with Ashman at which he must answer our questions candidly. If he does that, then we'll believe him."

"Seconded," shouted a bald man behind her.

"The motion has been made and seconded," said Terra Barr, the Mutant Union secretary. "All in favor?"

"Aye!"

The hall rang with the voice of the assembled mutants.

"Opposed?"

The only sound was that of a hundred hearts beating, a hundred mutants breathing as one.

"Is there any further business?" Wade asked. "No? Then this meeting is dismissed."

Jena hurried out of the building to wait by Wade's skimmer. Every group of mutants she passed was talking excitedly about Ashman. She heard his name mentioned in almost every sentence. When would she get to meet him? She couldn't wait.

Although Wade usually left these meetings promptly, he seemed to be dawdling. Impatiently, Jena checked her watch. Where was he? Finally, fifteen minutes later, Wade came around the corner of the building. But he was not alone. Kira was with him, laughing and walking very close to him. Too close. Jena recalled belatedly that Kira had managed to accompany the Mutant Union contingent to see Ashman.

"Wade, I'd like to talk to you," Jena said.

He frowned, turned to Kira, and said something softly in her ear. She nodded and hung back.

"Well?"

"Aren't you glad to see me?" She moved in close. To her dismay, he pulled away.

"I thought you'd decided to save your marriage." His tone was hostile.

"Well, yes. But I thought—"

"You thought you could have it both ways? I'm sorry, Jena. I don't want to be a plaything for a bored woman. We could have had a nice relationship if you'd been willing to take a risk. But that's over." He turned away. "And if you're so concerned about that husband of yours, you should be on the West Coast. From what I understand, this investigation is going to ruin him, poor bastard." Without another word, he got into his skimmer, Kira beside him.

"But—but . . ."

Open-mouthed, she watched them drive away. That son of a bitch. To humiliate her this way. She'd get even. Somehow.

Fuming, she drove home to find Herra's notescreen blinking: Gone to Treena's for weekend. Fine. She grabbed a hypo from the bar and jabbed it against her arm. A moment later, the warmth of the chemical had relaxed her enough to consider turning on the screen.

A Cable News jock with green hair was standing outside a low building at Armstrong Shuttlebase, giving a report on the Moonstation disaster investigation.

"Today's testimony was given by Marshall Kemp of Technar Industries and Michael Ryton of the embattled Ryton, Greene and Davis."

The scene shifted to the interior of a large, greenish room lined with long, faded draperies. The camera panned along the panel of congressmen and women. She saw her husband's face for a moment. Then, somebody else, familiar, from the past. Dark hair. Blue eyes. Kelly McLeod. And she was staring intently at Michael.

MICHAEL WALKED to a payscreen. He had half an hour before they resumed grilling him. Might as well check in on business. As he expected, the news was bad.

"We've had five contract cancellations," Penny confirmed. She looked more frazzled than he'd ever seen before. Her normally immaculate desk was covered with printouts. Even her shirt collar was askew, one yellow flap up, one down. "I don't have to tell you that the government accounts are running scared," she said. "And I don't even want to tell you what accounts receivable looks like. Serious cash-flow problems, Michael. Serious. We may have to consider layoffs to cut overhead." Her expression was partly annoyed and partly sympathetic.

Michael winced. "That's half the contracts for this quarter," he said. "Jesus, Pen. If it gets much worse, we'll have to declare Chapter 14."

She paused, jaw working. Then she lowered her eyes and spoke quickly. Nervously. "Or you take a leave of absence.

Let Dan Thomas run the company with Bill Sutherland. Take a vacation."

Michael stared at her in disbelief. "Are you suggesting that I go away?"

"Be reasonable, Michael. The media is howling for your blood. You're this season's sacrifice. Oh, it'll all blow over, just like it did in the eighties. But if you want to save your company, I suggest you take an extended vacation." She met his eyes reluctantly. "You'll stay on the payroll, of course."

"So long as I don't do any work." Michael sagged against the green payscreen shield. What choice did he have? He was tempted to stand and fight. But the price for that could be the loss of his company. His father's company. For a moment, the gray image of his father at Dream Haven flickered before his eyes. And then his mind was made up. "I'll take leave, Pen. Effective immediately. You're promoted to chief financial officer and acting chief executive officer. Put in Thomas as chief of engineering. And get to damage control as soon as possible."

"Right." She punched some notations into a notescreen. "Michael, as soon as you're back from Armstrong, we'll dot the *i*'s and cross the *t*'s. Don't worry. Within a year, you'll be back in the front office." She smiled gently. "I'm sorry we have to resort to such drastic measures right now. Take care of yourself, dear. Don't let the congressional wolves nibble off all your toes."

"Thanks, Pen. You're a good friend. I won't forget it."

His thoughts in turmoil, he turned away from the screen, and saw a woman dressed in purple fatigues standing as though waiting to use the phone. It was Kelly McLeod.

"What are you doing here?"

"I've been looking for you." Her face was pale and strained. "A message came in through the main switchboard. I heard you being paged, and when you didn't answer it, I took it. Something about your father. It's urgent that you contact a place called Dream Haven."

Fear gripped him with a cold hand. Dad. What now? He looked at Kelly, and for some reason, the sight of her enraged him.

"Don't you have to be someplace?" he snapped. "Getting into further space disasters and doing your part to ruin honest businessmen?"

"Michael, I—"

"Save it." He turned back toward the payscreen and asked for the Dream Haven code.

A big, swarthy male nurse answered. "Michael Ryton? Yes, we have a message for you. Some bad news, I'm afraid. Your father, James, was found before dawn, this morning, at the foot of a bluff. He'd fallen in the night."

"Is he alive?"

"Yes. In critical condition."

"How could he get out of his cabin?" Michael demanded. "Wasn't he watched?"

The mutant nurse stared at him impassively. "We don't know how he got out. We suggest the family come as soon as possible." The screen went dark.

Michael cradled his head on his arms. What else could go wrong? What else? He felt a hand gently rest upon his shoulder. He spun around.

Kelly.

"I thought I told you to leave."

Her look was sympathetic. "Come on. You need a drink."

Michael hesitated. His first urge was to hurry away, to get to Dream Haven as quickly as possible. But maybe he should stop at the office first . . . no, wait, he had to give further testimony, didn't he? His head was spinning. Maybe Kelly's suggestion wasn't such a bad idea.

He allowed himself to be led away. But instead of taking him to a bar, Kelly took him to a different building, up a flight of stairs and into a quiet hallway. The room they entered was furnished richly in soft blue and gray tones, with a spacious wallsofa and cushions.

"What is this place?"

"Counseling and meditation rooms for officers. Here." She turned from the roommech and handed him a glass of golden liquid. "Take a good sip. I imagine you need it."

"A meditation room with a mechbar?"

"Each to their own form of comfort." She smiled.

"Kelly, I—"

"Hush." She held her hand to his lips. Her touch was cool. She sat on the edge of the sofa and sipped a glass of clear liquor meditatively. "Poor Michael."

"I don't want your pity."

"How about sympathy?" Her blue eyes were candid. "I couldn't help overhearing that other call. When it pours, it pours."

Michael sighed as the liquor warmed him. "I don't even want to speculate how things could be worse." He looked down. "Forgive the self-pitying note. I promise to indulge for only two minutes."

"Take five." She smiled gently. "I certainly would if my life were falling down around my ears." Abruptly, she stood, walked toward the window, and looked out into the sheltered atrium at the crimson stalks of the bromeliads in bloom. She took another sip and slowly she nodded, as though she'd made a decision.

"Kelly, I should really contact my family. . . ."

"Hush." She sat beside him and took his face in her hands. Leaned close. Kissed him gently, once. Twice. The third time, the kiss was not as gentle, fueled by something warmer than kindness.

They broke apart, breathing heavily.

"This is a hell of a time for sentiment," Michael said.

"This isn't sentiment," she said. There was a fierceness in her eyes as she pulled him toward her.

He hesitated, holding her at arm's length. His father was hurt, his business in turmoil. There was no time for this. There never had been any time for him and Kelly.

"Michael?" Her blue eyes were luminous. Gently, she touched his face.

She was lovely. So lovely. He reached out and traced the outline of her lips with his forefinger.

"Gods, I've missed you," he whispered. Then she was in his arms and he kissed her hungrily.

"This time, I won't let you go," he said.

Smiling, Kelly shook her head. "Hush. Don't promise anything right now. Just use those magical mutant powers to dim the lights."

He did, and then there was nothing left to say.

12

THE MUSIC was high, sweet, almost ethereal.

Melanie watched the thin young man in brown leather coax note after magical note out of the blue glass claviflute. All thoughts of shuttle flights and deadlines had been dispelled by the cascade of fluid arpeggios.

He's wonderful, she thought. I've never heard anything like it. I could listen to him forever.

The music resounded in the small room, bouncing off the bronzed walls to form a counterpoint which Yosh incorporated into his song. His long, sensitive fingers danced along the claviflute's golden keys. His face was somber. Eyelids almost closed in meditation.

He has a beautiful face, she thought.

What was it about his face that so delighted her? The pleasing sun-browned color? Well, yes, surely that. And the way the sunlight gave green depths to his dark hazel eyes, warming them. The neat way his cap of dark hair fit his head, framing his face. The square jaw. The precise Fu Manchu mustache that lined his lips. And the lips—not too full, not too thin. Sensual. Perfect. To look at him was to desire touch. And more. Much more. Suddenly, she wanted to go beyond the swooping but superficial delights and terrors of this mating dance. To feel the pressure of those elegant fingers upon her. Pheromones, she thought. Wise up, girl. You've caught a bad case of chemical infatuation. But she couldn't take her eyes from his face. Infatuation—it was an alien feeling. But not unpleasant. Melanie relaxed and listened to his music.

When he finished, she applauded. "Play me something else," she said, leaning back against the cushions.

"All right."

He took off his jacket, slid down until he was inches away from her, and began a slow, intoxicating melody. His eyes never left hers. When the tune was finished, he put down his flute, leaned over, and kissed her.

This is crazy, she thought. I don't have time for this. But she was responding, kissing him back, wanting more.

"The door's locked," Yosh whispered.

For a moment, she was tempted. But then she remembered what she was there for. Who she was. Pulling back, she straightened her clothing. Shook her head.

"No. I've got to go."

The disappointment in his eyes was unmistakable.

Me too, she thought. Aloud, she said, "What about that tour you were promising? At least show me the way back to Mrs. Emory's office."

"Sure. Come on." He took her hand and led her out into the corridor. A right turn, then a left, and another right found them in the pink granite hallway that Melanie had first walked down—was it only hours ago? It felt like days. And Yosh's hand felt warm around hers. When he let go, she was sorry.

"Hmm. The door's closed," Yosh said. "That's strange." He put his hand against the palmpad. The door irised open with a hiss. But the room was empty. There was nothing in it but late sunlight slanting in through the windows.

"Tavia?"

Melanie stepped in after him. "Looks like Nesse's gone, too."

"Who?"

"My colleague."

"That bald one?" He made a contemptuous face. "I like hair."

"How do you know what she looks like?"

Yosh shrugged. "I was watching when you arrived." He turned toward the immense wallscreen. "Wonder where Tavia is. I'll try calling her."

He punched in a five-digit code.

The screen stayed blank.

"No answer. That's really strange." Yosh tapped in a different code. "Still no answer. I don't like it."

"What don't you like?" a light tenor voice inquired silkily from behind them.

"Ashman!" Yosh spat the name out. "Where's Tavia?"

The pale man floated across the room to lounge insolently in the bronzed leather chair near the alabaster desk. "I believe she's resting after a strenuous interview." He chuckled. "She said she doesn't want to be disturbed."

"The interview is finished?" Melanie said.

"Hours ago." Ashman turned and seemed to focus on her for the first time. His eyes were glowing silver. Melanie felt as though she were falling into them. Only the touch of Yosh's hand on her shoulder kept her steady.

"Are you all right?" he asked quietly.

She nodded. But her heart was pounding in fright.

Ashman stood up and walked toward her, a look of disbelief and apprehension on his thin, pale face. His ivory silk robes whispered as he moved.

"What are *you* doing here?" he whispered.

"What do you mean?" She backed away. Could he tell that she was a mutant? If so, she had to bluff.

His gaze never wavered. "I didn't expect to see you, or

anything like you, in my lifetime." He smiled coldly. "But it seems our calculations were off. By quite a bit."

That magnetic, silvery gaze had sent chills coursing through her, but Melanie ignored them and took a bold stance, hands on hips. "What are you babbling about?" she demanded.

Ashman stared a moment longer. Then he blinked. Shrugged. "Nothing, nothing. Mutant business. And you obviously aren't a mutant. Or are you?"

Before Melanie could respond, she felt the blue lenses covering her eyes lifting away, levitating out and upward like twin sapphires, to hang, sparkling, suspended in the glow of the overhead spotlights, just beyond her grasp.

Beside her, Yosh gasped. She knew he was staring at the mutant gold of her eyes. His look of horrified surprise was like a terrible blow. She hated this Ashman, whatever he was.

"A nice trick," she snapped. "But a telekinetic in any third-rate sideshow can do that."

Ashman bowed at the intended barb. "So you don't deny your heritage?"

"Difficult to do now, isn't it?"

"Then why don't you reclaim your disguise? Or compel me to return it?"

She gave him a contemptuous look. "If you really were a supermutant, you'd know why. I'm a null. And you're obviously a fake. Now give me back my lenses, damn you."

He stared at her in genuine surprise. "A null? I hadn't considered that." He nodded. "Yes, of course. It makes sense. Perfect sense." With a blink, he restored her blue lenses to her eyes.

"What's he talking about?" Yosh said. He looked confused, pale but determined.

"Nothing. Absolutely nothing. He's just playing hocus pocus."

"Why can't I reach Tavia?" Yosh demanded. "Where is she?"

"Who knows? I hardly keep tabs on her." Ashman shook his head. "Once that reporter left, Tavia disappeared. Told me to take charge until she feels better. Touch of the flu, probably." He gave Yosh a sharp glance. "You don't look so well yourself, musician. Are you sure you wouldn't like to go and lie down? I'll be happy to entertain your friend."

Melanie's heart beat faster. This Ashman gave her the creeps. She was thankful when Yosh took a step between her and the supermutant.

"I appreciate your concern, Ashman, but Melanie was just leaving. With me."

Ashman sank back into the chair and began buffing the nails of his right hand. "I don't think so."

"What do you mean?"

"I mean, dear Yosh, that it appears that all the building hydraulics have failed. It happened right after that newswoman left. No idea when they'll be fixed." He yawned. "Perhaps you'd both like to have dinner with me. Yosh, you could play the fiddle, or whatever it is you favor."

Yosh put his arm around Melanie. "Thanks. Maybe later."

He led her firmly out the door. Behind them, Ashman's laughter floated mockingly on the air, pursuing them down the corridor.

THE ROOM WAS DARK. Quiet. The red coldlight numerals of the bedside clock read 7:45. Still half asleep, Michael reached out for Kelly one more time. His hands closed on air. Beside him, the bed was empty. Where had she gone?

He padded into the bathroom. No sign of her. But he hadn't dreamt it. The memories of the evening clung to him. Somehow, they'd even managed to find his room, sometime in the middle of the night.

A yellow message light blinked on the wallscreen. *Had to go. On duty at eight. See you tonight?*

"Yes," he said. "Yes, yes, yes."

He pressed the wall panel. The heavy blue curtains sped apart, admitting filtered February desert sunshine to dance over the deep blue carpet. Another press of the trigger, and the mechmaid rolled out of its wall slot, green lights blinking, eight arms extended. With lightning speed it made up the bed while dusting the wallscreen and windows.

Whistling, Michael peered into the bathroom mirror as he applied depilatory cream. Then he took a sonic shower and dressed in a lightweight gray suit. So what if his life was shattered, he thought. Out of the ashes, he'd found Kelly. Better make a reservation somewhere for dinner, he thought. Champagne. Flowers. Then he hesitated. What the hell. Get room service.

The screen buzzer rang.

"Yes?"

"Dream Haven call for Mr. Ryton."

Michael froze.

The male nurse stared at him with open disapproval. "We'd expected to see you here," he said. "Your father's condition is worsening, Mr. Ryton. The family is advised to hurry."

"Thanks." His heart thudded. He had to call his mother right away.

The door buzzed and he hit the release key.

Jena stood on the threshold, eyes glittering. She was wearing an iridescent pink tunic and leggings, which, at first glance, gave her an ethereal appearance, as though she'd just stepped out of a soap bubble.

"Hello, dear." She pecked him on the cheek.

"What are you doing here?"

"You asked me to come. Or did you forget?" She brushed past him into the room, leaving a trail of musky perfume hanging in the air behind her. The mechmaid beeped with alarm and rolled out of her path, racing for the safety of the wall slot. "After all, in such a stressful time, a man should have his family with him. Aren't you happy to see me?"

"I thought you had 'business' at home. What happened? Get stood up?" He leaned back against the bar, arms crossed in front of him.

Jena's laughter ended on a high, uncertain note. "What are you talking about? I almost think you aren't pleased I came all the way out here to give you support."

"It's a little late, isn't it?"

Jena sat on the bed. "All right. Act hurt. I guess I deserve it. I should have dropped everything to come with you. But say you'll forgive me." She got up and walked toward him to embrace him. A wave of sensual images came dancing into his mind, projected from her. Michael turned away.

"Save it, Jena. I'm tired. And those adolescent mindshows don't exactly have the same appeal they did fifteen years ago."

"Fifteen years ago?" Jena's eyes narrowed with sudden suspicion. "All right," she snapped. "Where is she?"

"Where is who?"

"Don't play games with me, Michael. I saw you on the news last night. And I saw that pathetic normal, Kelly McLeod, too."

"So that's why you're here."

"What's so funny?"

Michael's smile broadened. "I actually was ready to believe you—that you were worried about me." He rubbed his eyes. "But all you're doing is protecting your property. Taking inventory. Jena, the good shopkeeper."

"How dare you talk to me like that!"

He shook his head in admiration. "Jena, you went into the wrong business. You're too good an actress to waste your life in a boutique, stocking shelves with reedglass." He reached for his jacket.

"Wait." There was panic in her voice. "Where are you going?"

"I've got to get to my father. He's been hurt. In critical condition. Not that you care." He didn't wait for her reply. The door hissed closed behind him and he was in the street. Time for dealing with her later. With the subcommittee. With everybody.

A pang of remorse hit him as he remembered the call from Dream Haven. What kind of son was he? His father was badly hurt. Possibly dying. And he'd taken time out for a sentimental reunion. His life was crazy. His entire world was crazy. He had to get to Mendocino right away.

He found a payscreen in the shade of the Armstrong Auditorium.

Kelly had told him about Melanie's reassignment. Maybe she was back in the office by now. "Cable News."

A receptionist appeared onscreen. Her hair was streaked with a blue and white zebra pattern.

"Melanie Ryton, please."

"I'm sorry, Ms. Ryton is currently on assignment."

"I'm her brother. It's urgent I reach her."

The receptionist stared at him—at his eyes—in amazement. Then she turned away, revealing an ear bristling with silver studs, selenium accuprobes, and pressure nodes. "Try code 9758321, area 712." The image faded.

Sighing, Michael reactivated his credit chip and punched in the code. The screen rang for half a minute before the busy signal cut in. Michael tried the call again. Busy.

He broke the connection, called Cable News, and left Melanie a message to contact Dream Haven.

Better try Jimmy next, he thought.

A minute later, his younger brother stared at him out of the screen.

"Bad news, Jim. Dad took a fall, and he's in serious condition. How soon can you get up here to Dream Haven?"

His brother's face paled. He looks so much like Dad, Michael thought. At least the way he used to look: same high forehead and long face.

"I can catch the next B.A.-Austin shuttle," Jimmy said. "Probably make it to the West Coast in three hours if I'm lucky." His golden eyes were wide with apprehension. "How bad is he, Michael?"

"I don't know. They just said come. And hurry."

Jimmy winced. "That's bad. Okay, I'll grab my bag and see you in California."

Michael stared at the buzzing screen with dread. Time to call his mother.

"Michael. I've been waiting to hear from you." Sue Li's Buddha face was a white mask. Her eyes looked glassy. "I didn't want to leave without speaking to you first. I'd tried to reach you. I knew you'd call."

"Mom, I'm sorry. I just talked to Jimmy. He'll meet us at Dream Haven."

"Have you found Melanie?"

"Tried. Left her a message."

"Good. How soon can you come?"

"Right away."

Sue Li nodded somberly. "I'll see you there."

Michael bought the last seat on a quickjet to Mendocino, due to leave in fifteen minutes. He was halfway to Dream Haven before he realized that he'd forgotten to leave a message for Kelly.

13

"I DON'T KNOW what you think you're doing, Victor." Tavia Emory stalked back and forth before the seated mutant, her bronze caftan fluttering like strange wings each time she moved. "You can't keep Narlydda here indefinitely. Surely you can see that."

Ashman toyed with a small, green embroidered pillow, humming. She wanted to bat it out of his hands.

"Victor, listen to me!"

"Oh, calm down, Tavia." He tossed the pillow into the air and left it there, floating lazily in an erratic orbit. "Narlydda will be grateful for the vacation. Besides, I think you're just jealous." Twisting like a cat in his seat, Ashman picked an invisible piece of lint from the shoulder of his blue silk tunic.

"Jealous? Are you insane?"

"Now, now." He shook a reproving finger at her. "No slurs, please. I fail to see why Narlydda should have a problem working here instead of in California. Besides, you want her to change the Moonstation commission, don't you?"

"And she's refused." Why was he being so obtuse? "You know she rejected the entire project. Victor, she wants to leave. Let her go." Her tone softened. "Please."

Ashman's smile lit up his wan features. "That's better. You're learning, Tavia." He picked up another pillow made of black and red kilim rug fragments and tossed it casually from hand to hand.

Wearily, Tavia sank down by his feet. He was becoming a stranger. She didn't know how to deal with him anymore. Gently, she touched the hem of his tunic.

"Victor, are you in love with Narlydda?"

The kilim pillow landed on the floor with a thud.

"In love?" He threw back his head and laughed. "Love? I've never loved anybody." He stopped laughing and fixed Tavia with a pure, silvery gaze that seemed to go right through her. "I don't know what love is. But I feel something powerful and compelling, for Narlydda. We're fellow travelers. I've been alone for my whole life. And so, I think, has she. She's the only one who could understand me. I won't lose that. Not now."

"Victor." Tavia choked on his name. He was beyond her control. A tear slid down her cheek, then another. She sobbed helplessly, defeated.

Ashman patted her hand. "There, there, Tavia. Don't feel sad. I owe you so much. You've taken me in, protected me. You know I won't forget that. We'll always be special friends. So stop worrying. I know what I'm doing." He gazed at her affectionately. "Now go to sleep." He began to hum a lullaby.

The tune pulled Tavia away from sorrow, away from her objections. He still liked her. She would always be his special friend. She sank happily into the warm comfort of slumber, her head pillowed against Ashman's knee.

KELLY STRIPPED OFF her uniform and stepped into the sonic shower. It was seven-thirty. There was no message from Michael but she assumed she'd meet him for dinner at his room. For a moment she hesitated. Wear a uniform? On a night like this? No.

Smiling, she selected a midnight blue deep-cut tunic and high-heeled boots. Crylight jewelry for her hair, and one earlobe. She nodded, pleased, at her reflection in the mirror. She felt like a young girl going off on her first date. But the face that gazed back at her was that of a woman going to meet her lover.

The desert twilight lasted long, even in winter. Humming to herself, she walked through the violet dusk. In five minutes, she stood outside Michael's room, pressing the palmpad for admittance. The person who answered the door was mutant, but female. A familiar, detested face. Jena.

"So, I *was* right," she said. "Come in, Kelly."

"No, I don't think so."

"I said, come in!"

Kelly found herself being compelled to cross into the room. The door slid shut behind her. "You realize that you are in violation of the Freedom Act," Kelly said. "I could have you arrested for this."

"You wouldn't dare. And who would believe you? Just two childhood friends having a reunion chat." Jena's eyes glittered in the dimness of the room. There was joysmoke everywhere. "So tell me, Kelly. Woman to woman. What do you think of Michael now?"

Kelly wanted desperately to reach out and slap that beautiful, feline face. But she was outgunned. She knew that Jena was a powerful mutant and potentially dangerous to a nonmutant. Best to do nothing. Play along. Dammit, Michael, where are you?

"Yes, where is he?" Jena said. Malice showed in her smile. "I couldn't help but catch that last thought. He left here this morning saying something about his father. Of course, you wouldn't know anything about that, would you?"

Kelly kept her voice level. "He received a message about his father being hurt. From someplace called Dream Haven."

"Dream Haven?" Jena was on her feet now. "Gods, it

must be serious. I should have known." She reached for her purse.

"What's Dream Haven?" Kelly asked.

"A mutant place," Jena said. "And none of your nonmutant business." She moved briskly past her.

The door closed, and Kelly was alone. She sagged wearily into a chair. Why had Michael left without a word? What was Jena doing here? And what in hell was Dream Haven?

Why had she ever allowed herself to get involved with Michael Ryton again? All he'd ever brought her was trouble and confusion.

For a moment Kelly was tempted to get gloriously, riotously, thoroughly drunk. To forget last night, mutants, and everything that had happened fifteen years ago. But she couldn't shake the memory of Michael's arms around her. The look in his eyes as he told her he loved her. She had believed him fifteen years ago. And she believed him now.

She turned toward the wallscreen and punched in Heyran Landon's private code.

The screen rang once. Twice.

Please be in, she prayed.

He answered on the fourth ring.

"Kelly?"

She took a deep breath. "I need to know about Dream Haven. What it is. Where it is."

"Why? Where did you hear about it?"

"From Michael Ryton. I mean, from his wife."

"His wife?" Landon's eyebrows shot upward. "I thought you wanted to avoid this Ryton."

"That was yesterday."

"Maybe you'd better meet me at the Officer's Other," Landon said.

"I don't know . . ."

"Well, I do." Landon's golden eyes held curiosity and amusement. "I want a full report in fifteen minutes. And that, my dear Kelly, is an order."

THE FRONT DOORS WERE LOCKED. The side doors were locked. Every blue-green acrylic door in Emory Foundation was locked. And Melanie believed that they'd tried them all. Wearily, she sat upon a pile of orange cushions in Yosh's studio, rubbing her feet.

"At least the screens still work," she said. "I managed to get a message back to Cable News. Maybe I'll keep my job."

Yosh was noodling with a keyboard in his studio, hardly listening. He looked worried.

"Maybe you should try Tavia again."

"I don't think she'll answer. And I can't get into the wing where her private rooms are."

"You think something's wrong?"

Yosh ran his hand through his hair. "I don't know. I'm trying not to get paranoid. But why isn't maintenance working on the door hydraulics? Where is everybody? The place seems deserted. Usually it's buzzing away. I'll bet Ashman could answer a couple of these questions, but I sure don't feel like talking to him about it."

"You don't trust him?"

"I don't like him."

"Neither do I." She shivered briefly, remembering the so-called supermutant's eerie gaze. He was a fake. He had to be.

The crystal clock atop Yosh's roommech chimed seven times. Yosh put his keyboard down and stretched lazily.

"Are you hungry?" he asked. "I'm no sushi chef, but I can whip up a tolerable soya casserole."

"You mean you're willing to feed a mutant?" Melanie's flippant tone covered her nervousness. Yosh had been shocked when Ashman unmasked her. She had to know how he felt now.

Yosh turned to face her. He was unsmiling. For a long moment he gazed into her eyes. "I'll admit it," he said. "I was amazed when Ashman pulled out your contact lenses. I've really had enough mutants to last a lifetime. Or so I thought." He smiled. Touched her cheek briefly. "Melanie, why don't you leave those things off? I'd rather see you as you really are."

"Do you mean it?"

"Of course."

Feeling shy, Melanie turned away, removed the lenses, and popped them into a lenspak in her pocket. How odd after all these years to be showing the mark of her mutancy. And to this man. At his request.

"There." She curtsied. "Just don't ask me to do any heavy lifting with the blink of an eye. I meant what I said about being a null."

"I don't require party tricks," Yosh said. "In fact, it's kind of a relief that you can't do any of them. But how are you with a wine cork?" He rummaged in a cabinet for a moment, then stepped back to reveal a bottle of chardonnay. "I can never open them properly."

"Don't you have a mech? Give me that." Melanie reached for the bottle and old-fashioned corkscrew. With practiced skill, she drove it into the cork, yanked the levers down, and pried the seal open. "There."

"The glasses are in the side cabinet. Give me five minutes, and we'll have something decent to eat."

As she poured the foaming, yellow-green wine into the delicate glasses, Melanie wondered why she felt so comfortable with this man. She barely knew him. But somehow, it didn't seem to matter. Well, it had been a strange day, and there was no sign of it getting any less strange now.

True to his word, Yosh whipped up a tomato and tofu loaf that had her asking for third portions. When they finished the chardonnay, he found a bottle of champagne, managed to open it himself, and filled her glass with the sparkling wine. And still holding the bottle, he leaned down and kissed her. Put the bottle down. Kissed her again.

It's about time, she thought.

Still kissing, they sank down among the pillows, fitting

together like two puzzle pieces. He pulled playfully at the neckline of her tunic, and she allowed him to loosen it so that he could move his hands underneath. A little later, they agreed that all their clothing was getting in the way and the only solution was to remove every stitch.

Gently, Yosh traced the curve of her shoulder, her breast, first with his hand, then his lips.

"Your skin is like silk," he whispered. "So smooth. So lovely." Slowly, his hands slid down her body, so slowly that she wanted to beg him to hurry. Clever musician fingers, stroking and probing, coaxing a theme out of her that she scarcely recognized. She hummed and moaned in ardent response to him, every nerve singing, her long-throttled emotions bursting upwards, free.

He was passionate, playful, and best of all, skillful. Eagerly, she rolled around with him on the soft orange cushions, making love until she was exhausted. Finally, they sank down sweatily in a comfortable heap.

"Mmm. So nice." She closed her eyes.

He caressed her sleepily. "Stay the night?"

Melanie chuckled. "As if I have a choice." She snuggled sleepily in his arms and was soon drifting into dreams. She was walking across the nighttime desert. Above, the stars burned with cold, remote light. The wind sent sparkling sand in looping whorls above her head and whispered secrets in her ears as it rushed past but she couldn't understand the words. She listened harder. The whisper became a mutter, then a scream that hurt her ears. Melanie sank down on her knees in the midst of the sudden, raging sandstorm. And across the shifting gray landscape, a green woman approached, fighting the wind and blowing sand, arms extended in supplication. Her mouth moved, but the gale tossed her words away. In frustration, the green woman grabbed Melanie and shook her.

"Stop it," Melanie cried. "I don't understand you."

She came awake to find Yosh gently shaking her.

"What's wrong?"

"Ooh." She leaned against him, her heart pounding. "Bad dream. Too much wine."

"Tell me."

"Weird. A green woman. On the desert at night in the middle of a storm. Asking for my help."

"A green woman?" Yosh's voice sounded suddenly alert. He sat up.

"Yeah. What's even stranger, I thought I saw her ghost. Or her sister's ghost."

"Ghost? When?"

"Today. Right before I met you."

"Where?"

"One of those screen rooms."

"Dammit. I should have known." Suddenly Yosh was on his feet. He pulled on a pair of leggings and grabbed a cold-light stick.

"Wait. Where are you going?"

"To see Ashman. Stay here."

"No way." She jumped up and started dressing. "I'm not staying in this spookhouse alone, Yosh. Where you go, I go."

"All right. But hurry."

"What's wrong?" she said, sealing her yellow tunic. "I didn't think you believed in ghosts."

"I believe in this one. Bad omen. If I'm right, a friend of mine may be in trouble."

"A friend? Who?"

"Just a friend, all right?" He waited impatiently by the door. "Come on."

She hurried after him into the hall. "Should we really be wandering around here in the dark? Do you think your friend is here someplace?"

"Yeah. And I've got an idea that Ashman will know where."

Melanie stopped in her tracks. "Yosh, do you really think we should go ask him about this? He doesn't seem, well, exactly stable to me. What if he gets upset? He's so unpredictable. And powerful."

"That's a good point." He paused. "Well, there's the empty wing. They haven't quite finished it yet. We could look around there."

He led her down a maze of hallways until her head was spinning. She felt as though they'd been walking for hours. Numbly she followed him along shadowy halls, lit by narrow pin spots and green sodium lamps. The building was silent, deserted. Melanie wondered where the security staff was. The place seemed as silent as Sleeping Beauty's castle.

Around one corner, down a left-hand corridor, around another corner, and through an atrium where the moonlight filtered spookily down through green glass. Spiky shadows revealed saguaro cacti reaching arms toward the stars.

I feel like I'm walking through a dream, Melanie thought. Holding Prince Charming's hand.

The new wing was barely finished. Blue carpeting lay piled in bolts against walls awaiting a final coating of enamel. The lighting here was raw, almost too bright after the gloom of the main building. Melanie blinked, watching dark after-shadows flare against her eyelids.

Doors all along the corridor yawned open into unfinished rooms. The night glowed softly through uncovered windows. Their steps echoed strangely along the uncarpeted hall.

"Yosh, there's nothing here."

"Shhh. Be patient," he said. "I've got a hunch. . . ."

They both stopped as the lights flickered, dimmed as though in warning, then came back up. And at the far end of the corridor, a door was closed. Melanie was almost certain it was locked.

Yosh pressed the doorpad. The door stayed closed. He pulled a circular clamp out of his pocket, punched in a five-digit code, then pressed it against the lock.

"Skeleton key," he said, grinning. "Tavia gave it to me as a joke after I accused her of living in a castle."

With a whir, the door irised open.

The room within was shadowy and the walls were an odd blue shade that gave the space the look of an undersea world. An aquarium. A figure lay curled, catlike, upon a low bed set against the far wall. Yosh flicked on the coldlight and trained it on the room's occupant. Slowly she sat up, rubbing her eyes. She had an angular face, golden eyes, green skin, and dark hair with a shock of white at her temple. It was the woman in Melanie's dream.

"Yosh," the green woman said. "Thank God."

14

NIGHTTIME in the desert. Cold. Stars harsh pin-
pricks in the black velvet sky.

Skerry ignored the chill. His cycle floated noiselessly over
the silver sand. The bulk of Emory Foundation's outer walls
came into view over the nearest dune, a shimmering curve of
green-black glass.

He turned off the cycle's motor and dismounted. From the
sack at his back he drew a pair of grapplers. Then he grabbed
the laser pistol from its metallic holster and started toward
the glass monolith.

Narlydda was somewhere inside. And supermutant or no
supermutant, he would find her and bring her out, or bring
the entire building down with him.

A cold gust of wind struck him in the face. He grinned at
the chill.

Good cold. Helps me think. He sent a cautious mental
probe out and felt it rebound back at him off the slick surface of the compound.

Just as I suspected, he thought. They've got some sort of
elaborate esper shield. Probably state-of-the-art. Generated
from inside.

He tried the main doors. They were locked. But no guard

came to investigate the stranger knocking to be admitted. Strange.

Skerry walked around the compound's perimeter until he came to the power plant. A watchman—a normal—was on duty outside.

Careless of them, he thought.

Skerry grinned and ducked out of sight. A quick probe told him that the man was mildly shielded. Now where did a normal get an esper shield? he wondered. There was something curious about the shield as well, but no time to analyze it now. He prodded the shield until he found its flaw. There was always an emotional weakness in esper shields. You just had to know where to look.

He took a deep breath and sent a directive mental thrust: *I wonder what Shayla is doing. She said she was going out to the breen show with friends. She should be home by now. But what if she's not? What if she lied? Maybe she's out with somebody else.*

He waited. The guard paced nervously. Skerry amplified the thought.

She'd better be home. Alone. The man looked to the right, then to the left. The remnants of his shield shattered, and Skerry slipped in easily to intensify his suspicions.

Maybe I should go home and see if she's there. If she's not alone, she'll be sorry. Shayla, and whoever she's with.

The guard nodded and hurried towards a dark skimmer parked at the side of the building. Skerry waved as he disappeared.

Good luck, Shayla, wherever you are, he thought.

The door to the powerhouse opened easily. Humming a tuneless song, Skerry walked inside, and locked the door behind him.

MICHAEL STOOD by the bedside, helplessly studying the still, gray face behind the dials and orange monitors, trying to recognize his father under the plaskin bandages. The golden eyes were tightly shut. Would they ever open again?

Despite the medical report, Michael was convinced that his father had tried to kill himself. A fall, the nurse had said. How could his father have fallen? He was watched almost every moment of the day. Medicated. Supervised. If somehow he'd managed to wrest a free moment away from his kindly captors, thrown off the drugs' sedation, and flung himself off a sea cliff, Michael didn't blame him. He'd probably have done the same. But how awful to have survived the attempt.

If I could help him go, I would, Michael thought.

The door opened and Sue Li walked in with Jena. The tension between the two women was obvious, and Michael wasn't surprised. Most people found it difficult to relax in his wife's company. Most women, anyway.

Michael kissed his mother, then turned to take his wife by the arm.

"Why are you here?" he said.

Sue Li turned to stare, her serene, controlled mask disrupted by his outburst. "She's part of the family, Michael." His mother's voice held a note of warning. "She belongs here."

To hell with tradition, Michael wanted to say. This woman has no business in this room. But there was his father's putty-colored face. There was his grief-stricken mother, dark circles under her eyes. He took a stronger grip on his emotions, forced himself to nod. "You're right," he said, voice tight. "Thank you for coming, Jena." Anything else he might have said was cut short, mercifully, by the arrival of his younger brother.

Jimmy smiled weakly and tried to straighten his jacket. He looked as though he'd been up for days.

"Mike, Jena." He gave them a nod as he hugged Sue Li. "Mom." Then he turned toward the bed. His face paled. "How is he?"

"Dying." Sue Li's voice was ragged with emotion.

Jimmy ran his hand through his hair. There was a look of helpless anguish on his face. "What happened?"

"Nobody knows," Michael said. "They found him at the foot of the bluff."

"How did he get there?"

"No one can answer that, either."

They jumped as a strident three-note alarm split the air. The main monitor over James Ryton's bed was flashing wildly back and forth across the spectrum.

"What's happening?" Jena cried above the din. "Is he dead?"

Sue Li gave her a venomous look. "Get the doctor."

Michael leaped for the door, but he was cut off by a mechnurse which rolled out of its wallslot, hypo poised in its foremost claw. In an instant, it brought the syringe down against James Ryton's arm. A quick hiss, and the alarm died away as the dial above the bed returned to orange.

"He can't last much longer," Jimmy muttered. He sank down wearily on a wallseat near the bed. Sue Li took a seat beside him. Michael was about to suggest that he go for coffee when the door opened. Melanie?

"What are you doing here?" Jena demanded.

Michael whirled and came face to face with Kelly McLeod. She was poised in the doorway, her cheeks pink with embarrassment.

"Michael . . . I'm sorry. I just had to come when I heard. Heyran Landon told me where Dream Haven was."

"Only mutants are welcome here," Jena said coldly. "Why don't you leave before you make things worse."

Kelly ignored her. Her eyes sought out Sue Li. "Mrs. Ryton . . . I'm sorry to interrupt you at a time like this. If there's anything I can do . . ."

"You're very kind," Sue Li said. "But certainly you didn't come all this way just to extend your sympathy?"

"No." Kelly looked at Michael for a long moment, then looked away. "No. I came because there's a warrant out for

for your arrest, Michael. You failed to appear before the subcommittee. You're in contempt of Congress. You've got to come back."

"A warrant?" Michael laughed harshly. "What else can they do? Throw me in jail? They're just going to have to wait until this is over. Then they can arrest me or hang me or do whatever else they want to me." He sat down. "Thanks for coming, Kelly. I hope this won't put you in jeopardy."

"I'll be all right." She looked around uncertainly. "I didn't mean to intrude—"

"Please, come and sit with us," Sue Li said. She indicated a place next to her on the wallseat. "You've come a long way to warn Michael. You must be tired. Rest awhile."

Jena's expression was explosive. She glared at Sue Li, then at Michael and Kelly.

"I'm going for coffee!" she sputtered, and slammed out of the room.

Jimmy turned to his brother. "What's she in a bad mood about?"

"She's very upset about your father," Sue Li said. "Now why don't we all just chant together for inner tranquility. It's easy, Kelly." She smiled. "I'll show you how."

MELANIE WATCHED the tall woman embrace Yosh. In the dim light, the greenish cast to her skin was barely apparent. She was an unusual mutant, but Emory Foundation was filled with mutants. Maybe there was an enchanted mutant princess behind every door.

"What are you doing here?" Yosh said.

"I never left. Ashman did something to me that put me to sleep. When I awoke, I was in this cell. And I've been here ever since."

"Alone?"

"Except when he visits me, or takes me out for a walk."

Melanie couldn't stand it any longer. "But I saw you," she

blurted out. "At least, I thought it was you. In the screen-room. Only you were transparent. Like a ghost."

"I thought it was a dream," the green woman whispered. "My esper quotient is so low, I didn't think I could project anything at all. Especially from that room with its neural dampers. But you say that you saw me?"

"It looked like you," Melanie said. "You tried to say something, but I couldn't hear you. Then you faded away."

The woman looked at her in surprise. "Who are you?"

Yosh hesitated and Melanie stepped forward. "My name is Melanie. Melanie Ryton."

The woman smiled. "Hello, Melanie Ryton. My name is Narlydda."

"The artist?"

She nodded.

Melanie felt the laughter building in her throat. She'd searched high and low for the elusive Narlydda, and where did she find her? On a midnight trek through an enchanted glass castle in the desert. The laughter bubbled up and out. She couldn't control it. She knew the others were looking at her as though they thought she was crazy. She didn't care. When the hysteria passed she wiped her eyes.

"If you only knew how long I've been looking for you, Narlydda," Melanie said. "I'm a reporter for Cable News. And even using the Census Net, I couldn't find you."

"Good. I had to pay a bundle to keep my address out of that data base. Hmmm. Melanie Ryton. I knew your name sounded familiar." The artist stared at her appraisingly. "Didn't you call me about a month ago? But your eyes were a different color then."

"So you *were* monitoring my call!"

Narlydda shrugged. "Even *I* feel curious occasionally." Her expression changed suddenly as her mask of indifference was swept away by something primal and immediate. Fear. Desperation. "Get me out of this place and I'll give you your interview, Melanie Ryton. Or anything else you want."

"It's a deal."

Yosh leaned against the door. "Aren't you forgetting something? The doors are all locked."

"What are you talking about?" Narlydda said.

"Ashman's got this place locked up tighter than a prison," Yosh said.

"That's a good word for it," the artist said. "Well, if we can't get out, isn't there someplace where we can hide?"

You can run, but you can't hide.

The mindspeech was deafening. Melanie grabbed her head with both hands. Yosh sank to his knees. Only Narlydda stood, strangely untouched.

"Ashman, get your volume under control," she said.

The supermutant slowly faded into view, like some old-time video. He looked displeased. "What are you all doing together?" he demanded. "Conspiring?"

"Conspiring? Against whom?" Yosh said. "You're the one who has us locked in."

Ashman stared at him fiercely. Then he smiled. It was almost a sweet smile.

"You look tired, Yosh. Sleep."

Yosh's eyes closed and he collapsed to the floor, curling into a tight, fetal ball.

"You've hurt him!" Melanie cried. She fell to her knees beside him. Yosh barely stirred as she touched his face.

"I haven't hurt anybody," Ashman said. "He'll wake up in a day or two, feeling like he's had a vacation. I just stimulated his sleep center."

"Victor, you can't go on behaving this way," Narlydda said. Her voice was low and hoarse. "Don't you see that you'll only hurt yourself?"

Ashman smiled brilliantly. "It means so much to me when you show that you care. But you'll wear yourself out worrying about unimportant normals. And I can show you things you've never dreamed of, even in your wildest artistic visions." He pulled her into his arms.

For a moment, Melanie thought he would waltz Narlydda around the turquoise room in his crazed exuberance. The artist rested listlessly in his embrace, head drooping. But Ashman seemed oblivious to her nerveless state. He held her close, crooning for a moment before he remembered that somebody else was watching them. With a jerk, he looked up and locked his brilliant, silvery gaze upon Melanie.

"Don't let me interrupt," she said. "I was just leaving anyway." She backed away toward the door.

"I think you could use a nap as well," Ashman said.

His eyes held her with hypnotic power. Melanie stared into their cool, shimmering depths and felt a strange compulsion to yawn. No. No, stay awake, she told herself. Get away. She shook her head, breaking the spell.

Ashman frowned, disconcerted. "I said sleep!"

"Try a lullaby," Melanie retorted. "I knew you were a fake."

"How strange." Ashman turned so that Narlydda could see Melanie as well. "Look, dear, she seems impervious to my charms." His voice was cold. "Well, Miss Melanie Mutant, why don't you perform for me, then? Narlydda has already given me quite a demonstration of her telekinetic skills—or tried to. How about you? Can you read my mind? Throw a mechmaid through the air? Juggle burning torches?"

"I'd rather just disappear," Melanie said. "That would be a nice old sideshow trick."

"Whatever you'd like, dear." Gently, he helped Narlydda onto a heap of cushions. She sat there passively, her hands resting in her lap.

"Don't 'dear' me," Melanie said sharply. "And I'm not interested in joining your mutant circus, Ashman."

"Oh, that's right. You're a null. I did forget that. My apologies." He gave her a peculiar look. "Would you like some mutant powers?"

Melanie froze. Was it possible? Could this madman give

her what she'd always dreamed of? To be able to levitate. Or use mindspeech. To participate fully at Mutant Council meetings and clan gatherings . . . she wavered. Then she glanced at Yosh, curled on the ground asleep. He had told her he preferred her as a null. And after all this time, how could she imagine that she would adapt to being an operative mutant? She wouldn't recognize herself. No. No.

She nodded toward Yosh. "Wake him up and let us out of here!"

"How disappointing." Ashman shook his head. "Oh well. . . ."

Narlydda seemed to divine his thoughts. She jumped up and reached for his hands. "No, Victor. Please. She hasn't done anything . . ."

Too late, Melanie heard the click of a mech behind her. As she whirled, she felt the sting of a hypo in her left arm. And then she was slumping to the floor, her mind a pleasant, warm red buzz, fading to black.

15

ASHMAN, DON'T—

The mindspeech cut through Skerry's telepathic shield like feedback, flaring oddly in clairaudient cadence. Despite the distortion, the intonation felt familiar.

Narlydda? Did he dare risk dropping his own shields to broadcast an inquiry? If Ashman was listening, he'd hear him immediately. Might be eavesdropping clairaudiently right now.

The cry he'd caught seemed to come from several floors above him. He was on the third level of Emory Foundation headquarters. Behind him was row after row of employees slumped at their desks as though enchanted.

This is worse than I thought. What has Rebekah gotten me into?

He paused near a pale woman. Her long red hair spread in a vibrant halo over her deskpad. The dim lighting gave her skin a bluish cast.

Face it, he thought. Rebekah hasn't gotten me into anything I haven't already chosen. If Narlydda's here, then I have to be here too. Love's a ball and chain, all right.

He blew a kiss toward the red-haired sleeper.

Need a lot of Prince Charmings to awaken this bunch, he thought. I don't know if my lips are up to it.

He turned and strode toward the stairs. The laser pistol swung from his belt. To his surprise, he climbed to the sixth level without obstacle. Either Ashman knew he was here and didn't care, or he was getting sloppy.

Hope it's the latter.

He emerged from the stairwell into a dim hallway. The starlight that entered through the filtered windows gave a cool glow but precious little illumination. Skerry cut his shields and risked a brief mental probe, aiming for subliminal resonance, below Ashman's notice. If Narlydda was nearby, she would reflect the probe by instinct. All Skerry needed was an echo or two. And there it was, bouncing back toward him from a far corridor to his left. He didn't like the stressful coloration of the reverberations, but there wasn't anything he could do about it until he found his lady.

He squinted down the dark corridor.

Ready or not, Ashman, here I come.

The mental echo danced tantalizingly in Skerry's mind. It led him into a wing of rooms that seemed partially unfinished. Carpeting lay piled high in bolts. He peered into one open chamber and saw a young Japanese man lying on a cot, fast asleep. He paused for a moment, then walked on into the next open chamber.

The walls inside were blue. The room was empty. He walked out and continued down the corridor, but found that every room he came to was empty.

Time to risk a probe again. The echo came back, stronger, this time, from the second blue room.

Lydda?

No answer, save for that faint, tantalizing echo: *Ashman, don't, don't, don't.*

Narlydda was here. That was the echo of her thoughts. Unmistakable. Skerry hurried into the chamber.

Ashman, don't— Too late, he saw the door close behind him, cutting off the brief connection. Narlydda's mindspeech had come from outside the room. But the echo had come from within. A trap.

He send a quick telepathic bolt against the door. It bounced back with lightning speed, causing him to jump out of the way to avoid getting seared.

Neural reflectors, he thought. This room is a cage for telepaths. And I walked right into it. Brilliant.

Cursing, Skerry sat down on the wallseat, and the bulky laser pistol scraped along his thigh. He fingered it, watching the door. Maybe he could burn his way out of here. It was worth a try.

The pistol had five settings. Try lowest first, he thought.

Taking careful aim, he depressed the trigger stud. A bolt of yellow light exploded toward the door. And bounced back at him. He ducked just in time. But it richocheted in his direction with blinding speed.

"Shit!" Skerry dropped to the floor as the laser bolt danced crazily from wall to wall before exhausting its energy and fading away.

Well, that was a bad idea too. Cautiously, Skerry sat up. He looked around the room. When he saw the mech and food supply, he cursed again and put his head in his hands.

At least he knew that Narlydda was here. But Ashman had been clever. And prepared. The least he could do was return the compliment.

Skerry took a deep breath, sat back against the turquoise wall, and closed his eyes. His pulse and breathing rate slowed as he counted. One, two, three, four . . .

Let Ashman keep him locked up. He could maintain at this level for twenty days. Almost three weeks in which he would still be a tiger, waiting for the zookeeper to open the cage.

NARLYDDA WATCHED ASHMAN fiddle with the wallscreen microphone.

"Isn't it a little late for sending messages?" she said acidly.

"Not to the West Coast," he said. "I promised to discuss my plans with Rebekah Terling, and I think that this would be an ideal time to chat with her."

"I don't know that she'd agree," Narlydda said. She sat down carefully on a pile of blue cushions. How long had she been here? Days? Weeks? She knew it was the middle of the night. But which night?

The wallscreen whistled strangely, as though bucking interference of some sort. Then the picture solidified and the Book Keeper of the Western Mutant Council stared from the screen with a wary expression.

"Rebekah, Ashman here."

"I know who you are," she said. "I'd expected that we'd talk face to face. . . ."

"We are," Ashman said pleasantly.

"I meant in person," she said sharply. "And not in the wee hours, either."

"I'm a nightowl."

"I'd expected to hear from Tavia Emory. I've left messages for her over several days."

Ashman shrugged. "She's been a bit under the weather. A touch of the flu. The doctor prescribed rest."

"I'm sure." The Book Keeper's tone was skeptical. "Well, what's on your mind, Mr. Ashman?"

"I've been considering how best to integrate me into your group."

Narlydda looked up in surprise.

"Yes, we'd all been wondering about that," Rebekah replied drily. "And what are your suggestions?"

"I suggest, my dear Rebekah, that you resign as Book Keeper in favor of my natural ascendance. I'll be making the same suggestion to Astori on the East Coast, of course, but I suppose that will have to wait until tomorrow."

Rebekah seemed speechless. Swallowing hard, she turned

away from the screen for a moment. Then she gave him a piercing look. Her golden eyes glittered.

"You can't be serious," she said. "Assuming we would countenance this change in the first place, it would have to be put up before the respective councils for a motion to request full-membership vote. We couldn't even begin to mobilize that before the summer meeting—"

"Why do you resist unification!" Ashman shouted. "Don't you see how fragmented you are? That you're being assimilated against your will even as you try to resist? You're growing weaker, not stronger. You need a central leader—a powerful one—to direct mutant affairs. Don't give me limp excuses about parliamentary procedures. You can call a plenary session any time if there's reason for it."

The Book Keeper's expression froze at his outburst. "I don't think this is a good enough reason," she said quietly. "I appreciate your concern for the mutant community. If you wish to work with us, Mr. Ashman, I suggest that you attend the next full council meeting, on *either* coast. You will be made welcome. Should you wish to discuss this or any other issues, you will be invited to put them before us at that time." She paused. "It seems to me to be in all our best interests that you make an attempt to join us before you attempt to own us."

Ashman cut the connection abruptly. "I knew she was against me the moment I met her," he said. "Well, she'll be sorry she resisted me."

"She's not resisting you," Narlydda said. "You can't expect to just walk in and take over. . . ."

"I can do whatever I want," he snapped. "Do you doubt it?" He swung around, his black tunic flapping. "I've completely controlled this entire complex. No one comes or goes, sleeps or awakens, unless I allow it. I've given those pitiful, puny lesser mutants the courtesy of an illusion that they have a choice." He laughed harshly. "They have no choice.

As they'll see, shortly. I'm their future, whether they like it or not."

Narlydda swallowed gingerly. She felt very tired, and her throat was dry. Ashman seemed to sense this and levitated a pitcher from the table near him, pouring a sparkling cascade of amber liquid into a tall, amethyst glass. When the glass was full, it floated into Narlydda's hand.

"Drink," he said. His tone was gentle. "I know you're tired. But please, just keep me company for a while longer, and then I'll let you sleep."

She wanted to dash the glass to the floor. To tell him he was crazy, delusional, and repellent. But there was something oddly touching about him in his crazed loneliness. She couldn't hurt him that way. Whether she would survive his affection, well, she'd worry about that later.

She tipped the glass up and took a sip.

16

REBEKAH TERLING tossed restlessly as the dawn light slipped through the window blinds to draw pink lines on the wall by her bed. She'd tried chants, warm milk, even valedrine, but sleep eluded her still. Ashman's call had confirmed her worst fears, and no amount of narcotic could quiet the tired, panicked voice in her head. The one that said Ashman was serious. And that he had the power to implement his desires, with or without the assent of the council members.

Enough worry, she thought. Furiously, she threw back the covers and turned on her bedside screen.

Damn. No message from Skerry. Where are you, old will-o'-the-wisp? In trouble? On the Moon? Should I send in help? I wish I knew what to do! I thought that Book Keepers always knew the right thing to do.

For a moment, she considered going to Scottsdale herself. With a high-powered laser rifle, she might be able to kill Ashman without coming in range of his powers . . . but no. She was fooling herself. She was no match for a man who could mindspeak across a continent. Their only hope was Skerry. If even he was strong enough.

She closed her eyes and made the chant against fear:

I am on a dark road.
Fear is with me,
and I have walked here before.
Life takes us to strange and lonely places.
Time moves us in ways we do not see.
Time moves
and we follow
until there is light ahead.
Step by step, the way is found.
Step by step, the way is made.
Alone, I will walk,
in the light,
to the end of the road.

Rebekah sighed and opened her eyes. That was better. At least she could think clearly now. She punched Chemen Astori's code into the screen. She wanted somebody to worry with.

The screen lit to show the Eastern Book Keeper in a blue suit. His dark hair was wet, freshly combed. The expression on his apple-cheeked face was one of surprise.

"Bekah?" Astori's throaty baritone voice sounded especially deep. "I was just getting ready to leave for work. I never expect you to call this early." He paused and stared at her intently. "What's wrong?"

"Can you shield this?"

"It's that important? You *are* worried." Astori looked away for a moment. "Done."

"Thanks. I can't help being paranoid whenever I'm talking —or thinking—about Ashman."

"You've got the supermutant blues?"

"Worse than that. You know that 'job' I mentioned?"

He nodded. "It's come to that?"

"I've sent Skerry. . . ."

"Skerry! Are you crazy?" Astori glared at her.

"Che, you know he's one of our strongest telepaths."

"And most unpredictable. By the Book, I thought you'd send a group of multis, at the very least. Not one crazy renegade!"

"A group would be too conspicuous. Besides, multis are usually weak telepaths, and with Ashman, we need esper power. I thought one clever telepath could handle it."

"But now you're worried. Well, I don't blame you."

Rebekah began to regret the call. But it was too late for regrets, wasn't it? "Che, I didn't call to debate this. I called because we need a contingency plan."

"In case this doesn't work?"

"Exactly. I'm beginning to think we'd better have a backup team ready in case Skerry fails."

Astori studied her silently for a moment. "You realize what you're saying?" he asked. "That would mean another aggressive assault against Ashman after he's aware of our intentions. God knows how he'd respond."

"All the more reason to be prepared for it," Rebekah said. "I'm going to call a few people here on the West Coast this morning. I suggest you do the same on your end."

"What about the nonmutants? The military?"

Rebekah shook her head. "Let's try to handle this in-house, first."

"I don't know. If we can't deal with Ashman, aren't we exposing the normals to a terrible risk without warning?"

"If I know my generals, they've been in meetings ever since Ashman revealed himself," Rebekah said. "They'll be as ready for him as they can be. No need to encourage them further. Just get our own teams ready."

"Right. And hope we won't need them."

"Amen. I'll talk to you soon, Che."

KELLY LEANED into the payscreen, waiting for her call to go through.

Come on, answer, she thought.

A mutant clad in bright green healer's robes floated by to her left. She moved closer to the screen, hoping for privacy.

She had to reach Heyran Landon before the warrant for Michael was activated. He had a grace period of twenty-four hours in which to comply. After that, he could be taken into custody at any time. She had a sudden crazy image of her fighting off the federal marshals, trading laser pistol shots. Michael's moll. Just what she'd always wanted to be.

"There is no answer. Do you wish to leave a message?"

"No. I mean, yes!" Quick. What to say? "This is Kelly McLeod. Urgent that Colonel Heyran deactivate warrant for Michael Ryton's arrest. I repeat—"

"Kelly?" It was Landon's voice. But the screen remained dark. Blocked.

"Yessir."

"Got me out of a sonic shower. This had better be good."

"Sorry, sir. Did you know they'd issued an automatic warrant for Michael Ryton's arrest?"

"Warrant? For Ryton? Why?"

"He left the investigation because of family business."

"So you told me. How serious is it?"

"His father is dying."

"I see." The irritation faded from Landon's voice. "Ryton's in trouble right up to his eyebrows."

"That's why I called." Kelly tried not to sound too eager. "I was hoping you could do something about the warrant."

"Do something? I'm not a magician," Landon said. "Kelly, are you certain that you want to get involved in this? I remember a couple of days ago you felt considerably different."

"I know." How could she explain how she felt? She wasn't even sure herself. "I'm already involved. Here."

"Where are you? Dream Haven?"

"Yes."

"Thought so. I'm surprised they let you in."

"I insisted."

178

Landon chuckled. "I'm sure you did. Okay, I'll see what I can do about this warrant, Kelly. But if Ryton didn't request that he be excused due to a personal emergency, I don't know that I can help him. So don't get your hopes up. But keep in touch. Landon out."

Keep my hopes up, Kelly thought. Yes. I'll try. If only I can think of some way to do that. Or maybe I can find some nice mutant around here to levitate them for me.

She turned from the screen phone and peered down the quiet, pink-tiled hospital corridor. A secret medical complex for mutants, she thought. For their old, their infirm, their dying clan members. What a strange place.

A nurse and an orderly, dressed in neutral blue tones, levitated past her toward the upper floors. Their golden eyes sparkled as they turned to stare at the nonmutant in their midst.

What am I doing here? Chasing a dream?

Slowly, Kelly wandered down the corridor until she came to a concession room. She moved through the sliding doors and walked toward the nearest empty table. Around her, mutants were sipping gem-colored stimulants or levitating food trays from dispensers to tables.

Kelly ducked as a plate of choba salad sailed toward her at eye level. This was all becoming a little too much. Not that she was a stranger to levitation. She'd floated herself, at zero-g. But a room full of mutants twirling glasses in midair made her feel as though she'd stepped into the center ring of the circus. She saw an empty seat and sat down gratefully. Right next to Jena Ryton.

Wonderful, she thought. Just who I was looking for.

Jena let her cup sink to the green table top with a clatter. Her eyes flashed angrily. "Why don't you get out of here?" she said. "I don't know why you bothered to come here to begin with. No one wants you here. There's really no room for you. Can't you see that? Aren't you embarrassed? I would be, in your place."

"Don't tell me how to act," Kelly snapped. "You have absolutely no idea how you'd react in my place. And I'll bet you don't really have much of a clue about how to behave given your own set of circumstances."

"What?!"

Around them, mutants turned to stare.

Kelly knew she'd gone too far. But Jena's baiting had pushed her over the edge. "Why weren't you with Michael at Armstrong?" she demanded. "Why was he all alone, in desperate trouble? How could you abandon him like that?"

"I don't have to sit here and be interrogated," Jena replied. "Especially by an outsider." She gathered up her jacket and walked out, head held high.

Kelly sank down into her hard acrylic seat, aware of every golden eye in the room trained upon her. Bravo, she thought. Open mouth and insert both feet. So speaks the hero of Moonstation. Perhaps it's time for me to go before I make things worse.

No. Please, stay.

Mindspeech.

Kelly looked around, but the mutants in the room were studiously ignoring her now. Try as she might, she couldn't locate the speaker.

"Who?" she said softly.

Sue Li. Meet me in the lobby in five minutes. Please.

"All right."

Gratefully, she hurried out of the room, eager to get away from the chilly atmosphere. For a moment she was tempted to keep right on walking out the front doors of the building toward the nearest taxi stop.

But no. Michael's mother wanted to talk to her. What did she want? Kelly decided to stay until she found out.

YOSH OPENED HIS EYES. He felt as though he'd been asleep for a week. His head was spinning. Gingerly, he sat up. This was worse than the worst hangover he'd ever had, and he didn't want to think about that, if he could help it. He stood up with extra care.

"Ooph!"

At least he was on his feet now, even if he was hanging on to the wall for support. Funny texture to the wall, though. Soft, almost velvety. He looked closely at it. Turquoise. He didn't remember any turquoise walls. The color made his head hurt even more. He looked away.

Where was he?

And where was Melanie? That pretty reporter. At least he remembered her.

I'm Yosh, he told himself. I'm a musician. I work for . . . for Emory Foundation. I must be someplace in the Emory Foundation headquarters. And I was with Melanie, pretty Melanie, when . . . what happened? Where is she? Where is everybody?

He remembered a bustling complex filled with busy golden-eyed folk and the noise of ringing screens. A sharp-faced woman with gold-tipped hair and glittering eyes: Tavia Emory. Where was she?

His legs felt rubbery and unreliable, but he managed to stumble out of the room and down the hall, moving slowly. He passed rolls of blue carpeting. Abandoned carpenter's tools.

I must be in the new wing. And that means I should be able to find my studio. Get some coffee. Clear my head.

He began to remember bits and pieces of what had happened. A man with silvery eyes and a tinny laugh: Ashman, the supermutant. A tall, elegant woman whose skin was light green. Narlydda. And with these memories came a growing sense of uneasiness. Something bad had happened. He knew it.

Yosh leaned heavily against a doorpad for support, then jumped with surprise as the doors sprang open.

"It's about time," said a sardonic male voice.

The voice's owner was a tall, muscular, bearded mutant.

He sauntered out of the room and sized Yosh up with a quick, surprised glance.

"You're not Ashman. Who are you?" he said. "And why aren't you asleep? Everybody else is."

Just what I need, Yosh thought. An angry mutant asking crazy questions. "I was asleep until a few minutes ago," he said. "My name's Yosh. I work for Emory Foundation. And who are you? What are you doing here?"

"Name's Skerry. I'm looking for somebody."

"So am I," Yosh said quickly. "You haven't seen a mutant girl around here, have you? Sort of Caucasian and Oriental mix. Her name is Melanie."

"No, I haven't. . . . Did you say Melanie?" The bearded mutant stared at him sharply. "What's her last name?"

"Ryton, I think."

"Jesus, it's old home week at the spook house," the stranger muttered. "No, I haven't seen Melanie Ryton for, let's see, maybe fifteen years. Since she was a kid. But I know her brother. Is she here?"

"She was. But she's not the one you're looking for, is she?"

"Nope. I'm interested in a tall, green lady. . . ."

"Sounds like Narlydda," Yosh said.

"You've seen her?" Skerry grabbed his arm. "How long ago? When?"

"Hey, go easy." Yosh winced and pulled himself free of the mutant's powerful grasp. "I think it was last night. But it could have been two weeks ago. I don't know how long I've been out of commission. Ashman . . ."

"Where is he?"

"Wish I knew. If I did, I'd bet we'd find Melanie and Narlydda. I think that he took them away after he knocked me out. How long were you in that room?"

"Hard to say, although I think it hasn't been longer than two days. Nice little mutant trap there."

"That's Ashman's doing. I'm sure of it."

"You've met Ashman?" Skerry asked.

"Oh, yeah." He shuddered at the memory.

"What's your take on him?"

Yosh rubbed his forehead thoughtfully. "He's unpredictable. Kind of high-strung. Arrogant. Those powers of his are hard to believe."

"But you've seen him use them?" The tall mutant stared at him intently.

"Yes. He seems very powerful."

"Let's hope he's not too powerful." Skerry smiled wryly. "How about we team up and look for him? Considering that he seems to have made off with both of our ladies."

"Fine with me," Yosh said. "But I'm not much use against a mutant or supermutant." He held up his hands. "I'm great with a claviflute, if that helps."

"Try this." Skerry handed him a laser rifle. "That's cocked for medium power. I'm going to try out a long-range esper probe. If Ashman comes running, I may not be able to hold him for long. Use your own judgment, but try to hit him, not me."

Yosh caught the matte gray metal weapon. It was so large that he could barely hold it with both hands.

"I've never used one of these," he said uncertainly. What was he getting himself into?

"They tell me the best way is to learn by doing." Skerry grinned. "Let's hope you don't need too many lessons."

He closed his eyes. Waited. Cursed. Opened his eyes.

"All I'm getting are echoes. They're not in this wing. Maybe not even in the building." He set off down the corridor at a good clip. "C'mon. If you're coming."

"Wait. Where are we going?"

"I caught a bounce off of some screen that was used recently. Maybe I can trace Ashman if I can get my hands on the screen data for the past forty-eight hours."

Yosh followed him through the corridors of Emory Foundation until they came to a large, screen-filled room.

"This is perfect," Skerry said. He reached for the keypad. Pressed it. The screens remained dark.

"Let me," Yosh said, and brushed past him. He tapped in Tavia's code. Oddly, only a partial menu came up. "Hmm. Strange. Something's blocking the main menu."

"Figures. Do we have any outside-access capacity?"

"I think so." Yosh punched in his own code. "Yeah. Here. We can call out on this."

"Good." The bearded mutant punched a special code in, waited, then smiled as his call went through.

"You have reached the home of Narlydda . . ." said a pleasant female voice. Yosh recognized it as the simulacrum that Narlydda had named Anne Verland.

"Code Y6Cadmium Blue," Skerry said.

"Your identity is confirmed. All data files are open," Anne Verland replied. "Data search available.

"Anne, can you work a screen-to-screen search?"

"Affirmative. Specify data requested."

"All activity on premises within past forty-eight hours."

"Working."

"And Anne?"

"Yes, Skerry?"

"What day is it?"

17

SENATOR ANDREA GREENBERG brushed a strand of dark red hair back into place, straightened her silver gray suit, and closed her screencase with a snap.

That's it for the day, she thought. And good thing, too. These committee meetings are deadly. It's a wonder I get any work done at all. I should have had my head examined before I agreed to serve on Appropriations.

With a wave to her staff she was out the door, and in seconds, the private elevator had whisked her up to the skimmer port. She walked out of the heated elevator cab into weak, wintry sunshine and a crowd of reporters. Her red hair danced in the chill breeze.

"Senator Greenberg, any comment on your connection to the Ryton, Greene and Davis spacedome snafu?"

"Senator Greenberg, are you worried that you'll be linked to the substandard production of dome parts?"

"Could we get a sound byte for the nine o'clock news in Brisbane, Senator?"

"Over here, Senator—"

"Please, Senator Greenberg, your opinion on Michael Ryton's attempts to undercut the space industry—"

Michael Ryton! My God, she thought, I haven't heard his

name in years. What in the world is going on here? Andie spun on her heel and stared angrily right into the heart of the braying pack.

"Now what's this?" she demanded imperiously. "And one at a time, please. If you can't run your ambush in an orderly fashion, I won't answer anybody's question."

A blond-haired, green-eyed woman stepped forward. Andie recognized her as the Tri-Com anchorwoman, Lucia Silva. "Please, Senator," she said, "we'd like your reaction to the revelations concerning the manufacture of substandard parts for Moonstation."

"What revelation?"

"Well, Congresswoman Kate Fisher said that Michael Ryton's testimony before the subcommittee was clearly self-incriminating."

"Congresswoman Fisher is well known for her antibusiness sentiments," Andie said. "I'm not familiar with her comments on this issue."

"But you are familiar with Michael Ryton?"

"Yes. I met him and his father during Eleanor Jacobsen's term of office."

"Do you support his efforts at deregulating safety measures?"

"What are these measures you're referring to?"

"The lobbying efforts to prevent additional safeguards—"

"That was more than fifteen years ago," Andie said. "And the legislation targeted was for a specific project, already well covered by safety measures. As I recall, it had nothing to do with Moonstation."

"Congresswoman Fisher says—"

"Kate Fisher should do her witchhunting someplace else, not on my time. And not with the taxpayers' money!" Andie regretted the words as soon as she'd uttered them. She'd let her temper get the best of her. Her husband, Joel, had warned her about that. But it was too late. Besides, Kate

Fisher was a thorn in her side, and had been since Andie had won her senate seat five years ago.

"Now, if you'll excuse me. I have nothing further to say." She whipped around and strode toward her skimmer, daring any foolhardy reporter to pursue her. Once safe inside, she locked the doors and leaned back on the broad, honey-colored leather seat.

"Home."

At the sound of her voice, the skimmer sprang to life, humming gently as it cleared the exit ramp.

Michael Ryton, she thought. What trouble have you gotten yourself into this time?

She sped past federal buildings, their pale marble looking ghostly in the fading sunlight. Traffic was unusually thin, and in minutes, she was pulling into the driveway of her Georgetown coop.

Joel was waiting for her in the kitchen. He was wearing a red sweater and jeans. His gray hair curled gently in a cap around his head.

She gave him a kiss and sniffed the air appreciatively. "Is that Thai garlic noodles I smell?"

"Your favorite."

"Remind me again to congratulate myself for marrying the *Post*'s food editor."

His green eyes sparkled with pleasure. Reaching for her, he pulled her close and held her in a brief hug. Then he turned back to the stove. As he swished the noodles around in the wok, he said, "I thought you might want a treat after the way those media vultures descended on you."

"You saw that?"

"It's already been broadcast. I made a tape for you."

"Thanks, sweetie." Andie dropped her fur coat on the back of the sofa, settled into the deep, soft blue cushions, and palmed on the screen. For a moment, all she saw was a flickering hail of orange and red specks. Then the image coalesced into blond, efficient Lucia Silva.

"Senator Andrea Jacobsen denies any connection to the Moonstation tragedy," the blond reporter said. "Although she acknowledged her link to Ryton, Greene and David, the firm identified with manufacture of the allegedly faulty dome parts—"

"My God," Andie said.

"—she denied that she had in any way conspired with Michael Ryton to bring about the fatal deregulation of the space industry, which many experts, including Congresswoman Kate Fisher, say led to this disaster."

The newscast cut to a commercial in which a large, bald man strapped to a white tuba and oxygen tank was floating through a long aquarium filled with office buildings and orange fish wearing gas masks.

Andie reset the autotape and shut off the screen.

"Here. Drink this." Joel handed her a dark vermouth on the rocks with a lime twist.

"Thanks." She finished it in three gulps and refilled the glass. "How could I have been so stupid?" She stood up and walked toward the table where Joel was setting down a steaming plate.

"I will not allow anybody to call my wife stupid. Even my wife." Joel said mock severely as he ladled out the noodles onto their green acrylic plates. "Come sit down and eat before it gets cold. There's nothing worse than cold, gluey noodles."

"Yessir."

The tangy food warmed her. As she ate, Andie relaxed and began to plot strategy.

"I'll call a press conference."

"Don't talk with your mouth full." Joel filled her plate again.

She made a show of swallowing. "There. Happy now? I'll call a press conference with statistics from the results of the so-called fatal deregulation. Show how safe everything has been for fifteen years. Then I'll find out what's going on at that damned investigation. Kate Fisher's media circus. That woman's priorities need rewiring." Andie stabbed with her chopsticks at a stray noodle as though she were working on Kate Fisher's priorities.

The screenphone rang and Andie turned to answer it.

Joel rolled his eyes. "Not during dinner," he said. "I thought we agreed that you wouldn't take calls during dinner. The machine can handle it."

"But it might be important." Andie gave him an apologetic smile. "I know how you feel about this, honey, but please understand—"

"I know, I know. A senator's never off-duty." He switched on the screen near the table.

The round face of Chemen Astori, Book Keeper for the Eastern Mutant Council, appeared. Andie had met him several years ago. A strong, trustworthy leader, as she remembered. And an amusing man, to boot. But he looked sober now. Grim, even.

"Che? I'm here," she said. "Just finishing dinner."

"Sorry to interrupt, Senator."

"What's the problem?"

"We understand there's a warrant out for Michael Ryton's arrest."

"What?" Andie almost dropped her chopsticks. "How? Why?"

"The Western Book Keeper, Rebekah Terling, just called me. Ryton didn't show up for the last day of his testimony at Armstrong. Family emergency. His father is dying."

Andie closed her eyes for a moment. She hadn't spoken to James Ryton in years. But even now, she could see his features: the golden eyes, the thinning blond hair, the determined jut of the jaw. Dying? It couldn't be. She opened her eyes as the Eastern Book Keeper continued.

"Kate Fisher demanded that a warrant be procured," he said. "And she knows how to keep the media salivating."

"Sounds just like her," Andie said. "But why can't Michael just request to be excused from the hearings?"

"He should have. I'm sure it would have been arranged. But he must have been so upset by the circumstances that he wasn't thinking clearly—his father was seriously injured in what appears to have been a suicide attempt."

"Gods!"

"And now that he's gone AWOL, Kate Fisher has whipped up the authorities to get them on his trail. She's determined to use this investigation to shut down the space industry. She seems to have some special bias against Michael's company."

"I always thought Kate was a bigot," Andie said. "She's terrified of mutants. And this is one way to hurt them—the space industry is filled with mutant engineers and designers. Poor Michael."

"Senator, is there anything you can do?"

Andie leaned back in her chair and studied the screen carefully as she weighed her answer. What to do? Michael was certainly in a mess this time. But what was she supposed to do? Become Saint Andie the Good, saddle up, and ride to the rescue of mutants everywhere?

"I understand your problem," she said. "I'm not sure there's much I can do to help. Not that I don't want to." She shook her head and a few strands of dark-red hair danced around her face. "I hate like hell to worry about political necessities. But I've learned to live with them and work with them. This issue may simply be too hot for me. I've got an election to worry about next year, and the media have already sniffed out my mutant connection."

Joel gave her a look sharp with disapproval.

Onscreen, Chemen Astori's eyes were wide, astonished. Obviously, he hadn't expected her reaction. "But Senator," he said. "We're not talking about political expediency here. We're talking about justice. About saving part of an industry vital to this nation's economic welfare. And what's more, we're talking about an innocent man being hounded by congressional wolves—"

"Che, I'm sorry," Andie said. "I've known Michael Ryton and his family for a long time. We used to be fairly close. But it's simply out of the question. If I want to accomplish half of what I've planned—and this affects mutants as well as nonmutants—then I must play by the rules. And that means getting reelected." She gave him a quick, pained look. "I'd like to help. But if Michael was absent without excuse, then I'm afraid he is liable. There's nothing I can do."

Chemen Astori golden eyes glittered with disdain. "I'd expected more of you," he said coldly. "You've always been a friend to the mutants. But I can see that's changed. I'm sorry to have disturbed you, Senator." He cut the connection and his image scattered into buzzing black and red lines.

"Shit." Andie chewed on the end of her chopstick. "You were right. I shouldn't have taken that call."

"Can't you do anything?" Joel asked. His eyes bored into her. "I've never seen you turn your back on a friend before, Andie. That's not like you."

She waved her hands impatiently. "I know, I know. But Michael's irresponsibility has not only put him at risk—it could yank me and possibly the entire space industry along with him. Consider that." She stood up. "Then you might agree I'm wise to stay out of it."

"Do you really believe that?"

"I have to. As ugly as that may seem to you. And as much as I'd like to help him." She stood up. "I've got some work to do. Don't wait up."

Sue Li nervously paced the length of the hospital lobby, oblivious to the bright blue and yellow tile on the walls, the soothing wordless chants issuing from the wall speakers, the passage of other mutants on their way to and from visits with patients.

Her footsteps rang to a grim, internal refrain: My husband is dying. My husband is dying.

Never had she felt so helpless. So fearful. So tired. And now there was this peculiar situation with Michael's old girlfriend. What was she doing here? Sue Li didn't really have the time to spare for a chat, but she'd caught the exchange between Jena and Kelly in the cafeteria. Seen the tension between them at James's bedside. She had a responsibility as the head of the family to deal with this, if she could.

The elevator door slid open and Kelly McLeod walked out, radiating nonmutancy. In her bright purple uniform, she looked like a visitor from another world. Well, and wasn't she?

"Come sit down," Sue Li said. "Something to drink?"

"Thank you, no."

Kelly shifted uncomfortably on the yellow wallseat cushions. Sue Li didn't blame her. This was a strange place. A place of endings. Who could feel comfortable here? Even mutants found it difficult.

"Mrs. Ryton, I'm sorry. . . ."

"I know," Sue Li said gently. "But you didn't come all the way here just to tell me that."

"No. No. In fact, I'm not sure anymore why I came at all."

"You still love him." There. She'd said it.

Kelly's blue eyes widened.

For a moment, Sue Li expected her to bolt. But the moment passed. Kelly relaxed, smiled a tiny smile.

"Am I that transparent?" she asked.

"Perhaps not *that* transparent," Sue Li said. "But it's fairly obvious to anybody with eyes to see."

"No wonder Jena is so furious I'm here."

"Yes. But I'm not sorry you've come," Sue Li said. She took Kelly's hand. "There's something—something important—I've wanted to say to you for years, and this finally gives me the opportunity."

The younger woman looked apprehensive.

Sue Li took a deep breath.

"I'm sorry," she said.

"Sorry? About what?"

"Sorry that I didn't take your relationship with my son more seriously, years ago. Sorry that I didn't encourage him to pursue his own path."

"But—"

"No." Sue Li held up her hand. "Hear me out. Please. I pushed him toward the conventional way because I was afraid of repercussions within the clan. And because I feared that he was heading for a lifetime of grief. I see now that I helped steer him directly into great unhappiness. Perhaps, with you, things might have been different. And now, after so many years, you have come a long way to try and help him. I doubt that his own wife would have done the same."

Kelly's cheeks grew red. "I guess I've wondered what it would have been like if we'd married," she said. "I hated the Mutant Council for coming between us. But it forced me to grow up and become responsible for myself." She looked up, met Sue Li's gaze. "Not that I'm satisfied with my life now. I wish it had more of an emotional center. I haven't had that for fifteen years." Her glance slid away into the past. "I loved Michael then. And yes, I love him now—and not all the years and miles I've put between us can change that fact."

"What do you intend to do now?"

"Keep running, I guess," Kelly said bitterly. "I don't see any other solution. But at least I've acknowledged what's chasing me now."

She's very pretty, Sue Li thought. I hate to admit it, but I like this young woman—and admire her—much more than my own daughter-in-law. What a fool I've been, she thought. Aloud, she said, "I'm sorry. I seem to keep saying that. But I hope you will consider me a friend, Kelly."

"That would be nice," Kelly said. "I'd always hoped, at the very least, to be your friend."

The two women smiled shyly at one another, all barriers down.

Sue Li Ryton. Urgent. Please return to Room Five-C.

The mental summons brought Sue Li to her feet with a gasp.

"James," she cried. "No. No."

"What's happened?" Kelly said. "What is it?"

Sue Li turned to her in anguish. "My husband. I have to go to him—" She staggered, uncertain of her footing.

Kelly grabbed her arm, steadying her. "Come on," she said staunchly. "We'll both go."

Upstairs, the grim faces gathered around the bed answered all questions. The monitoring dials were dark. With an anguished cry, Sue Li sank down across the coverlet, reaching for her husband's hand. Where, before, she had felt linkage there was now only dreadful, echoing emptiness and shadows that threatened to engulf and devour her. The dreadful echoes, mocking her. No. No. No. Please, James, come back. Don't leave me here, alone. Take me with you. Please. Please. A lifetime of regrets and pleasures welled up and overflowed, running down her cheeks in salty tears.

"Mom, Mom. Can you hear me?"

Hands were shaking her. A familiar face begged her to answer, to say something, Mom, please. Who was this young man? He reminded her of James when he had first courted her. Yes, of course. Now she remembered—it was their son, Jimmy. And he was crying. She must comfort him. She must comfort all her children. Take control.

"I'm all right." Sue Li put a hand on Jimmy's shoulder for support and rose to her feet. "Michael, lend me a handkerchief, will you?"

"Here."

She took it and wiped her eyes. He was a good boy, Michael. Always such a good boy. Too good, really.

"We must arrange for the funeral," she said crisply. She forced herself to concentrate on details. "Michael, you'll

contact the Western Mutant Council. I'd like Rebekah
Terling to officiate, if possible. And Jimmy, try to reach your
sister at Cable News. Jena, please notify Chemen Astori."
She paused for a moment and her gaze settled upon the
dark-haired nonmutant stranger in their midst. "And Kelly,
of course, will stay."

18

SKERRY studied the orange figures on the screen for one second longer. Then he turned away.

"Screen off. Thanks, Anne."

"You're welcome." The simulacrum vanished.

"What did you learn?" Yosh asked eagerly.

"Ashman called a taxi about two in the morning."

"But I thought the building hydraulics didn't work! How did he get out?"

The bearded mutant gave him a sharp look. "How did I get in? I'm just a clever telepath with a knack for breaking and entering. For a powerful telekinetic mutant, a jammed door is child's play. You should know that. And for a super-mutant . . ." He let the implication hang in the air.

"I see your point." Yosh slumped down in his seat. "So you think Ashman took Narlydda and Melanie someplace else?"

"Looks that way."

"Stupid. Ashman is being stupid. He's much better off here, where he knows how to control everyone and everything. Out there, he's completely exposed. And vulnerable."

"Maybe he doesn't know that," Skerry said. "Or believe it. At least, let's hope so." He grinned but the smile faded as he turned quickly, whipping about from right to left. "Strange," he muttered. "Very strange. I'm getting weird clairaudial resonances. There's something really odd about this place. I want to look down this far corridor."

"That's Tavia's wing," Yosh said.

"Mrs. Emory?" Skerry nodded with satisfaction. "Good. I think I'd like to snoop around her office. See what there is to see. You know the way?"

"Follow me."

Yosh led him along a gold-paneled corridor to Tavia's private entrance. But the door was sealed shut. Even his skeleton key couldn't budge it.

"There are times I wish I were better at telekinesis," Skerry said ruefully. "I've only got a vestigial touch of it. Can't even reach into a baby's cradle and steal his bottle." He looked chagrined.

Yosh gestured with the rifle. "What about this?"

"What's that door made of?"

"Molded ceramic polymer, I think."

"Perfect. Give it a shot."

"Okay." Nervously Yosh aimed the rifle and fired. The door seal melted under the blast.

"Nice going," Skerry said drily. He pointed toward the door, his finger inscribing an arc. "Now why don't you try to cut around the perimeter—unless you want to lock this place up tighter than a type-E dome."

"Sorry." Yosh took aim again and managed to direct a clear orange ray along the edge of the doorway. The door smoked, shuddered, and fell in.

Before the dust had settled, Skerry stepped into the room. Yosh hung back a moment until the tone of Skerry's voice brought him running.

"Jesus!"

"What is it?"

Skerry stood next to a couch, blocking Yosh's view. "Is this Tavia Emory?" he demanded.

In horror, Yosh looked down at the emaciated figure of a woman lying on the lush velvet cushions. She was clothed in fine bronze silk, but the finest cloth couldn't disguise the mantle of death upon her features. The lips were drawn back tightly in a grinning rictus. The eyes were tightly shut. Her hands were clutched, clawlike, upon her bosom. A sickly-sweet odor hung in the air. Yosh looked away.

Tavia. No. No. No.

Yosh staggered, caught himself, and stumbled blindly out of the room. When his hands touched the cool acrylic surface of the wall in the corridor, he stopped moving. Leaning his head against the reassuring solidity, he fought back the urge to gag, to sob in revulsion and fear. What was happening here? It was a nightmare. Had to be.

He felt a firm hand grip his shoulder.

"Easy," Skerry said. "Take it easy, if you can. Deep breaths. Slow." The mutant placed his palm against Yosh's forehead with surprising gentleness.

Gradually the horror and shock ebbed as though leached away by mutant touch. Yosh straightened his shoulders and lifted his head, meeting Skerry's golden glance.

"Thanks. What happened to her?"

"Some kind of intravenous poison, I think. She can't have been dead more than a couple of days. But no fresh corpse looks like that. Whoever did it used something ugly."

"I don't understand," Yosh said. "I can't believe she'd commit suicide. Maybe Ashman—"

"You think he did it?" Skerry said.

"I don't know. He was her friend. She sponsored him."

Skerry shook his head. "Mutants are tricky beasts. Volatile. Peculiar. You never know how we'll react, and to what. I guess that's why mutant councils were created. The power of the groupmind can compel even the worst renegade to clean up his act. But Mr. Ashman lives outside of the Mutant Councils' reach. I'd say he's spending most of his time in Edge City. And I'm afraid he's taken Narlydda with him."

"That may be a blessing," Yosh said. "Better than finding her here. Like poor Tavia."

Skerry rounded on him. "I don't want to hear that," he said with quiet menace. "Don't mention it. Don't even think it—remember, I can hear you think."

"Sorry." *I see what you mean about unpredictable,* Yosh thought.

"Good."

"You know, Tavia had a private shuttle."

"Rich lady."

"No, that's not my point," Yosh said quickly. "I'll bet Ashman took it. If we can check the log for it, we might find out where he's headed."

"I'll have to get Anne Verland back on line for that," Skerry said.

"Maybe not. We might be able to gain access from Tavia's screen."

"You really want to go back in there?"

"No. But if it means finding Narlydda . . . and Melanie, then I'm willing to do it."

"Okay." Skerry watched him carefully. "Want me to put an esper shield around Mrs. Emory? You won't even notice her."

"Can you do that?" Yosh asked.

"Sure."

For a moment, Yosh was tempted. What a wonder these mutant powers were. Then he smiled sadly. "No. I can take it now. Thanks."

Skerry patted him on the back. "Stout fellow."

Once more Yosh stepped into Tavia's chamber. He did not look at the still figure on the couch as he passed it. He tapped his code into the keypad of Tavia's wallscreen. It sputtered as stray images of yellow and green burst upon the screen for a moment like fireworks. Then it went dark.

"Shit. Well, maybe the deskscreen." Yosh turned toward the sleek gray screen, hesitated, then typed in Tavia's password. The screen flared to life as a mechanical voice inquired, "Menu?"

"Emory Fleet log," Yosh said.

"Getting," the screen announced.

As Yosh watched, a dizzying array of orange files sped past. And, just as quickly, stopped. The shuttle log revealed minimal activity save for one recent departure.

"Got it," Yosh said. "A shuttle left at four-thirty A.M. for Fac-2."

"Nice work." Skerry peered over his shoulder. "What's Fac-2?"

"Orbital factory producing polyceramics."

Skerry stared at the screen for a moment. "Any chance Ashman faked this to throw us off the trail?" he asked.

"Sure. Ashman's capable of anything." Yosh punched in a different code.

"Menu?" the screen asked.

"Visual on Emory Fleet status," Yosh said.

"Working."

The screen image swirled as the orange letters were replaced by a video image of a shuttle hangar. Two sleek orbital fliers sat snug in their berths, dark save for the blue, blinking eyes of maintenance mechs.

"More," Yosh said.

The image panned toward a third berth. It was empty.

"Request data on Shuttle 3," Yosh said.

"Orbiter is enroute Fac-2," replied the screen.

Yosh turned to meet Skerry's glittering gaze. "That's all the confirmation we're going to get," he said. "My guess is that Ashman is getting sloppy. Or tired."

"That's good enough for me," Skerry said. He gestured at the shuttles onscreen. "Can you fly one of those things?"

"No. But I can program the autopilot. I think."

"Let's hope so." Skerry shot him a sardonic look. "This orbital factory—does it have any personnel in residence? Anybody we can warn?"

"No. It's totally automated."

"What about domes—does it have any environmental domes?"

Yosh held his hands out, palms extended. What was Skerry getting at? "I suppose," he said. "After all, some repairs can't be done by mechs. But I never paid much attention to this side of the business."

"Pity. Well, if it's got type-E domes, then somebody can survive up there. Even if it's just one mutant lady artist and her supermutant captor. I guess we'd better suit up and go after them. . . ."

A shrill female scream cut through the room.

Both men turned to see Clara, Tavia Emory's personal assistant, sag in horror against the doorway. She was staring at the velvet couch.

"I was asleep," she said. "I was asleep at my desk and I woke up and buzzed Mrs. Emory. Tried to. My screen was dead. Gods, what have you done to her?"

Skerry took her hand. "Easy, cousin. We haven't done anything. Just found her ourselves."

"And what's happened to the door? What's going on?"

"That's kind of difficult to explain."

Tavia's deskscreen began buzzing. Apparently, people all over the building were waking up.

"Why don't you get that?" Skerry suggested. The tone in his voice made Yosh suspect that he'd given Clara a compelling mental push. She nodded dully and turned toward the desk.

C'mon, let's clear out of here before we have a crowd asking more questions. Skerry's mindspeech was curt and urgent.

"But . . ." Yosh allowed himself to be carried along in the mutant's wake.

They ran down the corridor, bolting into a side passage at the sound of voices, down a flight of stairs and out onto a gray, carpeted hallway.

"Where are we?" Skerry whispered.

"I think we're near the labs." Yosh peered down the corridor, looking for a landmark. He had rarely worked on this level.

"Any exits around here?"

"I don't think so. Security precautions."

"Shit. Let me send out a probe." Skerry closed his eyes, frowning. "Hmm. I'm getting another strange feeling. Or rather, a blank where I should be hearing esper echoes."

"Could be another shielded room."

"Or a null."

"Melanie!"

"Keep your pants on, Romeo. I haven't found her yet. I don't even know what I've found." Skerry gave him a wink. "But let's try this way."

They veered left, then right, until they came to a double sliding door.

"Got your key?"

"Right here."

The door irised open. Yosh gasped. A slight figure lay sprawled on the white tile floor.

"Sarnoff!" Skerry said.

"You know him?"

"Oh, yeah. Our man in Moscow. A dabbler in the darker scientific arts. Should have figured he'd have his Ukrainian fingers in this mess. From the looks of him, he put his nose in one test tube too many."

"Dead too?"

Skerry nodded. "Check out the lab," he said. "I'm still getting that funny nonecho."

Grateful to get away from the corpse, Yosh hurried out of the main room into a storage area full of screens and autoprobes. A closet at the far end of it was empty, save for lab coats and acrylic slides. But the room beyond that was closed and locked. Heart pounding, he pressed his key to the doorpad. With a swish the doors irised open. A slim figure in yellow with dark hair was lying on a low couch just inside the door. Melanie.

Please be alive, Yosh thought. Please. He sank to his knees beside her, reaching for her wrist and a heartbeat.

"Don't worry," Skerry said, coming up behind him. "She's okay."

Yosh gathered Melanie into his arms and buried his face in her neck. She, at least, was real in the midst of this bad dream. He felt her pulse throbbing against his cheek. A moment later, she began to stir. He looked up and saw her eyelids flutter, then open. Mutant gold shined up at him. He'd never been so glad to see that color.

"Hi," Melanie said weakly.

"Hi yourself." Gently, he tucked a loose strand of her dark hair behind her ear. "What happened?"

"Ashman tried to put me to sleep," she said. "It didn't work too well. So he hit me with a hypo." She yawned. "How long have I been out?"

"About twenty-four hours," Skerry said.

She looked up. Squinted. "Cousin Skerry?"

He bowed mockingly. "So nice to see you again after all this time. Think you can walk?"

"But—"

"I know, I know. A thousand questions. But we'll play catch-up later, Mel. Right now, we've got to find Ashman. And Narlydda."

"What?" Melanie sat up. "What's going on?"

"Ashman killed Tavia Emory," Yosh said quickly. "And Dr. Sarnoff. Skerry thinks he's taken Narlydda someplace in Tavia's shuttle. We've got to catch them."

Melanie stared at them both as though they were crazy. "Killed Tavia Emory? Kidnapped Narlydda on a shuttle?"

"Looks that way," Skerry said.

"You boys have been watching too many vids," she said, getting to her feet. She wobbled slightly, then gained her balance but continued to hold on to Yosh's arm. "And next, the Shuttle Corps will come over the dunes to rescue us, I suppose?"

"Well, toots, that would be nice," Skerry said, and grinned. "But I doubt it. So let's us rescue ourselves before it's too late and somebody here wakes up and calls the cops." He grabbed them both by the hand. "All tender reunions are hereby postponed until we're airborne. Come on."

NARLYDDA watched Victor Ashman twitch and mutter in uneasy slumber. He was securely webbed to a blue couch in the shuttle cabin, as was she. How long had she been out?

She sat up uneasily and stretched. Her neck was stiff, and her legs ached. The orange pressure suit she wore restricted her movements. When had she put that on? And how did she get here?

Memory seeped back slowly. Wait, she remembered that Ashman had drugged that reporter, Melanie Ryton, right after he had knocked out poor Yosh. Then the call to Rebekah Terling. His brief, angry consultation with that little mustachioed doctor. The taxi to Tavia's shuttle port. Then nothing.

The clang of metal on metal startled her. The shuttle seemed to be docking. But where? Montevideo? Yugoslavia? She couldn't tell. There were no windows. Was it day or night? The screen in the front wall of the cabin was dark, but there was something funny about the darkness. It was dappled with white specks.

Was that space? Were those white specks stars?

Narlydda's heart began pounding. Ashman hadn't taken her to some secluded Earthside hideaway. He'd kidnapped her into space.

Maybe there's a chance I can escape while he's asleep, she thought. At least try to stop him. God knows what he's got planned. Maybe the best thing to do would be to punch a hole through the shuttle wall and kill us both before he hurts anybody else.

She glanced at the sleeping figure and felt an odd mixture of fear and pity. He was so alone. So powerful.

And I'm no hero, she thought. I love life too much. And despite what he's done, I feel sorry for Ashman. I know what it's like to be alienated and lonely. I can't kill him. Or me.

"Thank you," Ashman said. He opened his eyes and stared at her bleakly. "I'm so glad you're here. And that you won't hurt yourself. Or try to hurt me."

He unstrapped himself from the webbing and floated up, out of his plush red seat, toward the ceiling of the cabin. His pressure suit billowed out around him like a clown's costume. Turning toward Narlydda, he grinned with delight.

"So this is what reduced gravity is like," he said, bobbing gently. "Probably the closest normals ever come to understanding levitation."

Narlydda silently chanted for composure.

"You're frightened," Ashman said. He hovered near her couch, an anxious look on his face. "Oh, don't be scared of me, Narlydda, please. What can I do to reassure you?"

"Take me back to Earth. Let me go home."

"But then I'd be alone."

"You killed Dr. Sarnoff," she said. "God knows what you've done with poor Tavia. Not to mention Yosh and Melanie. Why shouldn't I be afraid?"

Ashman gave her a twisted smile. "Don't worry about Tavia. It's too late for that anyway. And your little friends will be fine." He stopped smiling. "I see you think you should humor me."

"Stop reading my mind," she snapped. "Goddammit! Don't you know anything about common mutant courtesy?"

"I'm not a common mutant," Ashman said. His face was a sober mask. "Nobody ever taught me, no Mutant Council shaped me. I've always been alone. Always hiding. Poor and starving freak. But no more. No more." He seemed to be talking to himself, oblivious to her. "Poor Ashman. Hiding with the rats. Keeping to the shadows. And then Tavia dangled her riches and promises before me. So I let her reel me in." He looked up as though he'd just noticed her sitting there. "Do you know what it's like to be really hungry and afraid and alone?"

Slowly, Narlydda shook her head.

"Oh Narlydda, don't be scared." He grabbed her hands. "I promise to respect your privacy. I will. Besides, I can't completely read you. You're partially shielded, you know. Telekinetics sometimes develop that—compensation for a lack of esper power, I guess."

That's interesting, she thought. Thanks for the tip. But maybe it's time for a little distraction. Aloud, she said, "Where are we?"

"Docking at one of the Emory orbital factories, I think. At least, that's what I programmed this thing for."

"Programmed! You mean this shuttle is on autopilot?"

"Of course. You don't think Tavia kept a string of pilots on call, do you?"

"Surely, the Shuttle Corps is tracking us."

"Oh, as far as they're concerned, this is a standard supply run out to the factory to pick up product. And if anybody else is trying to track us, they'd have to cut through the radar shield—the late Richard Emory had this thing equipped with stealth capacity." Ashman giggled again. "Wonder what he was up to."

The shuttle shuddered once, twice. There was the sound of clanking metal, or wheels turning. The main door to the cabin clicked and slid open, revealing a metal grid walkway that led away through a large docking bay toward a sealed portal.

Ashman waved her through the door. "After you."

Narlydda stepped down cautiously.

"Don't be afraid. It's completely pressurized."

The walk to the bay door had a curious, dreamlike quality. I'd like to set this to music, Narlydda thought. And do a series of fiber acrylic sculptures. . . .

"Always the artist," Ashman said in an approving tone of voice. "I really envy your ability. But don't worry. Once we're settled here, you'll have plenty of time for your work. I promise you that. And whatever you need. All you have to do is ask."

"That's very kind." Narlydda said drily. She wondered if he could read her sarcasm beyond her supposed esper shield. She didn't really care if he could.

They moved through the pressurized portal and into a dome environment carpeted in soothing greens and blues. The cold white stars winked at them through the transparent dome casing.

"Home at last," Ashman said. He unzipped his orange pressure suit and gestured for her to do the same. "Would you like something to eat?"

"I'm not hungry." Her stomach felt like a leaden ball.

"Well, I'm starved." He straightened his gray pants and tunic. "Space travel must work up a hearty appetite."

She watched in amazement as he sauntered toward the mech wall and ordered a choba roll.

Doesn't anything bother him? she thought. A quick trip up in the shuttle and he's ready for lunch.

With a grinding whine, the mech extruded the food through a white acrylic nozzle. Ashman caught it telekinetically, unwrapped it, and popped one of the green rolls into his mouth. "Mmm. Pretty good." Munching contentedly, he wandered around the dome.

Why has he brought me here, hundreds of miles above the Earth? What was he thinking of, she wondered. Or was he thinking at all? Would he just lead her on a strange odyssey? What was next, the Moon? She was getting tired of being dragged around like somebody's baggage.

"Ashman, why are we here?" Narlydda demanded.

He looked astonished. "You're angry. Why? I just wanted to be someplace less public. Less accessible. And easy to defend."

"This is easy to defend?" She gestured skeptically around the room.

"Of course." Ashman sounded as though he were addressing a four-year-old child. "Richard Emory had all his factories equipped with state-of-the-art nuclears and lasers."

"What? He must have been paranoid," Narlydda said. "Besides, I thought private arsenals were outlawed years ago."

Ashman's laughter bounced around the dome.

"You know that the rich can always find or finance ways to circumvent the rules." He finished the last bite of choba roll and wiped his fingers fastidiously on a napkin. "And Mr. Emory didn't just circumvent the rules. He reinvented them. His factories are orbital fortresses. I don't even think Tavia knew to what extent her husband was prepared for Armageddon. How disappointed he must have been when it never arrived. And now it never will."

"You hope."

"I know." Ashman wasn't smiling anymore. "Once I've had a chance to rest and gain my strength, I'll make sure that I enforce a lasting peace. That was Tavia's intention for me, and I'd like to make it a kind of memorial to her."

"Memorial? Then you did kill her!"

"I didn't want her killed." Ashman frowned and his voice took on an earnest tone. "Truly I didn't. But Tavia can be so tiresome. So demanding. She'd never have left me alone. And her dreams of a pure, perfect peace led by the Mutant Council were pathetic. I thought maybe if I kept her asleep for a while, I could get away. That shot was supposed to simulate a comatose state. But Sarnoff overdid it, the idiot."

"So you killed him, too?"

"Stop interrogating me, Narlydda!" Ashman's eyes flashed angrily. "I had to get away. To establish myself."

209

"Gods, what have I done?" Narlydda cried. "I should have blown us both to hell and back when I had the chance."

"Don't be silly," Ashman said. "You'd have missed all the fun to come." His expression turned icy. "You know, I don't think you really value the opportunity I've given you. What artist doesn't want all the time and freedom there is to work? And you've always hated intrusions—or so you've said. You should be grateful that I've given you a haven from the annoying, noisy nonmutant world. Why should you need or want anything else?"

He walked into an adjoining domeroom, gesturing for her to follow.

"We'll sleep here," he said. "The workrooms are beyond, in the next domespace. I think there's a bathroom around here someplace."

"That would be useful." She gazed at the large couch in the middle of the room. Sleeping with Ashman? She shuddered at the thought.

He ignored her sarcasm. "And there's something I think you'd like to see." He beckoned toward a doorway, and despite her fear and irritation, Narlydda followed him. Peering through, she saw a large domeroom filled with glittering apparatus. It was a fully equipped robotic lab. As Narlydda watched, gleaming silver mechs shuttled between vacuum centrifuges and refrigeration units. She looked around quickly, but there didn't appear to be any exits.

"Eye of newt, toe of bat," Ashman intoned, rubbing his hands together. Then he stopped, piqued. "Aren't you going to ask me what's cooking?"

He really is crazy, Narlydda thought. Calm down. Play along. Maybe you'll find a chance to escape. She bowed cautiously, and said aloud, "A thousand apologies. And just what have you got bubbling on the stove?"

"It's a surprise," Ashman said gleefully. "What a shame that Dr. Sarnoff couldn't join us. But two's company. Luckily, he lent me his secret formula for enhancing mutant strength. Once you've had some, we'll be a perfect match."

"Had some?" She stared at him in alarm. "What is that stuff?"

"Think of it as mutant steroids," Ashman said. "It's wonderful. Just imagine the artwork you'll produce. Oh, you'll create quite a stir. I'm sure of it."

"No thanks." Narlydda began backing toward the door as fast as she could. Get to the shuttle, she thought. Get away. At least try.

"You are ungrateful, aren't you?"

Steely, telekinetic fingers gripped and held her, unmoving. In horror, Narlydda watched a hypo fill with silvery liquid and float toward her.

"No, Ashman. Please. Don't!"

The sting of the hypo cut off any further pleas.

The serum burned a path up her arm across her chest and along her other limbs, throughout her body, as though she were enflamed. If Ashman's telekinesis hadn't held her upright, she would have fallen to the floor.

"It's not supposed to hurt," Ashman said, sounding surprised and petulant. "It didn't hurt me."

"I'm not like you," Narlydda gasped, appalled. Her arms and legs were shaking, spasming. She was burning up, being consumed from the inside out. "No, no, no," she cried. "Make it stop. I thought you liked me, Victor. Help me."

But even as she reached toward him in her fear and pain, he seemed to recede, to melt and run along the edges as she watched, until there was just a puddle of Ashman in front of her, shimmering in tones of silver and gray. Then a dozen tiny Ashmans sprang up, a miniature supermutant army, and advanced toward her, each one of them grinning insanely. Terrified, Narlydda pushed them away with her mind, and they splattered against the dome like bugs on a windshield.

"Now you're getting the hang of it," Ashman's voice said approvingly. But it sounded odd, elongated and slow.

211

Narlydda's blood beat a ragged tattoo in her head, her neck, her wrists. The pain was receding now, and the fear with it, replaced by an electrifying surge of power and strength. She felt the insane urge to dance and caper in time to that compelling blood rhythm. To grab Ashman's hand and go waltzing around the room to a wild mutant two-step.

"I'm a nobody, who are you? Are you a nobody too?" she quoted. Then she giggled. The room needed flowers. Lots of flowers. She would cover the floor, the dome, blot out the cold, merciless stars with garlands of red, purple, yellow dahlias and moonflowers, fabulous blooms that she'd invent and then, maybe, Ashman would make them real.

Let there be flowers, she thought. And music. And sculpture. Lots of sculpture. She'd send for Anne Verland right away and tell her to clone all her sculpture. Maybe they'd need more dome space. Ashman would have to think about that.

"Whoa, now. Slow down," Ashman said, grabbing her hand.

But she didn't want to slow down. She could dance for days. All she needed were the musicians. She already had the crazy drummer beating away in her chest. When had she ever had this much energy? Didn't Ashman understand? He of all people should understand. They could rule the world, the two of them. The misfit duo: Ashman and the green lady. But his grip was annoying. And what was he saying to her? He was making too much noise, like a buzzing mosquito. She couldn't hear herself think. She needed space. Room. And most of all, she needed silence.

"Go!"

With a telekinetic snap, she shoved him away from her as easily as flicking an insect. How amusing to hear his astonished gasp, to see the horrified look on Ashman's face as he went staggering back toward the centrifuge. Only his own powers kept him from a nasty bump on the head. Narlydda giggled. And now he looked mad. Oooh. Look out, here he comes.

Ashman flew at her, his face boiling with rage.

Stop that. Now.

The mental command was sharp. Thunderous.

Narlydda ignored it.

"I told you to stop!" Ashman yelled.

"Now, now," Narlydda said, waggling an admonishing finger at him. "You ought to watch that temper. And really, you shouldn't mess in somebody else's kitchen. Especially if you're not a very good cook."

Instead of flying at her again in a rage, Ashman stood back pensively. "I see your point," he said. Behind him, another hypo filled with silver fluid. In two quick movements, he'd injected himself.

Narlydda stopped laughing.

Ashman's eyes glowed with cold silver fire. He blinked, and she went toppling backward, somersaulting across the room. With a crash, she came to rest against the panels of the refrigeration cabinets.

That son of a bitch! She sat up, shaking her head to stop its slow, dizzying spin. *How dare he!*

Narlydda cast around her for something to throw. Telekinetically, she yanked a stool out of its storage slot and heaved it at the supermutant. He ducked, but she changed the arc of the stool's trajectory and caught him with it at the knees. Ashman toppled, cursing.

Above their heads, a wallspeaker broadcast a burst of radio static. It was loud and annoying. Narlydda shut it off.

Ashman was on his feet now, glowering at her. "Don't make me do something I might regret," he said. His voice was very high and strange.

For answer, Narlydda shoved him into a bulkhead.

"Is this a private game, or can anybody play?" a familiar voice asked.

Ashman whirled to face the intruder. "How did you get in here?" he demanded.

"Just followed your breadcrumbs."

Narlydda knew that voice, that smile. It was her one true love, the man in the Moon, and he'd come all this way just for her. For little green her. She laughed with delight and triumph.

"Skerry!"

19

S KERRY PUSHED BACK the orange sleeves of his pressure suit and stood, hands on hips, glaring across the domeroom at Ashman.

"You left a tough trail for me to follow," Skerry said. "I'd have been here sooner, but cutting through that stealth field was a bitch, even for me. Lucky thing you left the front door to the factory open." He cast a sharp glance at Narlydda. "Lydda, you look funny."

"Ashman gave me some magic potion," she said happily. She hummed a song fragment as her gaze wandered around the room. "Hi, Yosh. Hi, Melanie."

"He what?" Skerry rounded on Ashman. "Are you crazy? What the hell did you do to her?"

"I never touched her," Ashman said. "And I don't have to answer any questions. Get out."

"Not bloody likely." Skerry moved toward him. His hands were balled into fists.

"Then I'll just throw you out," the supermutant said. His voice was thin and whispery but his eyes flashed with anger.

A green bolt of telekinetic energy slashed across the room toward Skerry.

"Melanie, Yosh, get behind me!" he yelled. "Get down!"

Yosh grabbed hold of Narlydda's hand and yanked her down with them.

Spitting green sparks and hissing angrily, the telekinetic bolt hit Skerry full on, knocking the bearded mutant backward as it washed over and enfolded him in a deadly corruscating net.

Melanie closed her eyes in despair. Skerry was dead. He had to be. Nobody could survive that voltage.

"No," Narlydda cried. She thrashed wildly in Yosh's arms. "No, no, no. I won't let you do it, Ashman." Yanking herself free, she reached, panting, toward Skerry.

"Gods," Yosh whispered. "Melanie, look at that."

She was lying flat on her face on the scratchy carpet, just behind Yosh. Carefully, Melanie opened her eyes. And stared in wonder. Like a serpent recoiling, the telekinetic snare was pulling back into itself, disappearing as it released Skerry from its malignant grip.

"What's that around him?" Melanie said.

"Protection," Narlydda said. She slumped down, pale and exhausted, every bit of energy spent fighting off Ashman's attack.

Skerry shimmered and glowed as though his skin were afire. A glittering esper shield stretched to cover him as he stood up and faced Ashman once more.

"I really don't like you," Skerry said, and his voice smoldered with rage. "You or your style." As he spoke, a dark cloud formed around Ashman like a suffocating gray caul.

The supermutant struggled as the walls of the esper field shrank around him. Staggering blindly forward, he tripped over a low table and cried out but managed to catch himself. The esper cloud darkened as it drained his telepathic energy, reducing all cerebral functions to baseline levels. Ashman moaned and fell to the floor, where he lay, a shrouded figure, unmoving.

"Time to go." Skerry grabbed Narlydda's hand and started for the door.

She hung back, gaping in distress.

"You hurt him. I didn't want you to hurt him."

Skerry shook his head. "I don't know what he gave you, Lydda, but whatever it was, it's definitely not endearing you to me."

"Sorry," she said. Her frown melted and she began to giggle. "I feel pretty strange."

"I can see that. Come on." He hurried her and the others into the shuttle bay, along the catwalk, and aboard the minishuttle.

"Quick, let's get out of here," he yelled, sealing the door then webbing himself into a couch with Narlydda.

Yosh punched in the autopilot, and ponderously, the shuttle began to move out of the bay toward the safety of space. Metal screeched, then was still as the orbiter pulled away and out into the vacuum. In moments, the factory was a speck on the cabin screen.

"That was fast," Skerry said with relief. He turned to give Narlydda a hug. His hands closed on empty air as she faded away, lingering a moment as a green ghost before disappearing completely.

"Lydda!"

"Gods!" Melanie said. "She turned transparent, just like in my dream."

The color drained from Skerry's face. He pulled free from the webbing. "Dammit!" He punched the cabin wall, no easy task in low gravity. "God damn me for a fool!" His third punch dented the mech dispenser. Pink liquid began spraying out into the cabin, forming into round globules, which floated languidly, splashed upon contact, and settled into a fine pink mist.

"What happened?" Yosh demanded. "She was right here!" He hit the mech disabler, halting the flood of pink fog.

"Calm down, Skerry," Melanie said. "Before you wreck

the cabin." She detached her webbing, pushed off from her couch, and grabbed for her cousin's flailing arm. "Listen to me! You've got to calm down."

"I knew it all seemed too easy," Skerry said. He floated by the wallscreen, Melanie clinging to his shoulder. "No, Yosh, I don't think Narlydda was right here. In fact, I'm not sure she was ever here at all." A cloud of pink liquid floated around his head like a halo. "This Ashman is much trickier than I expected. If he could convince me I'd knocked him out with an esper squeeze while at the same time deluding me that I'd rescued Narlydda, then we're in big, big trouble. I've never seen anything like it."

"What should we do now?" Melanie's voice was shrill with fright. She released her grip on Skerry and pulled herself back to her couch using the handholds which studded the cabin walls.

"We could go back to Armstrong Base," Yosh said.

"Oh sure. And whistle up the military," Skerry said. "Wouldn't they just love to get their hands on Ashman. Or die trying."

"Well, what's wrong with that?" Yosh said defensively. "You've just said we're in big trouble."

Skerry leaned over and grabbed the musician by the collar of his orange pressure suit. "Listen to me," he said. "That factory is armed to the teeth. If the military gets involved in this, they could blow the entire place up. And Narlydda with it."

"But what else can we do?" Melanie cried.

"We can turn around and go back to the factory," Skerry said.

Yosh carefully unhooked Skerry's fingers from his suit, one by one. "Sounds crazy to me," he said. "No offense," he added as the bearded mutant glared at him.

"Yosh is right," Melanie said. "We've already proven that one strong telepath, a null, and a nonmutant are hardly a match for Ashman." She waited for another eruption out of her cousin. To her surprise, he said nothing, looked away as though pondering the problem, then nodded.

"We're overmatched," he said sourly. "That's for sure. Now if your brother were here, I might stand a real chance," he said. "Together, a strong telepath and a multitalent telekinetic . . ."

"Well, he's not available," Melanie said.

"Then we'll just have to do our best," Skerry said. "But we are going back to that factory. Now."

For a moment, no one spoke. Then, slowly, Melanie looked at Yosh. He nodded. She knew she couldn't fight them both.

"All right," she said. "If that's the way you want it. Yosh, does this shuttle have an armory?"

"Probably," he said. "Emory Foundation seems to have equipped this private fleet with everything but an atom splitter."

"I'm not interested in physics experiments," she said sharply. "But I could use a gun. Or three."

She aimed herself toward the cabin screen but nearly overshot and bounced off the far wall before she grabbed a handhold. The screen buzzed with static. She switched it to internal mode.

"Blueprint, Shuttle-D," she said.

"Getting." A holo diagram in full color seemed to spring out of the screen. Melanie studied it impatiently, then nodded.

"Screen off."

She pushed away toward the back of the cabin. "Good thing you didn't dent *this* mech," she said to Skerry. She fiddled with the keypad for a moment, nodded, and typed in her request.

The mech whirred. A small door in the brown cabin wall swung inward and up, revealing a long white tray on which a sleek, gray laser pistol sat. Melanie reached for the gun and hefted it approvingly.

"Nice."

"When you're finished admiring that laser, I suggest you web yourself back in," Yosh said. "I'm going to call Armstrong and tell them if they haven't heard from us in two hours, they'd better send the fleet. The cavalry. Whatever it is they send to space stations to rescue mutants in distress." He stared at Skerry defiantly. "With or without your approval."

Skerry's eyes narrowed in anger. He began to disagree, then stopped and, raising his hands, shrugged. "I suppose you're right. If we can't stop Ashman, we can at least warn somebody else."

"Good." Yosh typed in the emergency request.

The screen image disintegrated into flickering gray and red static. Yosh tried it again. More static.

"I think we're being jammed," he said.

"At this distance?" Melanie asked. "I don't believe it."

"Ashman's very strong. Remember, it wasn't until he was in space that his control over Emory Foundation headquarters began to erode."

Skerry nodded. "Good point. Well, at least we know that he has some limitations. If only we could get far enough away from him. But no time for that. Can you reprogram the autopilot to take us back to the factory?"

"Sure. At least that works."

"Okay." Skerry turned to Melanie. "You know how to use that gun?"

"Yeah."

Yosh looked up from the autopilot in surprise. "You do? How come?"

"Well, I had to learn about it for a feature I did on lasers in the home."

Skerry gave her an approving pat on the back. "And I thought that all video jocks were just talking heads. At least now both of you have weapons." His smile faded. "For all the good it will do us."

The image of the factory grew in size, looming onscreen as they drew near it. Tensely, the three of them stared at it.

"Ready or not," Skerry said. "Here we come."

NARLYDDA LOOKED AROUND in confusion. Had she imagined that Skerry had been there? But she thought he'd walked in and smiled at her. Right before he faded away, leaving the stars to twinkle at her through the transparent domewall.

Ashman stood across the room, rubbing his throat. His attention seemed distracted.

"Victor?"

He ignored her.

"Victor, what happened to them?"

"Not now."

"Victor—"

"Dammit, I said not now!" He whirled, eyes blazing. "I'm trying to protect us from your so-called friends. Stop distracting me."

She jumped to her feet. "So Skerry was here!"

"Yes, and he'll be back, I'm sure."

"Good."

"You're a fool, Narlydda." Ashman was almost sneering in his anger. "I got a quick look at this rescuer of yours—he's an irresponsible renegade. Not exactly the kind of man who will stay in one place. Or with one woman."

"Go to hell," she snapped. "You're just jealous. Did I say that I wanted a man to stay with me? The reason I like Skerry is because he's unpredictable. Untamable. And terrific in bed." Her fear of Ashman was gone. She was angry, heedless of what she said.

Ashman reacted with all the rage she'd hoped for. Cursing, he smashed a storage unit into splinters with a rasping telekinetic bolt. "You're an idiot," he said. "You don't know what I'm offering you."

"You're offering me obliteration," she said. "Only you think it's intimacy." She ducked as a serving mech sailed toward her and over her head to lodge in the far wall dividing the domerooms. "And if you want to play rough, you've certainly equipped me to be your playmate."

As she spoke, Narlydda pulled a storage cabinet free from its housings behind Ashman and tipped it over onto the supermutant. While he was disentangling himself, she hurried into the next room, looking for a hiding place.

The bed, she thought. Get behind it. She used her new telekinetic power to pull the white acrylic headboard away from the wall and hollow out a space in it that just fit her. Gratefully, she crawled in and moved the bed back in place.

Skerry, get back here soon, she thought. I can't stall him or hide forever, and I'd prefer a ride home to floating back all alone.

Heyran Landon paced irritably before the screen in his office. He was beginning to wish he'd taken a job with the Navy. He liked the ocean. All that peaceful blue water. And the only things you had to worry about were colliding with another ship, shearing off a drilling platform, or drowning. Much easier than dealing with zero-g and vacuum environments. And much more appealing than rescuing rich socialites whose private shuttles had malfunctioned.

"I understand, General Cadston," he said, addressing the screen. "Mrs. Emory's shuttle has been docked at the orbital factory for hours, emitting a distress signal."

"Somebody's probably just leaning on the wrong switch," the Brigadier said, smiling his famous smile. "But since it's Tavia Emory's shuttle, we have to check it out."

Halfheartedly, Landon returned the smile. The last thing he wanted to do was rush out and jump-start a society matron's shuttle. Even if she was a bridge partner for Cadston. "Sir, have you tried to raise them by radio?"

The Cadston smile faded. "Of course. No luck."

"Odd. Have there been any reports from the factory?"

"Negative. And why should there be? That place is completely automated."

"No external screens? We could at least get a look at the shuttle before scrambling a flight."

Cadston nodded. "A Korean news satellite went past it about half an hour ago. No external signs of trouble, although there were some funny things on that factory the brass wants explained. And I want you to go, Heyran. ASAP."

"Yessir."

The screen went dark.

Who was available to scramble for a quick rescue? McLeod was on leave—he could recall her, but that would take too long. Well, there was Ethan Hawkins. He could borrow him from the *Brinford* until Kelly returned. A two-man mini would take them up quickly. Be back by dinnertime, if they were lucky.

20

MICHAEL ROSE from the cushions beside his mother and left her sitting in silent meditation by his father's bed. Jimmy was slumped in a chair nearby, eyes closed, weary with grief.

I feel so strange, Michael thought. I should be sad, or guilty, or something, but instead, I just feel relieved. And free.

He looked at the still face of his father. James Ryton had slipped quietly into death. How peaceful, Michael thought. Like a pale statue. Nothing to indicate that he'd spent his life like a clenched fist ready to punch out in anger at the rest of the world.

He stared at him a moment longer.

Goodbye, Dad.

Jena was sitting by the door on a pile of beige cushions. The color seemed washed out of her. Even her electric blue silk tunic was oddly subdued. As he walked past, she mindspoke him.

I've sent for Herra. Rebekah Terling is willing to officiate at the burial, but Chemen Astori has offered to fly out if you wish.

Michael nodded. "Let mother decide. I want to try and find Melanie."

And will you please get rid of Captain McLeod! I think I've been patient and understanding, but really, Michael—

He cut her off. "I'll take care of it."

Jena flashed him a furious look but said nothing more.

At his nod, Kelly stood up, shot the cuffs of her purple uniform, and followed him out into the hall. The filtered sunlight warmed the blue hospital tile. Together, they walked in silence. Michael had a sudden urge to put his arm around her, even here, in this private, mutant place.

Without another thought, he took Kelly's hand. She looked at him with surprise. Then she smiled.

"I assume you've been instructed to banish me?" she said.

"Of course. Do you want to go?"

She reached over to gently straighten his tie and her hand lingered on his shirtfront. "Only if I can't help you further."

"Don't you have to be back at Armstrong?"

"Not for another seventy-two hours." She met his gaze, held it.

"Then I'd like you to attend my father's funeral." He fought the temptation to pull her closer. To kiss her, there, in the hallway of Dream Haven. "It would mean a lot to me."

Kelly's eyebrows disappeared into her bangs. "Won't your clan be shocked? Sounds like you're asking for trouble."

"Who cares? I don't have to worry about offending my father any more. And you know how my mother feels."

"Well, I'd like to show respect," she said. "But I don't want to make trouble. I know how hard this is for your mother. For you and Jimmy."

"Less painful because you're here," he said, and gave her hand a squeeze.

"What about your wife?"

Michael shrugged. "She's furious that you're here, of course."

"I don't really blame her," Kelly said. "Especially after our hissing match in the commissary. I almost left then. But your mother stopped me."

"Mom did? Good. I knew she liked you."

Kelly smiled gently. The late afternoon sun slanted in through the clerestory windows, haloing her dark hair. "Michael, I think the best thing I can do is stay out of the way until the funeral. There's an inn in Mendocino I know, and I'm sure . . ."

She broke off, distracted by something behind him.

Michael looked over his shoulder. Two men, nonmutants, wearing identical dark gray suits, approached him.

"Excuse me, Mr. Ryton?" the shorter one said. He had a resonant tenor voice.

"Yes?"

He smiled and held out a holo card which read EDWARD GREEN, FEDERAL MARSHAL in bronzed three-dimensional letters.

"You are in contempt of Congress," Edward Green said in the same pleasant tone. "Please come with us."

THE FACTORY WAS SILENT, all activity stilled. The sound of Melanie's footsteps on the metal catwalk echoed loudly and set her nerves jumping.

Ashman is waiting for us in there, she thought. He's like a spider anticipating the tug on his web. One little tweak and he'll come scuttling. . . .

Hey, ease up on the melodrama, will you?

Skerry's mindspeech crackled with tension.

Melanie nodded. For the tenth time, she felt the laser pistol in her pocket. Flanked by her tall cousin on one side and Yosh on the other, she walked toward the main domerooms. Was Narlydda in there? Was she all right? Could Skerry tell?

Melanie, please, chant or something. At such close range, you're driving me crazy. And yes, I know. You're sorry.

Yosh glanced at them as though he was aware of some hidden communication taking place. But he glanced away again at the sudden sound of humming. With an eerie screech of metal, the factory had jolted back to life.

They walked past mechs churning and distilling the liquid

ceramic. The creamy mixture glittered in its extrusion tubes as the light caught trace elements of mica and selenium. It was almost pretty, Melanie thought.

At the entrance to the domerooms, Skerry paused and looked around cautiously.

He must be casting an esper probe, Melanie thought. She watched as her cousin listened carefully then shook his head. No luck. She didn't know whether that meant Ashman was blocking him, or that there was nobody alive beyond those gray metal doors.

Ready, folks?

They exchanged glances. Melanie and Yosh both pulled their laser guns out. Slowly, they nodded. Skerry pushed the doors open.

The domeroom was half-lit by pink spotlights. The cold white stars twinkled beyond the safety of the transparent dome walls. Even in the dim light, Melanie could see that the room was a mess. A major struggle had taken place here. Between whom?

Skerry drew his breath in sharply. Melanie followed his glance and saw a figure sitting propped up against a mech storage unit. Narlydda! Was she hurt?

As they approached her, Narlydda lifted her head, jerkily, as though it were being pulled by strings. Her eyes remained closed.

"I'm sorry," she said tonelessly, mouth working hard to form each word. "It's a trap. You should have gone home."

"Lydda!" Skerry reached for her.

A crackle of mental energy and a flash of blue light sent him flying through the air and into the far wall. Skerry sat where he'd fallen for a moment, heavily stunned. Then, shaking his head as though to clear it, he got to his feet.

"Ashman? I know you're here. You'll have to do better than that. Esper bolts are child's play."

For answer, a second bolt of mental lightning sizzled

through the air, knocking him to his knees. He stayed there, tottering.

Melanie swung her head from left to right: she could only see the four of them. She scanned the room again. The supermutant was nowhere to be seen.

Why did you come back? I let you go. Why make me kill you?

Ashman's mindspeech was loud, with strange echoes that distorted it from tenor to soprano and back again.

"You don't really want to kill us, do you?" Melanie said gently. "In fact, you'd rather be friends, wouldn't you?"

Don't be ridiculous. I'd just rather not have to make the effort it takes to dispense with you.

Come on, Skerry, she thought. Get up!

But her cousin was still on his knees, groaning. Got to stall, she thought. She looked at Yosh in desperation.

"Uh, Ashman, you know I've always liked you," Yosh said. "Why don't you show yourself? I'd like to talk to you about some ideas I have for the Moonstation statue—"

Stop improvising, musician. We were never friends. And now you're beginning to annoy me. Since you won't go back, I must make you go away. The telepath, first.

Skerry began choking as though the air was being pulled from his lungs. He collapsed onto his back, his hands clawing at his windpipe.

"Stop it! Ashman, don't kill him!" Melanie cried. A telekinetic wind came out of nowhere, the exhalation of some strange beast, and blew her head over heels across the room. The stars careened crazily before her eyes. She lost her grip on the laser pistol, and it went clattering across the floor.

"Melanie!"

Yosh moved toward her, but he too was suddenly forced sharply back against the wall, blown by an unseen hurricane. He hit hard, slid down to a sitting position, and stayed there, eyes closed, stunned.

"Victor, please," Narlydda said in the same flat tone as before.

Skerry struggled harder for breath. His face was bright red and veins bulged at his temples.

No, Melanie thought. No. No. No. She clambered toward the laser pistol. Behind her, there was a strange clicking sound. She whirled.

Ashman was slowly materializing in a cloud of silver smoke. He looked astonished, as though the effect were not of his choosing.

The radio in the wallscreen crackled to life.

"Emory Fac-2, this is shuttle *Anorik*. Repeat, shuttle *Anorik* responding to distress call from private shuttle. Please respond if you are able."

With a cry of anger, Ashman blasted the wallscreen to silence. Beyond the dome wall a government minishuttle could be seen orbiting the factory.

Distress call? Narlydda, did you do this?

She nodded, and her eyes opened, although they seemed focused on places far distant.

Now I've got to get rid of them, too.

"No!" Melanie said. "Ashman, please—"

He stared intently out the dome wall. Melanie could see the port engine of the minishuttle begin to glow bright red. Another moment and it would explode.

"Ashman, wait."

Something in her voice made him turn to look at her.

His eyes were peculiar. What was it? Their silvery glow seemed tarnished. Fading. In its place, the familiar golden glow of mutancy sparkled with new-minted glitter.

"Your eyes," Melanie gasped.

Ashman covered his face and turned away.

Skerry stopped choking and sat up. Without a moment's hesitation he sent a huge bolt of shimmering mental energy whistling toward the supermutant.

Ashman deflected it.

Skerry threw another.

Ashman caught it and bounced it back at him. It enveloped Skerry in a sparkling feedback field, draining his psychic strength. He gasped, twitching helplessly, caught in his own esper net.

Melanie watched in horror. Even with his strength reduced, Ashman was more than a match for them. He would kill her and Yosh. Skerry and Narlydda and the shuttle crew. And then what would he do to everybody else? Her family? Her friends? The only things in this world that she had ever really cared about? No. No.

Hands trembling, she raised the laser pistol. Ashman saw her and smiled derisively.

Do you really think that little toy can hurt me?

"No," Melanie said. "Not really." She aimed. "Goodbye." Fired.

The laser shattered the dome wall just behind Ashman.

No!

His mindspeech was a scream of terror.

The cold vacuum of space reached in through the jagged hole and seized the supermutant. He struggled desperately, clinging to the walls with such telekinetic fervor that the room began to deform. But the struggle was not one of equals. Space was stronger.

Spread-eagled, Ashman gripped the edges of the dome wall, oblivious to the blood trickling down his arms from wounds inflicted as he grasped at the jagged shards of acrylic. The cuffs of his blue flight suit turned purple, then crimson. He looked back over his shoulder, away from the void, toward Narlydda.

Help me!

Eyes tightly shut, the green woman shook her head.

And with a sigh, he was gone, sucked out of the dome into the cold lonely starlight. In a moment, his body had spun out of sight, beyond the factory's orbit.

In his wake, the room's atmosphere whistled past toward the freedom of space. Melanie felt herself floating upward and around toward the hole in the dome where the stars awaited her.

I'm dying, she thought. But at least I've taken Ashman along with me.

It felt easier and softer than she'd expected. Like falling into a snowbank. It was cool, not freezing. And somehow, she could still breathe.

Is this what death is like?

I hope not.

The mindspeech had a gentle, unfamiliar ring to it. It didn't sound like Skerry.

No, Melanie. It's Narlydda. Don't move. I can't maintain this stasis field with atmosphere if you move around.

Melanie floated a moment more, then settled to the floor. But what about Yosh? And Skerry? Where were they? Why can't I see anything but this pale blue cloud? Melanie felt blind and wildly frustrated by her own lack of telepathic skill.

Don't worry. I can hear you. But calm down, please. You're pulling a lot of energy from me. I think Yosh is all right. I don't know if you saved Skerry. I can't hear him. I should be able to, but I can't.

Melanie could feel the grief in her words. Skerry, dead? No. She couldn't believe that her renegade cousin had been killed, even by someone as powerful as Ashman.

Well, I'm glad somebody has faith in me.

Skerry!

Nice going, Lydda. I didn't figure you for such feats of telekinetic strength. And since when could you mindspeak?

I—I don't know. Maybe that potion Ashman gave me. I can't understand why he didn't save himself.

Too startled, probably. Nice shooting, Mel. Yosh is definitely impressed. And as soon as we get out of here, he'll tell you all about that—and other things—himself.

Yosh. Good. Melanie leaned back, relieved. If Yosh was all right, that was all that mattered. But now what should they do?

I hear the Anorik *docking. Must have seen the explosion. They should be able to get us into pressure suits and back on our own shuttle. Lydda, can you hold this field for another fifteen minutes?*

I don't know, Skerry. I'll try.

Give it your best shot, babe. I'm looking forward to holding hands again.

Me too, Skerry. Me too.

21

THE SLEEK YELLOW TAXI sped past the towering gray eucalyptus grove that marked the entrance to the Dream Haven cemetery. Engine whirring, it pulled into the parking area and stopped. Michael climbed out.

A group of mourners clad in somber tones was already assembled around the gravesite. He could pick out his mother, his brother, and even gray-haired Rebekah Terling dressed in the purple robes. But who was that standing to one side—the muscular man with long hair caught back in a ponytail? Skerry? And a tall, angular woman stood with him, holding his hand. Her skin was a strange, silvery-green hue. Next to them was a Japanese nonmutant with his arm around a young, dark-haired woman. Was that Melanie?

As Michael hurried over, his sister looked up, spotted him, and waved happily. Her eyes glittered with unmasked mutant gold.

"Michael!" She threw her arms around him. "I'm so glad to see you."

He hugged her. Hard. "Did you get my message?"

"Uh, not exactly," she said, and exchanged a quick, private smile with the Japanese man at her side. "But at least I got here. I was beginning to think *you* weren't going to make it. Mom said something about you being arrested?"

"Yeah. But thanks to Senator Greenberg, I paid my fine and got out in time for the funeral." Michael shook his head in relief. "I was preparing myself to rot in some Mendocino jail cell. Then Andie's lawyer showed up."

"As the saying goes, better late than never," said a warm female voice.

The face was familiar. The dark red hair pulled back in a severe chignon, save for a few loose strands. The warm hazel eyes, surrounded by a few lines now. The body, thickening a bit but fashionably clothed in a tailored fur coat and ivory silk suit.

"Andie!" Michael grabbed her hand and awkwardly pulled her into his arms for a quick, grateful embrace.

"Down, tiger." Andie chuckled. "I'm glad to see that Douglas got you here in time."

"He said he'd see you back in the office."

"Now *he's* a workaholic." Andie patted her hair self-consciously. "And you must be the famous Melanie." She reached out and took her hand. "I'm glad to meet you, finally."

"Finally?"

"Oh, don't look confused. You don't know me, really. But I know you. I'm Andie Greenberg. A friend of your late father's. And your brother's."

"No wonder you rescued him," Melanie said. She tugged the Japanese man forward. "This is Yosh. Yosh Akimura. My fiancé."

"Your fiancé!" Michael cried.

"Close your mouth and congratulate your sister," Andie said. "I think it's marvelous, Melanie. I recommend marriage highly. And while we're discussing life planning, Michael, I want you to come see me in Washington. I understand you're taking a small vacation. There are some people I can introduce you to on the Aeronautical and Space Sciences Committee. . . ."

"Andie, are you suggesting I become a part-time lobbyist?"

She smiled slyly. "I never said that. But come see me and . . ." Her voice trailed off as something caught her eye. The smile faded and a strange expression came over her face, one of recognition and nostalgia.

"Andie?" Michael touched her shoulder gently.

"I'm sorry," she said. Her cheeks were red. "Would you excuse me? I see another old friend, and I'd better catch him before he disappears. Literally." With a determined air, she set out toward Skerry.

Michael rounded on his sister.

"Marriage? Does Mom know?" he demanded.

"Yeah. But I haven't announced it to the Council yet." Melanie watched with obvious interest as Skerry enveloped Andie in a bear hug. "Was that *the* Senator Andrea Greenberg?"

"Of course."

"I didn't know you were such buddies. Gods, she'd make a great interview. Of course, I don't know if I've still got a job—"

"Worry about that after the funeral." Michael turned to Yosh. "Welcome to the family. Any fiancé of my sister's is welcome."

Yosh grinned. "Hope you feel that way after you get to know me."

"Where's Jena and Herra?"

"Probably fixing their hair one more time," Melanie said with a malicious grin. "No, there they are. Near Mom." She hesitated. "And Michael? Kelly's here, too."

"Good."

Melanie gave him a strange look.

"We'll talk later," he said. "Come on. I'm sure Rebekah wants to get started."

With Melanie and Yosh in tow, Michael took his place near his mother, behind his wife and daughter. He spied Kelly at the back of the crowd. She was dressed unobtrusively in a dark blue suit.

Rebekah held up her hands for silence and the crowd leaned in toward her. Opening the Book, she began to chant in her resonant alto voice.

> The community is a circle
> moving from birth to death
> to birth.
> Each life is a circle.
> We grieve with each loss.
> We rejoice with each death,
> for the end and beginning are linked,
> always, in our community.

Slowly, she closed the Book.

"Friends, we have come through a hard time," she said. "A dangerous time. James Ryton left us before the danger was past, but his passing has brought us together so that we may celebrate the freedom from fear, from false supermen and supermutants. Please join hands for a sharing in thanksgiving at our deliverance."

The groupmind took hold of each one there, mutant and nonmutant, floating them out of the lonely prison of their private thoughts into the warm, honeyed community of sharing. Each pain was eased, every thorny memory softened for the moment. Here was love. Understanding. Acceptance.

Together, they floated in harmony a moment longer before the sharing ended. Then silently, they all slid back into their own private concerns. But less alone. Less troubled.

"In James Ryton's name, let us give thanks," Rebekah said. "And let us go forth with hope—"

"I demand the right of hearing," Skerry said, cutting off the Book Keeper in midsentence. Around him, the clan whispered, stunned by his outburst.

Rebekah stared at him reproachfully.

"I'm sorry to interrupt you, Book Keeper," he said formally. "But I demand the right of meeting."

"Is it so urgent, Skerry?" Rebekah's voice was soft.

"Yes."

"Then right is granted. A plenary council meeting is called. All mutants come to the Dream Haven Council Rooms in ten minutes."

The crowd dispersed slowly as some clan members moved toward the main buildings and others unable to stay straggled toward their skimmers. Somehow, in the confusion, Andie found Michael.

"I can see Skerry hasn't changed much." She rolled her eyes in affectionate exasperation. "I'd love to see what he's going to pull, but I'm afraid I've got to leave."

"Can't you at least stay for the meeting?"

"Sorry. Wish I could. But duty calls." She gave him a quick kiss on the cheek. "Don't forget my invitation. Come see me. Soon."

He held her hand for one moment more. "I will. And Andie, thank you. For everything."

With a wave, she was gone.

"Michael, hurry up," Jena said, coming up behind him. "Otherwise, we won't be able to get seats together." Herra stood next to her with a sulky expression on her face. Their blond hair sparkled with white gold in the sunlight. They wore matching blue silk tunics. They could have been twins, he thought.

"You go ahead and save me a seat," he told her. "I really should say goodbye to a few people."

"All right. But make it quick." She nodded at her daughter, and together they walked into the building.

Mike searched for Kelly. The crowd was thinning fast, mutants hurrying down the hill toward the meeting hall. No sign of her near the building. Hold on. By the skimmer port.

A slim blue figure in high heels with dark hair walking toward a gray sedan.

"Kelly! Wait." Michael raced toward her. A couple of mutant cousins turned to stare. He didn't care.

He caught her as she was closing the door of her rental
skimmer. With telekinetic force, he held the door half-open.
She tugged at it in vain, then looked up.

"I should have known it was you," she said. She looked
half-chagrined and half-amused.

"Where are you going?"

"Back to Armstrong. My leave's just about finished."

Quick, think of something. Don't let her go. Michael's
head began to pound.

"Look," he said. "I realize it's inconvenient, but could you
wait just until this meeting is over? It won't take long, and
I've got to go back to Armstrong for the rest of the hearing.
I'd really appreciate it if you could give me a lift."

She frowned. "I don't know . . ."

"It won't take long." Please, Kelly, he thought. Say yes.
"Why don't you have lunch in Mendocino and meet me
back here at one o'clock?"

"If you're sure you want to do that."

"Positive."

"All right." She turned away, gripped the door handle,
then turned back to stare at him. "Michael, do you feel all
right?"

"Yeah. Fine. See you at one." He turned and scrambled
down the green hillside toward the council chamber.

The room was paneled in silvery weathered redwood, which
had been stenciled with holo patterns of the constellations.
There was a seat waiting for him next to Jena. He slid into it
quickly and gazed around the broad table. His entire family
was here. Even Yosh with Melanie.

"All come to order," Rebekah said. "We are meeting at
Skerry's request. Cousin, you have the floor."

"Thanks, Bekah. I want to wrap up a few things before I say adieu to Mutant Council business for good." Skerry stood up. His black leather jacket reflected the glow of the holo patterns on the wall behind him. "I'm getting too old for the kind of high wire act I just went through. This is my official resignation as unofficial clan troubleshooter." He leaned forward, palms pressed upon the table. "I mean it, folks."

"You're referring to the death of Victor Ashman, the supermutant?" Torey Summers said.

"The so-called supermutant," Skerry replied acidly. "We had a quick analysis done of Narlydda's blood after Ashman had injected her with some special serum. Among other things, there were traces of trioxpanphetamine keyed to heighten metabolic processes."

"Trioxpanphetamine?"

"In simple English, cousins, Victor Ashman was hopped up on speed. A special kind of speed that was designed to enhance mutant powers. My guess is, he was a multitalent outcast whose latent skills were superenhanced by this stuff."

"You sound pretty certain about this," said Chemen Astori. "I didn't think you had much background as a chemist."

"I don't." Skerry's eyes flashed angrily. "But something my cousin Michael told me convinced me that Ashman was not a real 'ubermutant.' When we were trapped in the domeroom with Ashman, he was trying to kill everybody, except maybe Narlydda. And he damned near succeeded, too. Until that shuttle showed up."

Melanie leaned forward eagerly. "That's right," she said. "He was cloaking himself in an esper shield. We couldn't even see him. I remember how frustrated I was—I had a gun, and no target to aim at. Then he materialized just as the shuttle radioed its position. He seemed kind of surprised. And another thing. His eyes were funny. They weren't silver anymore. They turned gold. Regular mutant gold."

"Exactly," Skerry said. "Mike told me that a multitalent can only maintain the coextension of his powers for so long before one of them weakens. So Ashman could support his shield, try to choke me, and subdue at least three other people with ease. But he couldn't do that *and* fight off a space shuttle at the same time. The key was to overbalance him, pile the weight on until his arms started shaking."

"Assuming this is true, and not just another of your wild stories, where would he have gotten such a drug?" Astori demanded.

"From our old friend, the late Dr. Sarnoff. With a little assist from Emory Laboratories."

"How could Tavia Emory have gotten involved in this kind of thing?" Rebekah said.

Skerry shrugged. "That lady wanted to be a mutant. Maybe she hoped to inject herself."

"No. I don't think so," Narlydda said. "I think she truly believed she was helping to create a marvel. She saw the supermutant as a perfect human being—a saint, really. Her intentions were good. Not that it matters now."

"What about Ashman's corpse?" Astori asked.

"Recovered by the military," Skerry said. "After they're finished with the official autopsy, I'm sure the Mutant Council could have it for the asking."

"Skerry," Rebekah said. "Thank you. For all of us, inside the community and out."

"Don't thank me. Thank Melanie." He nodded across the table. "And Narlydda. Without them, I'd have been dead. Or a vegetable. Which is why I want to quit while I'm ahead. Take some time off for what counts. Maybe do a little finger painting." He smiled at Narlydda. Then he stood up and walked around the table. "And while we're on the subject of billing and cooing . . ." He stopped behind Melanie's chair. "I think we should acknowledge that our cousin Melanie has returned to the fold, bringing her husband-to-be with her. Everybody, say hello to Yosh Akimura." He put his hand on Yosh's shoulder and nodded. "Yosh, say howdy to your new mutant cousins."

"What?"

"Impossible. He's not a mutant."

"You're just making more trouble—"

Rebekah rested her chin in her hands and smiled. "Skerry, I'm beginning to look forward to your retirement." She shook her head. "Melanie, is this true? You intend to marry him?"

"Yes."

"What about children?"

"There won't be any children," Yosh said. His cheeks were flushed. He turned to Melanie. "I didn't have time to tell you. And I'd hoped that it would be in more private circumstances." He paused to cast an embarrassed glance at the Book Keeper. "But I'm sterile. Tested and confirmed years ago. Mel, I'm sorry if that changes things between us. I hope it doesn't."

Melanie looked down at his hand covering hers, then back up to meet his dark hazel eyes. "Not really," she said. "I mean, I'd hardly been thinking about marriage before I met you. I haven't had a chance to let that sink in, much less consider children. And after all, I'm a null." She smiled bravely. "Not much genetic material worth preserving there, I guess."

Yosh squeezed her hand.

"Nevertheless," Chemen Astori said, "We wish to maintain the gene pool for the community. Melanie, are you willing to consider artificial insemination from the Council's sperm banks?"

"Artificial insemination? Boy, you folks certainly know how to take the romance out of things," she said. "I guess I don't have any objections." She turned to Yosh. "But how do you feel about it?"

He looked around the room as though counting the number of mutants there. Then he shrugged. "What's one extra pair of golden eyes around the house?"

"It's agreed," Rebekah said. "Good. As presiding Book Keeper, I sanction the betrothal of Melanie Ryton and Yosh Akimura. Welcome, Yosh. We appreciate your acceptance of our ways." She gave him a quick, humorous glance. "You have our blessing." The Book Keeper raised her hands and her tone became more formal. "We will offer a follow-up report of the Ashman incident at the summer meeting. In the meantime, if there is no further business, I think we can close."

That's it, Michael thought. And now, back to the real world of congressional hearings and unemployment. Out of the corner of his eye, he watched as Jena pulled a mirror from her purse and gazed into it, fussing with her long blond hair. Then she reached for a packet of lipstain.

A sudden pressure expanded to fill his chest, moving up his throat and into his head. Michael jumped to his feet. "No. Wait," he cried. "I demand a hearing." His heart was beating so hard that he felt dizzy.

Jena looked up in surprise from her mirror. Her upper lip was bright pink.

"Is it really that urgent?" Rebekah asked testily. "We've already had a funeral, a meeting and a betrothal. Can't it wait two months until the summer meeting, Michael?"

He slammed his palm against the table. "No, dammit. I'm tired of waiting. I demand the right to be heard."

Around the room, conversations halted. Every eye, golden or otherwise, was staring at him in amazement.

"Very well." Rebekah gave him a long-suffering look. "State your case. But please, Michael. Be concise."

He took a deep breath. Where to begin? "I hereby formally announce my intention to divorce."

The audible and mental gasps reverberated around him. Jena's mouth fell open. Beside her, Herra stared at her father, her eyes huge in disbelief.

"Is this really the time and place for such an announcement?" Rebekah said. Her tone was sharp. "Michael, I know you've been under a great deal of pressure—"

He cut her off. "Yes. I'm certain," he said. "Now. Here. Before I get sucked back into the machinery once again. I've been a good son, a good husband, a good father, and a good worker. I've done all that has been asked of me. And in return, I've lost my job and my self-respect. I married to suit the community and council." His voice rose. "But I can't endure a marriage that is empty and meaningless. Whether or not you grant me right of divorce, I will leave this marriage. If necessary, I'll leave this clan and community as well."

"How dare you?" Jena cried. "How can you embarrass me like this? Don't you care about me? About your daughter?"

"Michael, you know we frown upon divorce and prefer that you make other arrangements," Chemen Astori said.

"So you admit that you demand hypocrisy as well as loyalty?" Michael said. "Well, I've had it with your double standard. I've sacrificed enough."

"Why not wait six months," Rebekah suggested. "You've been under terrible pressure. Talk to the healers . . ."

"They don't have any cure they can offer me," Michael snapped. "I prefer to settle things now."

"Dad, I don't believe this." Herra's voice was flat. Stunned.

He stared at Jena as though she were a stranger. "Jena, you can have everything," he said. "I won't fight you. Just let me have my life back."

"So you can spend it with a nonmutant?" Her tone was bitter and her eyes sparkled with tears.

"Maybe. If she'll have me. But I don't know about that yet."

"I support my son's request," Sue Li said suddenly. She stood, a small, gray-haired figure in a wine-colored kimono. "He's shown good faith to the community. He has given his loyalty, his seed, his time. Surely he deserves something in return."

"He's out of his mind with grief," Astori said.

"No, he's not," Skerry retorted. "In fact, he may be thinking clearly for the first time in years. I move that permission be granted. Get that ball and chain off of him now."

"Skerry!" Narlydda shot him a furious look. "Stay out of this."

"Wish I could, Lydda. But I've known this joker for quite some time. Watched him screw his life up, and as I see it, this is his chance to set things right." Skerry leaned back in his seat. "My vote is for him."

Rebekah stared at Michael as though she thought he was crazy. "I feel this is most inappropriate," she said severely. "However, as you've demanded a ruling, I will give you one." She looked at Jena, then at Michael. "Permission is granted. Reluctantly."

Jena sank back in her chair and covered her face with her hands. Herra burst into tears.

Michael was aware of his mother beaming at him, of Skerry pounding him on the back, of his brother and sister looking at him with surprise. But he felt strangely distant from the noise and excitement, and a bit dazed. The only sound he heard clearly was the chiming of his watch. Like an automaton, he looked down at its blue enameled face.

One o'clock.

Kelly would be waiting for him. Outside.

He looked around the table one more time at his family, friends, all the familiar faces. Then, eagerly, he dashed from the room toward the skimmer port, and the rest of his life.

EPILOGUE

SCOTTSDALE SHIMMERED in the April heat: the deep green downtown spires of FujiBank seemed to waver in the sunlight. Despite the early hour, the temperature was already climbing toward ninety.

Melanie hurried into the chilled entrance hall of Emory Foundation, hoping that she looked cooler than she felt. Her red silk tunic had to last through the broadcast.

"Hi." Yosh was waiting by the reception desk. He caught her up in a bear hug. "Your crew's already here, setting up. Am I allowed to kiss Cable News's newest anchorwoman?"

"You'd better," she said. "Married for only a little over a month, and I haven't seen you in two weeks! In fact, you'd better do more than kiss me—when there's time."

Yosh made a mock growl and gently nipped her on the neck. "I thought you'd be accustomed to strange deadlines by now," he said.

"Sure. My own." Her eyes flashed gold. "Not my husband's. That's what I get for marrying a musician—especially one involved with Moonstation commissions." She glanced at her watch. "Come on, or we'll be late for the unveiling."

Hand in hand, they hurried through the maze of corridors on Emory Foundation's main floor toward the sculpture garden in the atrium.

"Nice of Randy C. to give you this assignment," Yosh said.

Melanie laughed. "Didn't I tell you? Old Randy was kicked upstairs to the Seoul home office. Nesse inherited his job. She's the one who decided that I had anchorwoman potential—provided I dispensed with the contact lenses."

"So mutant gold sells more news?"

"We'll see. She was certainly impressed by my solid gold connections to the new mutant administration of the Emory Foundation Trust."

"Are you sure that Rebekah can handle this?"

"Rebekah is so organized, I'm beginning to think she should run for President. With Andrea Greenberg—what a ticket." She paused, eyes shining.

"Whoa—take it easy." Yosh grabbed her. "One story at a time. And here's today's story."

The doors swooshed open onto the bright yellow and green vegetation in the atrium. Bromeliads in purple bloom encircled towering saguaro cacti. The atrium stretched across half an acre under a soaring, shielded roof through which filtered sunlight spilled down for five stories. The smooth stone floor bristled with metallic sculpture.

"Ernst. Trova. Picasso." Melanie sighed with envy. "A nice little collection."

And don't forget to add Narlydda to the list.

The mindspeech twanged with amusement and pride.

Skerry sauntered around a stand of euphorbias. He looked jaunty in a pleated purple suit and turquoise headband.

"Cousins," he said, nodding. "Good to see you. Yosh, I like that strange music you made for Lydda."

"Thanks. Where is she?"

"Primping. Come see the sculpture." He drew them toward the center of the garden. "Of course, it's just the maquette. Three-quarter scale. The full-size statue is still being soldered and chased at the foundry. Siting date is May 28."

Melanie gazed at the model with awe. It was a beautiful melding of textures, bronze and gold married to creamy ceramic, and all shaped in forms both abstract and somehow figurative. The sculpture was an expressionist mermaid—or was that merman? The face changed as Melanie walked around it, from male to female, from familiar to strange. Wait. Wasn't that Skerry's face smiling merrily at her now? But as she moved, the sculpture shifted, the face flowed and melted to reveal—could it be Tavia Emory? And then, yes, it had to be—Victor Ashman's hollow-eyed image gazed out sadly at her before subsiding into what could only be a sly self-portrait of the artist. A haunting melody seemed to emanate from the heart of the sculpture, elusive, at once sprightly and melancholy.

"Amazing," she said.

"And it's never the same," Yosh said. "I've walked around it until I'm dizzy. Sometimes I see me in it. And sometimes, even you."

"I expanded my concept somewhat," said a female voice drily. "It seemed appropriate after everything that has happened."

Narlydda walked toward them with stately grace. She wore a silvery wide-brimmed hat that framed her face nicely, adding contrast to her dark hair without obscuring the flash of white at her temple. Her gown consisted of layers of silk gauze in shifting tones of violet, green, and yellow. Her face was clear, unadorned.

"No mask?" Yosh asked.

"No mask," Narlydda said, smiling.

"Congratulations," Melanie said. "It's wonderful."

"I'm glad you like it. I didn't know if I ever wanted to see Ashman's face again. But somehow, it felt appropriate."

Yosh grinned. "I'm just glad he turned out to be a regular mutant on drugs. Otherwise, I think we'd all be space dust by now." His smile faded as he gazed at Narlydda's sculpture. "Wonder what a real supermutant would be like."

"Gods," Melanie said. "Didn't we come close enough to finding out this time? I think the whole idea of an evolved supermutant is just Mutant Council mumbo jumbo."

Skerry frowned. "I wish I shared your opinion," he said balefully. "But nature is relentless. There will be an evolved mutant, sooner or later. You can count on that."

"Then let it be later rather than sooner," Melanie said. "I'm sorry I brought up the subject."

"Amen," Narlydda added. She gave Skerry a sharp, silencing look. "By the way, Mel, I haven't had a chance to congratulate you both on your marriage. Or to ask about your brother—"

"Have you heard from Mike?" Skerry said eagerly. "I wanted to tell him what a great exit he made from that meeting. Warms my heart just to think about it."

"Just an e-mail note from Bali. He's there. With Kelly." Melanie smiled. "I still don't believe it."

"You and me both." Skerry looked away toward the door. "Lydda, the governor just arrived. It's time to get rolling."

"See you later. And Melanie, I haven't forgotten my promise about that interview." With a wink, Narlydda was gone.

Melanie scanned the atrium for her crew and found the bright red eye of the video camera blinking, at attention, by the sculpture. But she wasn't ready to get on with business. Not quite yet.

"Yosh?"

"Yeah?"

"The sculpture is wonderful. And I may be biased. But I think that the music makes it even better."

He smiled. "Let's go home soon," he said.

And as the camera rolled, he kissed her jubilantly in the spring sunshine.